Midnight Breed
Compilation

Also from Lara Adrian

Midnight Breed Series
A Touch of Midnight (prequel novella FREE eBook)
Kiss of Midnight
Kiss of Crimson
Midnight Awakening
Midnight Rising
Veil of Midnight
Ashes of Midnight
Shades of Midnight
Taken by Midnight
Deeper Than Midnight
A Taste of Midnight (ebook novella)
Darker After Midnight
The Midnight Breed Series Companion
Edge of Dawn
Marked by Midnight (novella)
Crave the Night
Tempted by Midnight (novella)
Bound to Darkness
Stroke of Midnight
Defy the Dawn
Midnight Untamed
...and more to come!
Also:
The Midnight Breed Series Coloring Book

The 100 Series (billionaire contemporary romance)
For 100 Days
For 100 Nights (forthcoming)
For 100 Reasons (forthcoming)

Masters of Seduction Series
Merciless: House of Gravori
Priceless: House of Ebarron

Phoenix Code Series (with Tina Folsom)
Cut and Run (Books 1 & 2)
Hide and Seek (Books 3 & 4)

Historical Romances

Dragon Chalice Series
Heart of the Hunter (FREE eBook)
Heart of the Flame
Heart of the Dove
Dragon Chalice Boxed Set

Warrior Trilogy
White Lion's Lady (FREE eBook)
Black Lion's Bride
Lady of Valor
Warrior Trilogy Boxed Set

Standalone Titles
Lord of Vengeance

Midnight Breed Compilation

3 Stories by

By Lara Adrian

1001 Dark Nights

EVIL EYE
CONCEPTS

Midnight Breed Compilation
3 Stories by
Lara Adrian
ISBN: 978-1-945920-63-9
1001 Dark Nights

Published by Evil Eye Concepts, Incorporated

Sign up for the 1001 Dark Nights Newsletter
and be entered to win a Tiffany Key necklace.

There's a contest every month!

Go to www.1001DarkNights.com to subscribe.

As a bonus, all subscribers will receive a free
1001 Dark Nights story
The First Night
by Lexi Blake & M.J. Rose

Table of Contents

One Thousand and One Dark Nights

Once upon a time, in the future…

*I was a student fascinated with stories and learning.
I studied philosophy, poetry, history, the occult, and
the art and science of love and magic. I had a vast
library at my father's home and collected thousands
of volumes of fantastic tales.*

*I learned all about ancient races and bygone
times. About myths and legends and dreams of all
people through the millennium. And the more I read
the stronger my imagination grew until I discovered
that I was able to travel into the stories… to actually
become part of them.*

*I wish I could say that I listened to my teacher
and respected my gift, as I ought to have. If I had, I
would not be telling you this tale now.
But I was foolhardy and confused, showing off
with bravery.*

*One afternoon, curious about the myth of the
Arabian Nights, I traveled back to ancient Persia to
see for myself if it was true that every day Shahryar
(Persian: شهریار, "king") married a new virgin, and then
sent yesterday's wife to be beheaded. It was written
and I had read, that by the time he met Scheherazade,
the vizier's daughter, he'd killed one thousand
women.*

Something went wrong with my efforts. I arrived in the midst of the story and somehow exchanged places with Scheherazade – a phenomena that had never occurred before and that still to this day, I cannot explain.

Now I am trapped in that ancient past. I have taken on Scheherazade's life and the only way I can protect myself and stay alive is to do what she did to protect herself and stay alive.

Every night the King calls for me and listens as I spin tales. And when the evening ends and dawn breaks, I stop at a point that leaves him breathless and yearning for more. And so the King spares my life for one more day, so that he might hear the rest of my dark tale.

As soon as I finish a story... I begin a new one... like the one that you, dear reader, have before you now.

Tempted by Midnight

Acknowledgments from the Author

Several years ago, my editor at Random House forwarded me an email from a reader who'd just discovered my books and then tore through the entire Midnight Breed series in a matter of a week. Those are my favorite kinds of emails, and what made this one even more special was it came from the wife of a bestselling thriller writer whose books I also happened to love!

What a thrill and an honor it is to now call the lovely Liz Berry a dear friend, and a wonderful colleague. I'm delighted to be part of the 1001 Dark Nights collection with this novella in my Midnight Breed vampire romance series. My thanks to Liz, MJ Rose, Jillian Stein, my fellow authors and friends in this collection, and everyone else working behind the scenes to make the project possible. Can't wait to do it again next year!

Heartfelt thanks, as always, to my family, friends, and colleagues, and to my readers. None of my books would be possible without all of you!

With love,

Lara Adrian

CHAPTER 1

He had lived for more than a thousand years, long enough that few things still held the power to amaze him. The sea at night was one of those rare pleasures for Lazaro Archer.

Standing on the third-level bow deck of a gleaming, 279-foot private megayacht off the western coast of Italy, Lazaro braced his hands on the polished mahogany rail and indulged his senses in a brief appreciation of his moonlit surroundings.

Crisp, salty Mediterranean air filled his nostrils and tousled his jet-black hair. The late summer breeze was cool tonight, gusting rhythmically toward the Italian mainland. Dark, rippling water spread out in all directions under the milky glow of the cloud-strewn moon and blanket of stars. Far below, waves lapped fluidly, sensually, against the sides of the yacht where it floated, engines silenced as it waited at its destined location on the Tyrrhenian Sea.

Lazaro supposed the luxurious vessel he stood aboard would take the breath away from just about anyone—human or Breed. Being born the latter, and first generation Breed besides, one of the vampire nation's eldest, most pure-blooded individuals, Lazaro had known his fair share of wealth and luxury.

He'd once had all of those things himself. Still did, if he could be bothered to care.

He left everything he once had back in Boston twenty years ago, after the most precious things in his long life had been taken from him. His blood-bonded Breedmate, his sons and their mates, a houseful of innocent children...all gone. His only surviving kin was his grandson,

Kellan, who'd been with Lazaro the night the Archers' Darkhaven home was razed to the ground in a heinous, unprovoked attack by a madman named Dragos.

Lazaro exhaled deeply, no longer feeling the raw scrape of grief whenever he thought of his slain family. The anguish had dulled over time, yet his guilt was always with him, scarred over like a physical wound. A hideous, permanent reminder of his loss.

Of his life's greatest failure.

If his existence had any meaning now, it belonged to his work with Lucan Thorne and his fellow Breed warriors of the Order. As the commander of the Order's operation in Rome these past two decades, Lazaro had little time for self-pity or personal indulgences. He had even less opportunity for pleasure, rare or otherwise.

Which was the way he preferred it.

He dealt in justice now.

At times, he dealt in death.

Tonight, he was representing the Order on a less official basis, on the hopes that he could facilitate a secret meeting between two of his trusted friends. One of them was Breed, a high-ranking American member of the Global Nations Council. The other, the megayacht's owner, was human, an influential Italian businessman who also happened to be the brother of that country's newly elected president, a politician who had won his office with tough talk against the Breed. If the meeting with Paolo Turati took place as planned tonight and was deemed a success, it would be the first step toward forging an alliance with one of the vampire nation's most vocal detractors.

As for Byron Walsh, the Breed male had been one of Lazaro's colleagues in the States, even before the GNC had tapped Walsh for his current diplomatic post. As leader of his own Darkhaven in Maryland, Walsh's social circle had occasionally intersected with Lazaro's in Boston. There had even been a time, one bitter winter, that Walsh's family came to visit Lazaro's at their Back Bay mansion.

A long time ago, back when Lazaro had a Darkhaven. Back when he still had a family kept safe under his protection.

It had been even longer since Lazaro Archer had played emissary for any cause. He hoped like hell this clandestine introduction wasn't a mistake.

Seventy-odd miles behind him was the seaside town of Anzio,

where Lazaro had joined Turati on his yacht a couple of hours ago. Up ahead of them, an even farther distance, the island of Sardinia glittered with light against the darkness.

A smattering of other large yachts and watercraft bobbed in the vast space between Turati's vessel and the island, but it was the low drone of a motorboat that captured Lazaro's full attention. The size of a small cabin cruiser, the yacht tender had departed from an idling vessel in the distance and was heading Lazaro's way. He watched the chase boat approach from out of the inky darkness, its navigation lights dimmed as instructed, flashing three times as it crossed the water toward them.

His Breed colleague from the States did not disappoint. Byron Walsh was arriving as promised, and right on time.

Lazaro nodded, grim with relief.

He turned away from the rail and headed down to the yacht's main deck salon where Turati waited. On Lazaro's directions and assurances, the gray-haired billionaire had brought just two men from his usual security entourage. The yacht's crew of fifty had been reduced to a bare dozen, just enough personnel to operate the vessel.

At Lazaro's entrance to the lavish salon, Turati glanced up, wiry brows lifting in question. "He comes?" the old man asked in his native tongue.

Lazaro answered in Italian as well. "The boat is on the way now." As tonight's host did not speak English, Lazaro would personally translate for the duration of the meeting, if only to ensure that the conversation didn't inadvertently stray into unfriendly waters.

Paolo Turati was one of a small number of humans Lazaro considered a friend. He was also one of the few humans who didn't look upon the Breed as a race of monsters in need of collaring at best, or, at worst, wholesale extermination.

Granted, the fear wasn't without cause. For millennia, the Breed existed in the shadows alongside their *Homo sapiens* neighbors. In the twenty years since Lazaro's kind was outed to man, trust between the two races on the planet had been anything but easy.

That trust became even more complicated a couple of weeks ago, when a violent cabal calling themselves Opus Nostrum smuggled a bomb into a very important summit gathering of Breed and human dignitaries.

If tonight's introductions went well, the Breed would gain a supportive voice and a much-needed ally in their efforts to keep the peace between man and vampire all around the world. If it went poorly, the Order's efforts to broker peace could ignite the smoldering war that Opus Nostrum seemed to want so badly.

"I hope your friend from Maryland comes to this meeting with the same intentions as I do," Turati said, apprehension in the flat line of his mouth, even though the old human's eyes held Lazaro in a trusting look. "If I like what I hear tonight, I will do what I can to persuade my brother to at least entertain the idea of talks with the GNC and Lucan Thorne. After all, everyone's goal is peace, not only for ourselves, but for our generations to follow."

"Indeed," Lazaro replied. His acute Breed hearing picked up the faint, approaching growl of the boat carrying Byron Walsh. "He's arriving now. Wait here, Paolo. I'll go down to meet him and bring him up."

Turati frowned then shook his head. "I will join you, Lazaro. It seems only proper that I greet Councilman Walsh personally and welcome him aboard along with you. I would do no less for any invited guest."

Lazaro inclined his head in agreement. "A fine idea."

He waited patiently as the old man stood and smoothed his custom-tailored navy suit and creamy silk shirt. By contrast, Lazaro was dressed in what he'd come to regard as *Order casual*—black slacks, light-duty combat boots, and a fitted black patrol shirt.

And although he was first generation Breed and more than deadly with his bare hands alone, he carried a blade concealed in each boot and had a semiautomatic 9mm pistol strapped to his right ankle. He didn't expect trouble from either of the two men or their few staff present at tonight's meeting, but he'd be damned if he didn't come prepared for it.

Together, he and Turati left the grand salon on the yacht's second level, making their way down a polished brass stairwell that spiraled elegantly onto the lower deck. The boat carrying Walsh was coming around the stern as Lazaro and Turati arrived on the aft deck to meet it.

A suited bodyguard stood at attention on the motorboat, just outside the cabin's hatch. He was Breed, as big and menacing as any one of Lazaro's kind. Turati's steps hesitated at the sight of the unsmiling guard. The two men comprising the Italian's own security detail now stood behind their employer, pulses spiking with a tension Lazaro felt as a palpable vibration in the air.

He gave a solemn nod of greeting to Walsh's guard, the signal as good as his word that Walsh would be safe among friends tonight. The guard turned, opened the hatch to murmur an "all clear" to the boat's occupants.

Byron Walsh appeared in that next instant. Dressed less formally than Turati, the Breed diplomat emerged from the cabin in a crisp white shirt with rolled-back sleeves and fawn-colored slacks. Although Walsh was formidable-looking, over six feet tall and heavily muscled, like all of their kind, his relaxed attire softened his edges.

As did the smile he gave as he disembarked from his tender and stepped onto the deck of Turati's yacht. Walsh's friendliness seemed genuine, even if his smile didn't quite reach his eyes. There was an undercurrent of anxiety about him, as if he hadn't yet decided if he was stepping onto safe ground or a nest of vipers.

"Lazaro, my old friend, it's been too long. Good to see you," he greeted briefly, then extended his hand to the evening's host. "*Signor Turati, buona sera.*"

"Paolo," Turati offered as the two men shook hands.

"Thank you for agreeing to this meeting," Walsh continued in English. "And please forgive the cloak-and-dagger aspect of our introduction tonight. Unfortunately, there are those who might prefer to keep our people at odds, rather than embrace the peace that you and I both hope to achieve."

Lazaro murmured a quick translation, to which Turati smiled and replied in kind. "Paolo says he is honored to have the opportunity to talk and share ideas with you, Byron. He would like you and your men to be comfortable as his guests inside now."

Walsh held up his hand, gesturing to wait. "A moment, if you will. We're not all present just yet." He pivoted to look at his pair of Breed bodyguards behind him. "Where's Mel?"

"Right behind me a second ago," one of his men answered.

Lazaro scowled, confused, and not a little concerned that Walsh had apparently brought a third member of his entourage when the agreement had explicitly called for balance on both sides of this informal summit. He shot a questioning glower at his friend—just as a head emerged from the cabin below.

A head covered in long, luscious waves of fiery red hair.

"I'm sorry," the woman offered hastily as she made her way out. "I had to sit down for a second. I'm afraid I'm still trying to find my sea legs."

She came out of the cabin completely then, and every pair of eyes on deck rooted onto her like the tide pulled toward the moon. Not even Lazaro was immune.

Christ, not even close.

"Ah. There you are, darling." Walsh pivoted to assist her off the smaller vessel.

Darling? Lazaro vaguely recalled hearing that Byron Walsh had lost his mate in a car accident three or four years ago. Had he taken another lover so soon? Whether she was a Breedmate or human female, Lazaro couldn't be sure.

More to the point, what the hell was Walsh thinking, showing up with her unexpectedly to a meeting of this importance? Lazaro had worked on Paolo Turati for months before the man finally agreed to open the door to talks with a member of the GNC. Walsh himself had been reluctant to trust the kin of a government leader who made no secret of his suspicion and distaste for the entire population of the Breed. Lazaro could not imagine what had possessed Walsh to treat this unofficial summit as a goddamned pleasure cruise.

If grabbing the Breed male by the throat and demanding an answer to that very question wouldn't turn an already awkward situation into a potential disaster, Lazaro might have uncurled his fists at his sides and done just that. Instead, he stared, silent and fuming. He'd deal with his friend's apparent lapse in judgment later.

"Careful now," Walsh cautioned his uninvited companion. "Watch your step, sweetheart."

Hell, every male present was watching her step. She was tall, elegant, with bountiful curves that filled out every body-skimming line of a conservative—yet damned sexy—charcoal gray skirt that skimmed her knees and showcased her long, shapely legs. She wore a garnet-colored silk blouse unbuttoned midway down her sternum, just low enough to tease at the generous swell of her bosom.

At the base of her throat was a small scarlet birthmark in the shape of a teardrop falling into the cradle of a crescent moon. So, the voluptuous beauty was a Breedmate, Lazaro noted with displeasure. Had she been simply human arm candy for the councilman, Lazaro would have no qualms at all about turning her sinfully formed behind right back around and sending the motorboat away with her inside.

But a female born with the Breedmate mark commanded deeper respect than that from one of Lazaro's kind. And although he was more warrior now than gentleman, there was still a part of him that held rare females like this one in high regard. And if she was in fact mated to Byron Walsh, then Lazaro had no bloody right to stare at her with a smoldering crackle of interest heating his veins.

As her slender-heeled pumps settled gracefully on the deck, she lifted her head and glanced up to look at him and the other men. Her mane of lustrous, flame-bright hair framed a delicate oval face dominated by large green eyes and soft, sensual lips.

She was, in a word, stunning.

The face of an angel and the kind of body to tempt a saint.

And based on the sudden hush of focused male interest on the deck of Turati's yacht, there was hardly a saint among them.

Lazaro shut down his own awareness of her with abrupt, violent force.

Walsh took the woman's hand and led her forward. "Lazaro, you'll remember my daughter, Mel."

In a flash of memory, Lazaro envisioned a gangly tomboy about seven years old who'd come with her adopted parents to the Archer Darkhaven one winter. Freckle-faced, scrawny, and possessed of more courage than good sense, the way he recalled it now.

Nothing like the curvaceous, poised woman he saw before him here.

"Melena," she corrected her father gently, her lush mouth bowing in a polite smile as she offered her hand in greeting first to Turati, then to Lazaro. "I'm my father's personal assistant. Tonight I'll also be translating for him." She turned the full strength of her smile on Turati, speaking now in flawless Italian. "I hope you don't mind. Between you and me, Daddy's Italian is only slightly better than his French, which isn't saying much."

Turati chuckled, his aged eyes twinkling as he drank in the sight of Melena Walsh. The pair immediately began a light, effusive chat about Italy and its numerous areas of superiority over all things French. Lazaro didn't want to be impressed with the young woman, but he couldn't deny her language skills—or her charm. Paolo Turati was no pushover and it had taken her less than a minute to have the old goat eating out of the palm of her soft white hand.

Still, this wasn't a social call.

There was real business to be done tonight.

Lazaro cleared his throat in effort to break up the uninvited distraction. "Your offer to translate is appreciated, Miss Walsh—"

"Melena, please," she interjected.

"But it won't be necessary," Lazaro finished. "As this meeting is confidential and a matter of global security as well, all interpretation will be handled personally by me. I trust you understand."

She glanced at her father, an anxious flick of her eyes.

"I'll be more comfortable knowing Mel is nearby," Walsh replied. "As you say, Lazaro, there is much at stake in the world, and I would hate for my clumsy words to convey anything less than what I truly mean. Likewise, before I leave tonight, I would like to be sure that I've understood everything Paolo intends me to know."

"You don't trust that I am capable of assuring you of both those things?"

"Melena's come all this way to assist me, Lazaro."

"And she's welcome to wait on board in one of the other salons until the meeting is finished." Lazaro met his old friend's gaze, tried to decipher some of the apprehension he saw in the Breed male's eyes. "If you don't like my decision, take it up with Lucan Thorne when you return to the States."

Turati was frowning now, lost by the rapid back-and-forth in English. "Something is wrong?" he asked, directing his question to Lazaro in Italian, even though he could hardly tear his gaze away from Melena. "Tell me what is going on."

"Miss Walsh will join us after the meeting concludes," Lazaro informed him. "She was unaware of the sensitive nature of this arrangement and has agreed that I should provide the necessary translation assistance as planned."

Melena glanced down, and Turati's face pinched into a deeper frown. He stepped toward her, his mouth pursing under his silent contemplation. When she looked up at him, the old man grinned, hooking a thumb in Lazaro's direction. "Shall we ask him to join us after the meeting instead?" he whispered in Italian. "I would much rather listen to your voice for the next few hours than his, my dear."

She smiled but started to shake her head. "Thank you, Mr. Turati, but I cannot—"

"You can, and I insist that you do. You and your father are both my guests here tonight. I'll banish neither of you from our meeting." Turati slanted a sly glance at Lazaro. "I won't banish you either. Come, let's go inside now."

Lazaro sent the motor boat away with a dismissing wave as he waited for the Walshes, Turati, and the two pairs of bodyguards to head back up to the yacht's main salon. Then, with a low curse and a vague, but troubled, niggling in his veins, he fell in behind them.

CHAPTER 2

The meeting was going far better than they could have hoped. Especially considering Melena had nearly been banned from the room before it even started.

Her father and Paolo Turati had talked without interruption for a couple of hours—serious conversations ranging from cultural misconceptions among the Breed and mankind, to the volatile political climate that existed between the two races. They'd discussed their hopes for a better future and confessed their shared worries about what that future might look like if the mistrust that festered on either side of Breed/human relations were allowed to continue.

Or worse, if it were encouraged to spread—something the failed terror act at the GNC peace summit in Washington, D.C., two weeks ago had seemed orchestrated to do.

The two men hadn't solved the world's many problems in the space of two hours, but they did seem to be forming a genuine respect and fondness for each other. With the heavier subjects behind them, Melena happily translated as they moved on to trading anecdotes from recent travels they'd both enjoyed and talk of their children. Mundane, comfortable conversations peppered with easy smiles, even bouts of laughter.

If her father had reservations about his trip overseas for this covert audience, those concerns seemed all but evaporated now. And he had been more than apprehensive, Melena had to admit. He'd been on the verge of paranoia in the days leading up to this meeting.

He worried that betrayal awaited him around every corner—not so much groundless panic, but a hunch he couldn't shake. Born with limited precognitive ability, her father's hunches, good or bad, all too often proved to be fact.

Every Breed vampire was gifted with a preternatural talent unique to himself. The same held true for Breedmates like Melena, women who bore the teardrop-and-crescent-moon mark and had the rare genetic makeup that allowed them to blood-bond with one of the Breed in an eternal union and bear his young.

It was Melena's specific extrasensory ability that brought her along with her father tonight, more so than her translation skills. She'd needed to see Paolo Turati in person in order to assure her father of the human's intentions. And she'd been satisfied in that regard. *Signor* Turati was a good man, one who could be trusted at his word.

Melena was glad she could be there to allay her father's worry, even if her presence had met with the glowering disapproval of the Breed male who'd arranged the important introduction.

For the duration of the meeting so far, Lazaro Archer had loomed in brooding silence at the peripheral of the megayacht's opulent main deck salon, as distracting as a dark storm cloud. While he'd allowed her to translate as Turati insisted, it was obvious the raven-haired Gen One Breed male wasn't happy about it.

No, he was furious. He wanted her gone. And she didn't need to rely on ESP to tell her so.

From the sharp stab of his piercing indigo gaze, which had been fixed on her each time she dared a look in his direction, Melena guessed it wasn't often he found himself not in absolute control of any given situation.

She could personally attest to Lazaro Archer's commanding, take-charge demeanor. She had witnessed him in action firsthand once. She'd been just a child, but to say he left an impression was an understatement.

Memory yanked her back to a cold winter night and a foolish dare gone terribly wrong. She could still feel the frozen water engulf her. Could still see the blackness that filled her vision as her head struck something hard and sharp with her fall.

Idly, Melena ran her fingertips across the scar that cut a fine line through her left eyebrow. She didn't realize she was being spoken to until she saw both her father and Paolo Turati looking at her in expectation.

"Oh, I...I'm sorry," she stammered, embarrassed to have been caught drifting. Especially with Lazaro Archer there to notice it too. "Would you repeat that last part for me, please? I want to be certain I get it correct."

Her father chuckled. "Sweetheart, I just asked if you might like to take a short break. We've been going on for hours without a rest. I'm sure we all could use a few minutes to relax a bit."

"Of course," she replied, then pivoted to translate for their smiling host.

As she rose from the antique sofa, both men politely stood with her. Lazaro Archer took the opportunity to stalk out of the salon. She watched him disappear into the darkness outside.

"Would you like some wine?" Turati asked her, his Italian words infused with pride as he gestured to a collection of bottles encased in a lighted cabinet the length of one entire wall of the salon. "My family owns three vineyards, one dating back nearly a thousand years. I would be pleased if you would join me for a glass of my favorite vintage."

Melena smiled back at him. "I would enjoy that very much, thank you. But first, may I ask where I might find a restroom, please?"

"Certainly, certainly." Turati snapped his fingers at the pair of bodyguards who'd been hanging back obediently for the duration of the night. Continuing with Melena in Italian, he said, "There is one just through that door and down the passageway, my dear. Gianni will show you—"

"No, that's okay." She shook her head at the approaching guard, unaccustomed to so much fawning and more than capable of finding her own way. "Thank you, but I'm sure I can find it on my own. Will you all excuse me?"

With a reassuring glance at her father and a nod to Turati, Melena headed out of the salon and into the passageway. The private restroom at the other end was every bit as sumptuous as the salon, with gilded trim and elegant millwork, gleaming mirrors, and a wealth of original art on the walls.

As she came out of the single stall a few moments later and washed her hands, she couldn't help but pause to check her reflection in the polished glass. Her light copper hair was wind-tossed and thickened from the humidity of the sea. Her skin was milky beneath the freckles that spread out over the apples of her cheeks and marched across the bridge of her nose. And the aura that radiated off her was imbued with shades of green and gold.

Hope.

Determination.

She tried not to notice the faint pink glow that simmered beneath the stronger colors of her psyche. Her curiosity about Lazaro Archer had no place here. Her awareness of him as a dark, dangerously attractive male, even less. She'd come to assist her father; that was all.

And besides, the grim representative from the Order had given her no reason to think he'd even noticed her tonight, other than as a nuisance he was eager to relieve himself of at the earliest opportunity.

Every time she looked at him, he'd been cloaked in a haze of unreadable, gunmetal gray. Coupled with his intimidating gaze, the effect should have been enough to make her keep a healthy distance.

Instead, as she left the restroom, rather than returning straight to the salon again, Melena pivoted in the opposite direction. Toward the aft deck, where she'd seen him go.

He stood alone at the rail in the dark, a stoic figure, unmoving, forbidding. His large hands were braced wide before him. His immense, black-clad body leaned slightly forward as he gazed off the stern of the yacht over the endless blanket of rippling water beyond.

Melena took a silent step toward him, then hesitated.

This was probably a bad idea. She should go back inside and focus on what she was supposed to be doing. She had no business with Lazaro Archer, even if there was something she'd been wanting to say to him all night. For much longer than that, in fact.

But from the rigidity of his stance, she could see that he was in no mood for conversation. Probably least of all with the interloper who'd shown up uninvited and inadvertently defied his authority over the meeting.

Her feet paused beneath her, Melena started to pivot around to leave him to his solitude.

"You're doing well in there." His deep voice arrested her where she stood. He didn't bother to look at her, and although the compliment was completely unexpected, it came out more like a growled accusation.

"Thanks." Tentatively, since there was no point in trying to avoid him now, she crossed the deck to join him at the railing. "I like *Signor* Turati. And I have a good feeling about this meeting. I think my father has made a true friend here tonight."

Lazaro grunted. "I'll be sure to inform Lucan Thorne that you give your blessing."

Melena exhaled a short sigh. "I'm not trying to minimize the importance of this meeting. I understand what's at stake—"

"No. You couldn't possibly," he replied, finally swiveling his head to look askance at her.

And oh, Lord. If she thought Lazaro Archer was intimidating from across the room, up close he was terrifying. His midnight-blue eyes glittered as dark as obsidian in the moonlight, ruthless under the ebony slashes of his brows. His strong nose and sharp cheekbones gave him a ferocity no human face could carry off, and his squared, rigid jawline seemed hewn of granite.

Only his mouth had an element of softness to it, though right now, as he looked at her, his broad, sensual lips were flattened in an irritated scowl.

"How old are you?" he demanded.

"Twenty-nine."

He scoffed, his dark gaze giving her a brief once-over. Based on the fierce ticking of a tendon in his already ironclad jaw, she guessed he didn't particularly like what he saw. "You've barely been out of diapers long enough to understand how important it is to have peace between the Breed and humankind. You were only a child when the veil between our world and theirs was torn away. You didn't wade through the blood in the streets. You didn't see the death, the brutality inflicted on so many innocents by both sides of this war." He blew out a curse and shook his head slowly back and forth. "You can't possibly comprehend how thin the thread is that holds back an even uglier war now. Nor can you know the lengths to which some people will go to rip that thread to tatters."

"You're talking about Opus Nostrum," Melena said quietly. A flicker of surprise in those narrowing indigo eyes now. "As my father's personal assistant, he trusts me completely with all of his GNC business. I collect data for him. I summarize reports. I attend most of his meetings, as well as compose the majority of his speeches. I'm also his daughter, so of course, I'm well aware of the attempted bombing at the summit he attended a couple of weeks ago. I know Opus wanted to take a lot of lives at that event—Breed and human. I also know the Order's primary objective now is to unmask the members of Opus's secret cabal and take the terror group down."

Lazaro grunted but seemed less than impressed. "If you came out here to recite your credentials, Miss Walsh, let me spare you the effort."

"You all but challenged me to tell you," she pointed out.

"And all you've done is confirm what I already knew about you. I have a job to do here too, and you've been standing in my way all night." He glanced back out at the water. "I'm sure your ample charms will find a far more receptive audience back in the salon."

Ample charms? Was that a cut on the fact that she actually had curves and a figure, or could he possibly mean he found her even a little bit interesting?

"I didn't come out here to...Jesus, never mind," she stammered. "Forgive me for disturbing you." Frustrated, Melena pushed back from the railing. She started to pivot away, then paused. Glanced over at him one last time, her own anger spiking. "We've met, you know. You don't remember me."

Why she felt stung by that she really didn't want to consider. When he didn't respond after a long moment, she decided it was probably for the best. God knew, she would be better off forgetting the night she nearly died too.

She turned and headed back across the deck.

"I remember a reckless child doing something stupid," he muttered from behind her. "A silly little girl, being somewhere she damned well didn't belong."

Rather like the way he seemed to regard her now, she thought, bristling at the comment.

"I was seven," Melena replied, swinging a look over her shoulder at him. Lazaro hadn't moved from his position, was still staring out at the black water. "I was seven years old, and you saved my life. I'd be dead if not for you."

"Saved you? Christ." He exhaled sharply, as if the idea annoyed him. "I'm not in the habit of saving anyone."

Something about the way he said that, the quieting of his tone, and the almost raw edge to his words made her drift back toward him. She rubbed a chill from her arms as the recollection of her accident washed over her with fresh terror.

"Well, you did save me. You pulled me out of that frozen pond and you saved my life." He didn't look her way at all, hardly acknowledged she had returned. "My family was in Boston, visiting at your Darkhaven. A bunch of us kids were playing outside that night, mostly boys—your grandsons and young nephews and my older brother, Derek. Unlike me, they were all Breed, and as the only girl with them besides, it took all I had to keep up."

Sometimes she felt as though she were still competing, still struggling to prove her worth in everything she did. She realized she held others up to her same impossible standards too. Her parents had pointed it out to her on numerous occasions. So had more than a few of her exes.

Now here she was, making a point to remind this arrogant man of the stupidest thing she'd ever done in her life.

Melena let out a soft sigh as she stood next to Lazaro once more. "The boys didn't want me there with them at the pond, but I followed them anyway. They started daring each other to walk farther and farther out onto the ice."

"Idiots, all of them," Lazaro grumbled. "Winter came late that year. The pond hadn't yet frozen toward the center."

"Yes," she agreed. "And it was very dark that night. I didn't realize the ice wouldn't hold me until I was already too far out. I stepped onto a thin section, and it broke away underneath me."

The curse Lazaro uttered was ripe, violent. But the look he finally swung on her was oddly tender, haunted. To her complete shock, he reached out and grazed the pad of his thumb over her scarred eyebrow. "You'd hit your head on something."

"The edge of the ice was jagged," she murmured, her throat going a bit dry for the mere second his touch had lingered on her face. When his hand was gone, she shivered, though not from anything close to a chill. "I went down very quickly. God, the water was so cold. I could hardly move my limbs. I panicked. I couldn't see anything. When I tried to swim back up, I realized I was trapped under the ice."

Lazaro was listening intently now, his expression impossible to read. His aura forbade her too, the dull gray haze blurring the edges of his broad shoulders and strong arms, haloing his dangerously handsome face like a brooding cloud against the darkness of the night that surrounded him.

"I remember everything started to go black," Melena said. "And then...there you were. In the water with me, pulling me to the surface. You dived into that frigid pond and searched until you found me. Then you brought me back to your Darkhaven."

"You were bleeding," he said, his gaze returning to the scar above her left eye.

Melena nodded. "Your Breedmate, Ellie, helped my mother patch me up."

Both women were gone now. Melena's adoptive mother, Byron Walsh's mate, Frances, had been killed in a senseless car accident a few years ago. Lazaro's kind-hearted, beautiful Breedmate, Eleanor, had suffered a far more brutal end. Killed just a couple of years after Melena had met her, along with the rest of Lazaro's family who'd been home at his Boston Darkhaven the night of an horrific attack.

His gaze hardened, going distant at the mention of his lost mate. It took nearly all of Melena's self-control to keep from reaching out to offer comfort to him now.

If she didn't think he'd snap her fingers off at the roots, she might have braved it in spite of his forbidding glower.

And yet, there was something more in his eyes as he looked at her. As much as she was drawn to him tonight, she couldn't help feeling that he was aware of her too. Not as the hapless girl he'd fished out of a frozen pond, not even as the grown-up daughter of a colleague and friend.

He was annoyed with her tonight, no question. Given a choice, he'd probably still prefer her gone. But Lazaro Archer was also looking at her the way a man looked at a woman. And she couldn't deny that his interest made her pulse trip into a faster tempo.

"What are you doing here, Melena?" His gruff question caught her off guard.

Did she even know the answer to that? She shrugged lamely. "I guess I just...I don't think I ever got the chance to thank you—"

"No." He cocked his head slightly, those unsettling eyes narrowing shrewdly now. "I mean, what are you doing here at this meeting? As skilled of an interpreter as you are, I think we both know there's something you're not saying."

She stared at him, wondering how he'd gone from looking at her like he wanted to touch her—maybe even kiss her—to pinning her in a suspicious glare. Maybe he hadn't been ignoring her all evening, but silently assessing her, even now.

Part of her wanted to tell him the truth. That she'd been a psychic insurance policy, to make certain her father wasn't walking into a trap with Turati or his men, regardless of the Order's assurances. Lazaro would be furious to hear it, no doubt. That she and her father had defied diplomatic protocol to insert her into a top secret meeting without the knowledge or permission of the Order or the GNC? She didn't even want to consider the ramifications of that, for her or her father.

And anyway, it wasn't her place to publicly voice her father's fears or suspicions, not even to Lazaro Archer. If any of Byron Walsh's colleagues knew how paralyzing his paranoia had become lately, he would surely lose his position on the Council. Her father lived for his work, and Melena would not be the one to jeopardize that for him.

"I don't know what you mean," she murmured, hating that she had to deceive Lazaro. "And I really ought to get back inside now."

"You're protecting him. From what?" Lazaro took hold of her by the arms, preventing her from escaping his knowing stare or his questions. His large hands gripped her firmly, strong fingers searing her with the heat of his touch. "What is your father trying to hide?"

"Nothing, I swear—"

He wasn't buying it. Anger flashed in his eyes. Behind his full upper lip, she glimpsed the sharp points of his emerging fangs. "Tell me what he's afraid of, Melena. Tell me now, before I go in there and haul his ass out here to tell me himself."

"It's nothing," she insisted, finding it impossible to break Lazaro's hold or his stare. "It doesn't matter anyway. He had no reason to be afraid tonight. Turati's intentions are good, he means no harm to—"

She wasn't able to finish what she was saying because in that same instant, Lazaro tensed. His head snapped up, eyes searching the dark sky. Some of the blood seemed to drain out of his grim face in that fraction of a second.

"Fuck," he snarled, his grip tightening on Melena's arms. *"Goddamnit, no."*

He lunged into motion, yanking her against him protectively. His arms wrapped around her. He then tumbled her over the railing of the second-level deck along with him...

Just as a screaming object arrowed down from the sky.

It hit the yacht, a direct, dead center strike.

The vessel exploded. On the deafening boom of impact, Melena crashed into the hard waves with Lazaro. Engulfed by the cold, horrified by what she was seeing, all the air left her lungs on an anguished cry. She tried to break away, but Lazaro held her close, refusing to let her swim back up to find her father.

Together she and Lazaro sank deep into the water, falling down, and down, and down...

Far above them, a hellish ball of flame had erupted on the surface. Fiery chunks of debris dropped into the sea everywhere she looked.

There was only ruin left up there.

The yacht and all of its occupants obliterated in an instant.

CHAPTER 3

By Lazaro's guess, they had been in the water roughly two hours before Anzio's cliff-edged shore was finally within sight. Bleeding from shrapnel wounds and battered by the long journey, he was close to exhaustion—even with the preternatural strength and speed of Breed genetics at his command.

Melena was faring far worse. She was limp against him, having fallen unconscious somewhere around the halfway point of their swim. Although she wasn't entirely mortal either, her human metabolism could not cope with the prolonged exposure in the cold seawater.

In that regard, Lazaro was doubly fortunate. Being Breed had given him another advantage. The same one that had allowed him to pull Melena out of the frozen pond twenty-two years ago. His ability to withstand extreme temperatures had given him the strength to search for her under the ice and pull her to safety before she drowned.

He hoped he hadn't lost her tonight.

Lazaro held her close at his side as he paddled the last few hundred yards with his free arm. As soon as his bare feet were able to touch ground, he repositioned Melena in both arms and ran her toward the empty, moonlit beach.

The bulky cliffs that lined the shore loomed just ahead. Several large caves were burrowed into the rock—black, yawning mouths that had once been part of an ancient Roman emperor's crumbled stone villa that was a thousand years in ruin. Lazaro carried Melena inside one of the caves, past a littering of rough rocks and pools of tidal water, to a spot where the sand was soft and dry underfoot.

As he set her down, he couldn't help revisiting the night he'd carried a lifeless little girl into his Darkhaven in Boston. He'd remembered every minute of it, despite the indifference he'd feigned with Melena earlier on the yacht. She had been a seven-year-old child that first, and last, time he saw her before tonight. Back then, she had been as helpless and fragile as a baby bird to his mind. He'd rescued her the same way he would have done for any innocent child.

But now...

Now, Melena Walsh was a grown woman. She was as enticing a woman as he'd ever seen—even more so, with her lovely face and thick red hair, and all of her soft, feminine curves that drew his eye even as he carefully arranged her unresponsive, alarmingly chilled body on the sand.

And as fiercely as he'd wanted to save her life in Boston, he wanted to save her now.

Not the least of his reasons being his need to know what secret she was keeping from him. She'd been on the verge of telling him in the seconds before the yacht was blown to pieces. If that secret had anything to do with the attack tonight, he was going to see that Melena answered for it.

Lazaro felt in his bones that Opus Nostrum was behind the brazen act. Whoever did it knew just who and where to strike. But how did they know? Both parties were meticulously screened by the Order. Lazaro had personally vetted everyone in attendance, right down to the last man on the vessel's crew tonight. He'd approved them all.

Except Melena Walsh.

He gazed at her in the cave's darkness, his Breed eyes seeing her as clearly as if it were midday. She was beautiful, stunningly so. She was poised, intelligent, erudite. And he'd seen her wield her charm without effort over Turati and the rest of the men at the meeting.

Lazaro couldn't deny he'd been equally affected. More than affected, despite his unwillingness to give it reins. A woman like Melena would make a deadly asset, if allied with the wrong people.

He didn't want to think she might be his enemy, intentional or otherwise.

The fact that she'd nearly gotten killed tonight along with everyone else made it impossible to imagine her presence on the yacht could have had anything to do with the catastrophe that followed.

She would give him the truth, but first he had to make sure she stayed alive to do so.

Lazaro scowled at her sodden, bruised condition. Her skirt was shredded, her shoes lost like his somewhere between the yacht and the shore. Her blouse was in tatters, the burgundy colored silk dark with seawater...and blood. Fortunately, most of it was his.

Her hair drooped lifelessly into her face. Lazaro smoothed away some of the drenched red tangles, letting out a low curse when he saw how white her skin was. Her lips were slack, turned an alarming shade of blue. She had contusions on her forehead and chin. Blood from a scalp wound trailed in a bright red rivulet down her temple.

Fuck.

His vision honed in on that thin scarlet ribbon, everything Breed in him responding with keen, inhuman interest. The fact that she was a Breedmate made her blood an exponentially greater temptation to one of his kind.

Melena's blood carried the subtle fragrance of caramel and something sweeter still...dark cherries, Lazaro decided, his lungs soaking in a deeper breath even though it was torment to his senses.

His fangs punched out of his gums, throbbing against the firmly closed line of his lips. His vision sharpened some more, his irises throwing off a rising amber glow that bathed her paleness in warmer light. His own skin prickled with the sudden surge of heat in his veins.

If Melena opened her eyes now, she'd see him fully transformed to the bloodthirsty, otherworldly being he truly was.

If she opened her pretty, bright green eyes, she would know that his desire for her didn't stop at just her blood. He didn't want to think what kind of base creature he was that he could feel lust and hunger for a bruised, bloodied woman who'd just lost her father and nearly her own life too.

The truth was, he'd felt these same urges back on the yacht too. He hadn't wanted to admit it then either.

For all he knew, she could belong to another Breed male. Hell, she could already be blood-bonded to someone, a thought that should've relieved him rather than put a rankle in his brow. It would be pointless to let himself wonder, then or now. He wasn't about to act on either of his unwanted needs. Least of all with a woman bearing the Breedmate mark.

Since Ellie's death, he'd found other women to service him when required. Humans who understood the limits of his interest. More importantly, humans he could feed from without the shackle of a blood bond.

Instead here he was, shackled to the rescue and safekeeping of a woman he didn't fully trust and had no right to desire.

On a rough curse, ignoring the pounding demands of his veins, he stripped off his ragged black combat shirt and hunkered down in the sand alongside Melena. She moaned softly as he wrapped his arms around her. Her raspy sigh as she instinctively settled into his heat was an added torment he sure as hell didn't need.

Jaw clamped tight, pulse hammering with thinly bridled hunger, Lazaro gathered Melena to his naked chest to give her body the warmth it needed.

CHAPTER 4

She woke from an endless, cold nightmare, a scream lodged in her throat. She couldn't force out any sound, and when she dragged in a sudden gasp of air, her lungs felt shredded in her breast.

No, not her lungs.

Her heart.

All at once, the details flew back at her. The explosion. The fire and debris. The cold, black water.

Her father...

No, he couldn't be gone. Her kind and decent father—that strong Breed male—could not have been wiped from existence tonight.

Betrayed, murdered. Just as he'd feared.

Her father was dead.

Some rational part of her knew there was no other possibility, but accepting it hurt too much.

She tried to move and found herself trapped in a cocoon of warmth. Thick arms encircled her. Arms covered in Breed *dermaglpyhs.* The elaborate pattern of skin markings could only belong to one man.

"You're all right, Melena." Lazaro's deep voice rumbled against her ear. "Lie still. You need rest."

She felt him breathing, felt his large body's heat all around her. And God, she needed that heat and reassurance. Every particle of her being wanted to burrow deeper and just close her eyes and sleep. Try to forget...

But her father was out there in the dark. Left behind in the frigid water, while she was safe and protected in the shelter of Lazaro's arms.

She opened her eyes and took in her surroundings as best she could in the lightless space around them. She smelled the sea and wet rock. Felt soft sand beneath her.

"Where are we?" Her words came out like a croak. She swallowed past the salt and soot, attempted to extricate herself from the comfort she couldn't enjoy. She ached all over. Could barely summon strength to move her limbs.

"I brought you to Anzio. We're in a cave at Nero's villa ruins."

She had no idea where that was, only that it had to be a good long distance away from the yacht. "How long have we been here?"

"A few hours."

An irrational panic crushed down on her. "Why did you let me sleep for so long? We should be out there, searching for them!"

His answering curse vibrated against her spine. "Melena—"

"I have to get up. We have to go back for him, Lazaro. For all of them."

On a burst of adrenaline, she managed to slip out of his loose embrace. She sat up, registering dimly that her clothing was damp and ruined, torn open in more places than it was held together.

And Lazaro was only half-dressed. Just his black pants, clinging to him in tatters as well. No shirt on his bare, *glyph*-covered chest and muscled arms. There were numerous bruises on his torso and shoulders. When he sat up too, she noted that a healing gash in his thigh had bled through the material of his pants.

"There's no reason to go back, Melena. There's no chance of survivors."

She didn't want to hear him confirm the terror churning inside her. "No. You're wrong!" She made a clumsy falter to her feet. Lazaro stood with her, catching her by the arms before her sluggish legs could buckle beneath her. She didn't have the strength to break out of his hold again. "You *have* to be wrong. I have to go back and find him. My father—"

Lazaro shook his head. His handsome face was grim with sympathy and something darker. "I'm sorry, Melena. The missile strike was a direct hit. There was nothing left."

Some of her hysteria leaked out of her under his grave stare. She couldn't hold back the grief, the tears. It all flooded out of her on an ugly, shuddering sob. And then her knees did give out, and she sank back down to the sandy floor of the cave.

Lazaro's warm hands were still clasped on her arms as he crouched down in front of her. She couldn't stop the wracking anguish, no more than she could keep herself from pitching forward into his arms, clinging to him as she wept.

He held her there, for how long, she didn't know.

She only knew that after she didn't think she could cry anymore, or hurt any worse, he was still holding her. Still keeping her upright when the rest of her world was crumbling all around her.

"Why?" she murmured into his bulky shoulder. "My God, he knew this. He was so afraid he was going to die soon. Who would do this to him? Why?"

Lazaro gently pulled her away from him, his ebony brows knit in a tight scowl. "Your father feared for his life?" Confusion flashed across his features, then settled into suspicion. "Damn it. Why didn't he tell me this? We spoke several times before the meeting. He had plenty of opportunity to say something if he felt he was in danger in any way."

Melena shook her head, heartsick. "He didn't know who he could trust. He'd been having premonitions, sensing some kind of betrayal. He knew he was going to die soon. He didn't know when, or where the betrayal would come from. He wasn't sure of anyone anymore."

"Not even me," Lazaro replied. "Jesus Christ, why didn't he cancel the damned meeting? He could have made any excuse."

"I told him the same thing. But it was too important to him. And he didn't know what would happen tonight. Neither one of us knew." She thought back on the time she and her father spent with Paolo Turati. She had detected no hidden agendas. No duplicity or harmful intent in any one of them.

Lazaro was studying her in unreadable silence. "You need to tell me the truth, Melena. Beginning with why your father brought you with him tonight."

She gave him a weak nod. There was no more reason for her to keep it from him. Her father was gone. He had nothing left to lose if word of his paranoia became public. Melena no longer needed to protect him. "I've been traveling with him everywhere for months now. He can't bear to go—he *couldn't* bear," she corrected herself quietly, "to go anywhere unless I was there to assure him no one meant him any harm."

"How so?"

"You were right that it wasn't only my translation skills that brought me here tonight. It was my ability to see people's auras. I can tell at a glance if someone's intentions are good or not."

"Your Breedmate talent," Lazaro murmured. There seemed to be a trace of relief in his tone. "So, when you looked at Turati and the others on the yacht tonight?"

She shook her head. "There was nothing to fear from any of them."

"Did your father voice his concerns to any of his colleagues in the GNC?"

"No."

"Anyone outside the Council?"

"No one," she replied, certain of it.

Lazaro grunted, and she could see his gaze go distant as his mind began to churn on the information. She knew he and the Order would not let this attack go unmet, and there was a vengeful part of her that longed to see the guilty tortured to within an inch of their sadistic, cowardly lives.

"Make them pay, Lazaro."

"They will," he answered solemnly. "Whoever had a hand in this, they will be found. There will be justice."

Her tears started up again, but they were quieter now, filled with more rage and resolve than bereavement. She hadn't been prepared for Lazaro's tender touch. She held her breath as he caught her chin on the edge of his fingertips and lifted her gaze to his. He stroked her cheek, his thumb sweeping away the wet trail of her tears.

She could sense his tenderness went deeper than mere concern.

She could see the evidence of that truth in the crackling sparks of amber that were lighting in the deep sapphire of his irises. She could see it in his *dermaglyphs*, which surged with dark colors across every muscled inch of his torso and arms, the intriguing swirls and arcs of the *glyphs'* pattern changing hues before her eyes.

And if all of that weren't enough, she could see his intent in his aura, which formed a smoldering glow around him now, confirming the astonishing fact.

Lazaro Archer wanted her.

No sooner had the thought entered her mind than he leaned down and brushed his lips over hers. Her breath was already shaky and thin, but as his mouth pressed against hers, her lungs dried up on a slow moan. The kiss was tender, careful, no doubt meant to console or soothe her.

It did both, but it also inflamed her.

Heat raced through her at the feel of his mouth on hers. She didn't want to feel it—not now, not when her heart was breaking over the loss of her father and fear still held her in a firm grasp.

But Lazaro's arms were stronger than any of that. His gentling, but arousing, kiss made her melt against him with a desire she could hardly reconcile.

And he broke away much too soon for her liking.

His Breed pupils had narrowed to the thinnest vertical slits. And when he ground out a vivid curse, the tips of his fangs gleamed white and razor-sharp.

"Fuck." He let go of her. "That shouldn't have happened. I apologize."

"Don't," she murmured, her voice a raspy whisper. Desire was singing through her veins—uninvited, maybe, but too powerful to be denied. "I didn't mind, Lazaro. I...liked it."

"Christ, don't say that." He blew out a harsh breath, then drew back from her as though she had scorched him too, and not in the good way he'd ignited her. "You do not want to say that to me, Melena. For the good of both of us."

He got to his feet in abrupt, stony silence. As he stood, she noticed that the gash in his thigh was still bleeding. While he'd been looking after her these past few hours, he'd neglected his own injuries. He seemed oblivious to it, walking over to examine a comm unit that lay on a nearby rock. He shook the device, swearing as water dripped out of it.

"That wound on your leg needs attention, Lazaro." He was Breed, Gen One besides. She knew his body would heal itself, but even a vampire needed help sometimes. "You need to feed soon."

"Is that an invitation, Miss Walsh?" The comm unit clutched in his fist, he snarled down at her, baring his teeth and fangs. God, they were huge. Terrifying, and he damned well knew it. His aura seethed as menacingly as the rest of him. When she shrank back a little where she sat, he gave a dark chuckle. "No, I didn't think so. Smart girl. Do us both a favor and don't concern yourself with what I need."

His anger confused her, almost as much as his unexpected tenderness of a moment ago. And the fact that he wanted to push her away when he was the only reason she was alive right now kind of pissed her off too. She stood up, refusing to be cowed by his bluster.

"Why shouldn't I be concerned? You just saved my life—for the second time, in fact. So, forgive me if that makes me care about you just a little bit."

When he scoffed and took a long stride away from her, she followed after him. When she put her hand on his shoulder, he rounded on her with a hiss. "Just because you're alive, doesn't mean you're safe with me. Don't make the mistake of thinking I'm some kind of hero."

He didn't give her the opportunity to reply. On a furious glower, he pivoted to stalk toward the mouth of the cave. "Stay put. I'm going to see about sending a signal and getting us out of here."

Melena watched him prowl out into the darkness, his kiss still warming her lips and his harsh words ringing in her ears.

Don't make the mistake of thinking I'm some kind of hero.

Didn't he know? She'd been thinking of him that way for most of her life.

CHAPTER 5

One of Lazaro's comrades showed up less than an hour later to retrieve them in a big black SUV. Melena had hardly been introduced to the Breed warrior who drove them—a towering male with a mass of loose golden curls and a dimpled, quicksilver smile that instantly softened his strong, square-cut jaw. She thought he'd said his name was Savage, but in her opinion, he looked more like a fallen angel. If fallen angels wore combat patrol gear and bristled with blades and heavy firearms.

The warrior seemed already aware of who she was and how she'd come to be in his Order commander's company, although he didn't so much as try to ask. It was obvious from Lazaro's menacing silence during the ride to wherever they were heading that conversation with her was neither welcomed nor encouraged.

Where they'd been heading was Rome.

More specifically, the Order's command center in that city.

Melena tried not to gape when she realized that's where Lazaro had brought her. Neither the late-night sight of the illuminated Colosseum nor Pantheon had inspired more than a lingering look as they passed the monuments, but when the SUV approached a gated, secured mansion compound nestled in the heart of the sprawling city, Melena couldn't help but sit up a little straighter in her seat and draw in her breath.

The stately white brick mansion with its elegant, carved marble detailing and old bronze fixtures looked as timeless as the city around it.

But it didn't take long to understand that the structure's antiquity ended at the street. This was a modern fortress, beautiful and sturdy and impenetrable. Inside the massive gates, motion sensors followed the SUV's progress toward an underground parking garage around back.

Once they got out of the vehicle, Lazaro sternly instructed her to follow him. The warrior who drove them lingered behind, leaving her alone to his commander's dubious care.

Lazaro took her not into the living quarters of the compound, but to another wing of the estate that seemed to be where the warriors conducted Order business. She heard two male voices in one of the rooms they passed along the corridor, but her escort didn't slow his pace at all.

Actually, it didn't seem that he could get rid of her fast enough for his liking.

A few minutes later, Melena found herself abandoned to a vaguely medical-seeming room. The small space contained the hard bed she sat upon, and next to it a single chair. Glass-fronted cupboards mounted to the wall opposite her appeared to house bandages and other field dressing supplies.

She wasn't sure how long she sat there, feeling awkward and unwanted in Lazaro's domain. At some point, she dozed, still exhausted from her ordeal and the raw grief that clung to her. A couple of times, she'd glanced toward the window in the infirmary room door and saw one of the warriors stride past. The gorgeous blond who brought her there had smiled through the glass as he walked by. Another Breed male, a mean-looking warrior with a shaved head and a jagged facial scar that made him more suited to the name "Savage" than his friendly comrade, spared her only the briefest, disinterested glance.

But it was a different warrior altogether who finally came into the room. Hulking and immense, he had a mane of shoulder-length brown waves and skin the color of sun-kissed golden sand. Arresting sky-blue eyes scrutinized her from within his ruggedly handsome, exotic face. "Melena. How are you feeling?" As big and imposing as the Breed male was, he somehow moved with the easy, feline grace of a jungle cat as he approached. His voice was rich and deep and cultured. "I am Jehan."

"Nice to meet you," she replied, her manners on automatic pilot.

"Commander Archer sent me to see if your injuries need tending. I must apologize that we're not equipped for treating wounds outside of the Breed, but I can get you medicine for your pain. There are ointments I can prepare to make the contusions heal faster."

Melena shook her head. "Thank you, but no." Compared to the pain of her grief and fear following the attack, and the lingering exhaustion from what she suspected had been hypothermia back in the cave, her assortment of cuts and bruises were a minor issue. "I'm okay."

He eyed her skeptically, folding his *glyph*-covered muscled arms over his chest. "You've endured quite an ordeal. You're certain there is nothing you need?"

Melena gave a vague shrug. She wasn't certain of anything at the moment. Part of her wanted to bolt for the door and find the fastest way out of this nightmare, back home to Maryland. Another part of her just wanted to crawl under the covers of the bed and scream.

"I know this can't be easy," Jehan said, genuine concern in his low voice. "And I am sorry for your loss."

"Thank you." Although she was well-versed in multiple languages, she couldn't quite place his unusual accent. His name was old French, if she wasn't mistaken, but the formal way he carried himself and the way he spoke had her curious. "Where are you from, Jehan?"

"All around," he answered cryptically. "But it's Morocco you hear in my voice. My father's homeland."

That explained it. He had the kind of voice that made her imagine moonlit desert plains and the spicy fragrance of incense and woodsmoke. "Your mother wasn't Moroccan, though?"

"Born and raised in Paris," he confirmed, his sensual mouth curving at the corners. "She and my father met in France. After they were mated, he brought her back with him to our tribe's Darkhaven in his country."

"Your tribe?"

Jehan's dark brows quirked. "A relic of a term." He shrugged it off, but something mysterious flickered in his mesmerizing gaze. "My father's Breed line is very old. Its roots go deep into Moroccan soil. Burrowed in almost as stubbornly as the old man's heels."

"What about you?" Melena asked, genuinely curious.

Jehan inclined his head, almost courtly in its tilt. "To my father's eternal regret, his eldest son's feet refused to stay put. Despite the shackle of obligation he's tried to affix to them."

As they spoke, the door opened again and the blond warrior came in. He grinned, his hazel eyes bouncing off Jehan for a second before fixing on Melena. "I see Prince Jehan is already trying to dazzle you with his long, boring pedigree."

Melena swung a questioning look on the enigmatic warrior. "Prince?"

Jehan grunted under his breath, but didn't deny it. "What are you doing here, Sav? You know damned well Lazaro's orders were that no one enter this room or speak to Melena without his permission."

Melena wanted to be offended by the news of that domineering command, but her two visitors were a welcome distraction from everything else going on. Not the least of which being Lazaro Archer's stinging rejection of her in the cave. A sting that hurt all the worse for his tenderness when he touched her...kissed her.

"We weren't properly introduced," Sav said. "Ettore Roberto Selvaggio."

His dimples deepened along with his heart-stopping smile. His Italian accent seemed to deepen as well, the kind of accent that probably ensured he never wanted for female company.

"Melena Walsh," she replied. "I thought I heard Lazaro call you Savage."

"Lazaro?" he echoed.

She felt color rise to her cheeks. "Your commander. Mr. Archer. Whatever I should call him," she muttered. The man who saved her life, awoke an irresistible desire in her, but made her feel as if he might have rather left her behind in Anzio a few hours ago. "I think he despises me."

The two Breed males now exchanged a look. Jehan was the first to talk. "Don't let him scare you. It's just his way."

"Come on, man," his comrade said. "It goes a bit deeper than that."

Melena glanced at them both. "What do you mean?"

"The way I heard it, Archer's never been the same since he lost his family back in Boston twenty years ago," Sav said. "He blames himself, I imagine."

"Why would he do that?" She couldn't begin to guess how Lazaro could hold himself even the least responsible for what happened to his kin. "The Darkhaven was attacked while he wasn't home. It was razed to the ground."

"Yes," Jehan agreed soberly. "And now imagine you have the

incredible gift of walking into even the most extreme temperature and emerging wholly unscathed. But you're not there when the attack on your own loved ones takes place."

"You have the ability to save some of them—maybe all of them," Sav added. "Instead, you lose them all in one fell swoop."

Melena couldn't speak. She wasn't even sure she was breathing as the weight of what she'd just heard settled on her.

She hadn't known about Lazaro's Breed gift. Now it made sense, of course. His ability to search for her for so long in the frozen pond all those years ago. The fact that he'd swum across nearly half of the Tyrrhenian Sea to save her tonight, impervious to the cold, unlike her.

He'd saved her twice, but had been unable to save the ones he loved. Including his blood-bonded Breedmate.

"He will not be pleased if he knew we told you," Jehan warned grimly.

Sav gave a nod. "Probably want to stake both of us out in the sun. Or worse." He glanced at Melena. "So, not a word, yeah?"

"Okay," she murmured woodenly. But oh, God, her heart ached for Lazaro now.

"Enough about him," Sav said, grinning as if he wanted to lighten the grave mood. "You asked about me, if I recall. So, to answer your question, yes. Most people who know me call me Savage."

She took his bait, needing to put her sympathy for Lazaro on a higher shelf. He wouldn't want it anyway. "Why do they call you that? You seem nice enough to me. Are you usually mean or something?"

"Or something," he said, the glint in his eye and the playful, seductive hue of his aura providing all the correction she needed.

Jehan snorted. "He's a legend in his own mind. Pay no attention to him."

Sav barked a laugh. "Envy isn't a good look for you, Highness."

"And you may kiss my royal ass, peasant."

Melena found herself smiling with them. She took in their banter and warm, welcoming faces, not realizing until then how much she needed to feel she was among friends.

She needed her family, which was now reduced to just one other person. Her Breed brother, Derek, had been living in Paris for the past year, bouncing between England and France on one business venture or another.

Melena hadn't seen him since he left, hadn't even spoken to him for several long weeks. She couldn't imagine the anguish it would cause him to learn their father had been killed. Before he heard it anywhere else, she wanted to be the one to break the news to him. She wanted to spare him the unnecessary grief of thinking she had died along with everyone else tonight.

"Do you think it would be possible for me to try to reach my brother somehow?" she asked the two warriors. "He's traveling and I need to let him know—"

"Is there a reason half my team is not where I expect them to be?" Lazaro's deep, furious growl interrupted the conversation without warning. He stood in the open doorway, looking every bit as ferocious as a Gen One Breed male could. His sapphire eyes were thunderously dark, except for the flashes of amber outrage sparking in their depths. "Out. Both of you. Now."

Sav and Jehan departed on command.

Leaving Melena to face Lazaro's rage by herself.

She waited for him to lay into her too, but he didn't. He merely stared at her, a tendon ticking hard in his jaw. His aura was as stormy as his glower, back to the gunmetal haze that she found so difficult to read.

His animosity seemed clear enough. He didn't want her in his command center any more than he'd wanted her in his presence on the yacht or at the cave.

And she wanted to be somewhere safe now, even if that meant returning to her father's empty Darkhaven in the States. "I don't want to be here," she murmured. "I need to get in touch with my brother Derek, and I need to go home."

"Out of the question." His answer was firm, flat. Unyielding. "I've spoken to Lucan Thorne. Before you go anywhere else, he wants me to bring you to the Order's headquarters in Washington, D.C. He'll talk with you there, debrief you."

"I already told you everything I know. What more can I tell him?"

Lazaro didn't answer. "We leave tomorrow evening, Melena." He started to go, then pivoted back to her. "In the meantime, I won't have my team distracted by the fact we have a Breedmate underfoot. I'll make a place for you in the villa. You'll stay there until we depart for D.C."

CHAPTER 6

Melena had been moved out of the command center's infirmary to the living quarters of the mansion hours ago. Lazaro's team had gone back to their business as instructed. The morning passed with discussions of Order objectives and priorities. Chief among those priorities being to ensure that reports of the tragic, "accidental" explosion on board Paolo Turati's yacht didn't brush up against the truth that it was, in fact, a stealth missile attack.

And while no one yet had stepped forward to publicly claim responsibility, there wasn't a shred of doubt among the Order's entire organization that the killings were surely instigated by Opus Nostrum.

Halfway through the afternoon in Rome, the warriors were now dispersed to prepare for their patrols that coming evening, everyone focused on task and ready to carry out their missions.

And yet the female under their roof remained a distraction.

For Lazaro, that is.

He made his way through the corridors in a foul mood. He didn't want to think about her. He didn't want to think about his irritation over finding Sav and Jehan chatting her up earlier, making her smile in spite of everything she'd been through. He didn't want to think about the anger that had shot through him in that moment—the blast of pure male possessiveness that he had no right to feel.

And he sure as hell did not want to give another moment's thought to the kiss he stole from Melena back in the Anzio cave. He'd had no right to take that liberty either. But was the kiss truly stolen if she didn't seem to mind that he did it?

She'd told him she enjoyed it, for fuck's sake.

His blood rushed a bit faster, disturbingly hotter, at just the thought. And a lot of that blood was making a swift run south. It pounded through his veins like liquid fire, settling in his groin when he recalled how soft and inviting her mouth had been under his.

Melena had more than liked his kiss. She'd welcomed it. Wanted more.

Wanted him.

Christ, he couldn't get away from her fast enough after that kiss. He still couldn't put enough distance between them for his peace of mind. How he was going to manage the long hours between now and their departure for D.C. tomorrow evening, he had no damned idea.

More than likely, he'd be spending that stretch of time with a constant hard-on and a fevered hunger that bordered on madness. He needed to exorcise that hunger, and soon. He was on his way to the weapons room to sweat out some of his aggression with his blades and pistols when one of his men met him in the corridor.

Trygg had been the only one of the unit with sense enough to avoid their pretty, uninvited guest. The bald, menacing looking Breed male carried a long, cream-colored box in his arms. "Package you ordered this morning just arrived."

Lazaro grunted as he took the box from the most intimidating member of his team.

"You want me to deliver it to her?" Trygg suggested.

"No." The reply came out too quickly, too forcefully, but there it was. Melena had been through enough of a scare already; she didn't need a brutal killer like Trygg showing up at her door, even if he did it with an unlikely gift in his hands.

Besides, Lazaro had placed the order for her as something more than just a courtesy. He supposed he'd been hoping it would also serve as some kind of apology. He'd been a warrior for twenty years, but he liked to think there was still some sense of decency in him. Given the way he'd treated Melena so far, she might be hard-pressed to agree.

"I'll bring it myself," he told Trygg. The vampire merely stared, his shrewd eyes unblinking, far too knowing. Lazaro tucked the long box under his arm. "There is something you can do. Locate Derek Walsh. Melena said her brother's been spending his time between Paris and the United Kingdom. When you've got a bead on him, let me know."

Trygg gave a slight nod. "Done."

Lazaro stalked through the command center to the attached, four-story residential quarters. The Roman villa had ten bedrooms, but Melena had been placed in the largest suite in the estate. It was also the one place where he knew neither of her newest admirers would be tempted to seek her out.

Paused outside the closed door of his private quarters on the top floor, Lazaro noted she'd left the tray of food he'd delivered hours earlier untouched. It didn't appear she'd even come out to look at it.

He listened for movement on the other side. Hearing nothing, he rapped his knuckles on the carved wooden door. He waited, feeling both awkward and annoyed.

When he knocked again and got no response, he started to get concerned.

He opened the door and peered inside. "Melena?"

His suite spanned the entirety of the villa's fourth floor. He didn't see her anywhere, not even in the spacious bedroom. He dropped the box on the end of the king-sized bed, then noticed the door to the en suite bath was cracked open.

Through the thin wedge, he saw her slip into a terry robe, apparently having just stepped out of the tub. He caught an unexpected glimpse of her bare skin—delectable curves, lovely breasts peaked with dusky peach nipples...the hint of dark curls at the V of her creamy thighs.

Ah, damn, she was gorgeous.

Everything male in him responded as swiftly—and as obviously—as everything Breed in him. His pulse jackhammered, the drum filling his ears with a rush of hot need. The tips of his fangs dug into his tongue, and as he stared at her, his gaze grew heated as his pupils thinned with his hunger and his cock thickened with desire.

Until he spotted the bruises that still lingered on her. His own wounds had healed, thanks to his Gen One metabolism, but Melena still carried numerous contusions on her ribs and delicate belly.

"Fuck." Lazaro's growled reaction made her look up sharply. Too late to pivot around and leave. Too late to pretend he hadn't just crept into the room and stood there ogling her in open lust. Or to hope she wouldn't notice how powerfully she affected him.

Her expression was guarded, wary. She opened the door wider, but he noticed how tightly she now gripped the edges of the robe at her chest. When Lazaro took a step toward her, she slipped out of the bathroom and into the larger space of the bedroom.

With some effort, he curbed the presence of his fangs. His vision was still awash in amber, but he could feel his pupils resuming a less feral state. And as for the state of his arousal, that was a more difficult thing to hide, let alone suppress. But while his body was still thrumming with awareness—and want—of her, his primary interest in that moment was Melena's well being.

"Jehan was supposed to look after your injuries when you arrived," he muttered angrily. "He's skilled with ointments and herbs. He should've given you something to help you heal."

"I told Jehan I was fine. And I am...or at least, I can try to be, once you and the Order allow me to go home."

Lazaro ignored the pointed complaint, even if it had merit. "I see you didn't eat anything either."

"What do you care?" she tossed back, her fine auburn brows pinched together.

"I care, Melena. For now, you're under my watch. It's my responsibility to ensure that you're comfortable and healthy. That you're fed and clothed." He gestured toward the boutique box on the bed. "I arranged for some things to be sent here for you from one of the local shops."

She cast a sidelong glance toward his gift, then back toward the bathroom where her ruined skirt and blouse lay in rags on the tile floor. Warily, she drifted over to the bed and lifted the lid off the box. She glanced inside, then one by one, pulled out the skirt and pants, then the blouse and sweater he selected for her.

"I didn't know what you'd prefer," he murmured.

She lifted the charcoal gray, fine-gauge sweater first, then the pair of black slacks. The understated classics of the collection, which didn't surprise him. She glanced at the two pairs of shoes he'd purchased as well, taking out the elegant Italian flats. "These are all in my sizes. Perfectly in my sizes." She slanted him a guarded look. "I wouldn't think you'd paid attention long enough to notice."

"I noticed." Lazaro slowly approached her near the bed. "I should be focused on a thousand other things right now. Instead, here I am. Noticing everything about you, Melena."

If she had flinched at all when he came to stand beside her, Lazaro would have somehow found the strength of will to leave her in peace.

If she had resisted even a little when he lifted her chin on his fingertips and drew her gaze up to his—if she had looked into his transformed Breed eyes with anything close to fear or uncertainty—he would have forced himself to let go of her and refrain from ever touching her again.

But Melena did none of those things.

And when he slowly lowered his mouth to hers, this time, not even he or his iron will could pretend the desire that arced between them was anything either of them would be able to deny.

He kissed her, hard and hungry. Any illusions he might have had for taking things slowly with her, or giving her a chance to get away before he pounced, were all but obliterated once their lips and tongues had come together.

A fresh surge of molten need scorched through his veins, and all at once it didn't matter to him that getting involved with Melena Walsh was the last thing he needed to be doing.

He wanted her.

She wanted him—he knew that even in the cave.

And the fact was, he'd already let himself get involved, whether or not they allowed this undeniable, if untimely, desire for each other to flare any further out of control.

Melena awakened a need in him that he hadn't felt in a long time. A new kind of need, something white-hot and irresistible. She had done in less than a day what no other woman before her had managed to do in two decades.

She made him feel alive again.

Lazaro growled and took her mouth in a deeper kiss. She moaned, reaching up to burrow her fingers into the short hair at his nape. Her soft curves felt like heaven against him, even through the barrier of their clothing. Her mouth tasted warm and sweet. Her body arched into his, pliant, consenting.

Welcoming.

Hot with need.

He smoothed his hand down her throat, breaking their kiss as his thumb grazed over the Breedmate mark nestled in the hollow between her collarbones. He lifted his head to look at it—to remind himself of what she was and why he could not allow himself anything more than this desire they shared.

"I should ask you if there is someone else," he uttered thickly. He dragged his smoldering gaze back up to hers. "I should ask, but right now I don't think I'll give a damn if you say there is."

"No." She gave a faint shake of her head, her breast rising and falling with each rapid pant of her breath. "There's no one. Not for more than a year. And even then, I never wanted anyone like this..."

He registered that sweet confession with a growl that vibrated deep in his chest.

He kissed her again, gathering her face in his hands while his mouth moved intensely, hungrily, over hers. Being Gen One, his appetites were stronger than most. With Melena all but undressed and willing in his arms, those appetites were on the verge of owning him. It was only the dim knowledge of her lingering injuries that kept him in check.

And she wasn't helping in that regard.

Meeting each thrust of his tongue, parting her lips to take him deeper, she stoked his arousal even further. Her body pressed against his, heat igniting everywhere they touched. He couldn't resist the loosened opening of her robe. His hand slipped inside to feel the softness of her skin. Her pulse banged against his fingertips, strong and certain. Erotic and primal.

Melena groaned in pleasure. Her voice rasped sensually against his mouth. "I like the way you kiss me, Lazaro. I like the way you touch me."

Holy hell. Her words made fire erupt in his already molten blood.

With fangs filling his mouth and his cock gone hard as granite behind the zipper of his pants, Lazaro moved his hand to cup the buoyant underside of her breast. A hot, pent-up sigh gusted out of her as he caressed her bare skin beneath the slackened robe. Her nipple was pebbled and erect, a temptation he lightly tweaked, then rolled between his fingers. Melena's grasp at the back of his neck tightened, her fingers curling into his hair as a moan leaked through her parted lips.

Every taut fiber of his being ached with the need to put his mouth on her silken skin, to feel all of her. Taste all of her.

His hands obeyed that need, reaching up to gently ease the robe off Melena's shoulders. It slipped down her arms, baring her to the waist. She was so lovely. Porcelain skin dusted with a smattering of sweet, peachy freckles and lush, feminine curves that begged to be savored.

The purple contusions and mending cuts on her torso and abdomen drew his eye just as intensely. Rage for whoever did it swirled through him like a fierce tempest. When he thought of how close she'd come to being lost in the explosion along with everyone else, that rage turned murderous and black.

But tenderly, he let his fingers light on a couple of her worst bruises. She flinched a little and some of his fury snarled out of him. "It hurts?"

"Only a bit." When he drew his hand away, she caught it, placed his palm atop her bare breast. "I don't want you to stop touching me."

His cock jerked in response, more than eager for him to oblige her. He filled his hand with her breast, then took her mouth in another deep kiss.

But feeling her, kissing her, only made him ache to explore some more.

His entire Gen One being throbbed with the need to claim, to possess.

He drew the robe off her completely. Let it fall in a pool at her feet. For one indulgent moment, he soaked in the sight of her through his amber-drenched, fevered eyes.

Then he lifted her off her feet and spread her out beneath him on his bed.

CHAPTER 7

Melena sank down onto the soft mattress and watched, wide-eyed and trembling, as Lazaro prowled up the length of her naked body.

It wasn't fear that gripped her. Nothing even close to fear.

Her every nerve ending had come alive—gone dizzyingly electric—under his careful, caressing touch and the sensual promise of his lips and tongue as he'd tenderly explored her skin.

Now, lying exposed to him completely on the bed while he remained clothed, she wasn't uncomfortable in the least. And whether that made her a wanton harlot or a daring fool, she didn't know. Nor did she care in that moment.

She wasn't nervous or uncertain about anything she was doing with this man.

She wanted more.

He sent the boutique box to the floor with a sweep of his strong arm, making more room for them. She jumped, breath catching at the animalistic power that poured off Lazaro in palpable waves. She'd never felt so much energy and heat focused on her.

In her handful of failed relationships, no other man—Breed or human—had stirred her passion so easily, so masterfully. *Difficult to please*, more than one lover had called her. And they'd been right. None of them had taken her breath away. None of them had been able to hold her interest, in or out of bed, for more than a few months.

Then again, they weren't Lazaro Archer.

She'd never been in the presence of a Gen One male with carnal hunger in his eyes.

And Lazaro's hunger was intense.

His eyes were twin coals, locked on her as he positioned himself above her, braced on his strong fists on either side of her head. His fangs gleamed razor-sharp, enormous and fully extended.

And while his *dermaglyphs* were obscured by his black shirt and combat pants, she knew they had to be vivid with deep colors—not unlike the pulsating, blood-red aura that radiated from him as his consuming gaze drank in her nakedness from forehead to ankle.

He spread her legs with his thigh, nudging her open to him. As he covered her, the rigid length of his arousal ground against her hip. Her pulse sped up, tripping as he gave her a meaningful thrust of his pelvis, those smoldering amber irises burning her up.

He took her mouth in a slow but demanding kiss. He took her lip between his teeth, sucked her tongue deep into his mouth. Kissed her until she was panting and writhing beneath him, grasping at him with needy hands. "Now, I'm going to taste you, Melena," he murmured against her slack mouth. "Every last creamy, delectable inch of you."

And then, heaven help her, he proceeded to do just that.

He started with a maddening sweep of his tongue just below her ear. She shivered, even though her blood was on fire for the heat of his lips and the gentle, but unmistakable, rasp of his fangs as he dragged his mouth down to the curve where her neck and shoulder met. He suckled and nipped, working his way to her breasts. Kneading them in strong hands, tonguing the tight buds at their peaks, he didn't move on until she was moaning with pleasure and aching for more.

Her back arched into him as he began a slow and steady exploration of her rib cage and abdomen. He took care around her bruises, astonishing tenderness from a Breed male who had lived ten lifetimes and counting, whose own otherworldly body was virtually indestructible. Yet he navigated her minor wounds as though he were handling glass.

That moved her deeply, even more than his passion had overwhelmed her.

Melena reached down, cradling his dark head in her hands while his kiss traveled lower.

Across her stomach, onto each hip bone, over the quivering tops of her thighs. She trembled as his mouth blazed a slow path down the entire length of her right leg and ankle, then returned up her left calf, to her knee and the tingling flesh of her inner thigh.

If he wanted to make her wet and vibrating with the need to have him inside her, Lazaro could have stopped right after their lips had met for the first time here in his bedroom.

But it was patently clear from the wicked look he shot up the length of her nude body that he was only getting started.

His head lowered between her spread legs. When the heat of his breath rushed out against her sex, she shuddered. When his lips touched down and his hot, silky tongue cleaved into her slit, she let out a strangled cry.

Fingers gripping the coverlet on each side of her, she held on for dear life as Lazaro licked and kissed and fucked her senseless with his ruthlessly skilled mouth.

She came in mere moments, pleasure shooting through her in wave after glorious wave. She didn't know if she sighed or screamed or both. She only knew that while her body was still floating in a million tiny shards of bliss, Lazaro started climbing back up to her on the bed.

He stroked her face, watching her—smirking in obvious satisfaction, for God's sake.

Then his grin was gone as quickly as it had arrived, and he covered her mouth with his, kissing her hard and deep and wild.

He drew back on a curse, his breath sawing in and out of his lungs. He stripped off his clothing and boots in mere seconds. Then he pivoted back to her, gloriously naked. He found his place between her thighs again and held himself there, unmoving, watching her. Considering her in some way.

His big body threw off waves of heat and power. The *glyphs* that traced his bulky shoulders and muscular arms continued onto the contours of his chest and rippled abdomen. They pulsed vividly on his skin, alive and flooded with color.

Those Gen One skin markings trekked farther south as well. The thick, long shaft of his cock was circled with *glyphs*, their hues flushing even deeper as Melena admired him with unabashed approval.

God, he was immense. Magnificently so.

And sexy as hell.

She rose up to touch his face, cupping his stern jaw in her palm when a scowl thundered across his expression. "It's been a while for me too," he said, then gave a small shake of his head. "I'm not sure I can be as gentle as I'd like for you. The last thing I want to do is hurt you."

Melena saw the torment in his aura, even if his body was being driven by a stronger need now. He didn't want to let her in, but he couldn't shut her out either.

He cared, even though he wanted to deny it.

She thought back to what he said to her in the cave. That just because he'd helped her stay alive, didn't mean she was safe with him.

Melena had never felt more protected or secure with anyone in her life.

And she'd never known anything so raw and consuming—so impossible to deny—as how it felt being with Lazaro.

She wrapped her hand around his nape and pulled him down in a deep, scorching kiss. With her other hand, she sought out his cock and grasped it firmly, pumping his length in sure, steady strokes. She didn't let go of his mouth or his penis for a good long moment. When she did, she gave him a smile against his parted lips and the fangs that now filled his mouth even more than before. "See?" she told him. "I'm not going to break."

He uttered a low, vicious curse that sounded to be half relief and half anguish.

Then he positioned himself at her body's entrance and drove home, deep and slow and long, all the way to the hilt.

He filled her so completely she could hardly summon her breath. Then he started to pivot in and out, rolling his hips in controlled, tantalizing swivels that dragged a curse out of her too. Sweet pressure spiraled within her core as he pushed her toward another climax. He didn't go gently, instead driving into her so far and fully, it was all she could do to hold on to him and let her body shatter in his arms.

Lazaro watched her as she came, his eyes locked on hers. She couldn't look away. The power of the connection was too intense. He felt it too—he had to have felt it.

As his own release built, then broke on a coarse shout, he kept his gaze fastened on hers too. It was so intense, so startlingly real, this thing coming to life between them.

If anything had the power to terrify her, it was this.

The feeling that she had already given herself to this man. A man who had pretended he barely remembered her when he first saw her on Turati's yacht.

A man who warned her not to get close to him, all but threatened that he would only hurt her.

And here she was, giving him her body.

Staring into his eyes as she surrendered the most intimate part of herself to him, and imagining that she could so easily let herself fall. That maybe she already had. Maybe the men in her past had been right. They would never have been good enough for her.

Because all along, what she wanted them to be was someone like Lazaro Archer. Brave. Loyal. And yes, heroic, even if he refused to accept that truth.

She didn't need him to be perfect, because even through the haze of affection and searing desire, she knew he would never be perfect. He didn't need to be. Not for her to want him like she did. Not for her to feel so right, so safe and contented in his arms.

Oh, God...could she be falling so fast?

Did she dare?

Melena finally broke his gaze then, turning her head away from him to the side, bewildered by her epiphany.

Her heart was pounding hard, making her carotid tick palpably in the side of her neck.

She didn't have to look back to him to know that Lazaro's amber eyes had drifted to that fluttering vein. She felt the heat of his stare. Then she heard a dangerously low growl curl up from the back of his throat.

She went very still, terrified he might bite her.

Terrified he wouldn't.

"Lazaro?" she whispered, uncertain what she was about to ask him to do.

She slowly pivoted her head back to look at him and saw torment in his handsome, otherworldly face. And fury. He drew back from her on a hiss.

His expression was wild looking, intense...and his smoldering aura told her he was balanced on the razor's edge of a rigidly held, but tenuous, control.

* * * *

What the fuck was he doing?

Lazaro came to his senses as if physically struck. He was still buried inside Melena's hot, wet heat, his pulse still charged and racing. His cock was still hard, still greedy, even after the climax that had ripped through him with brutal ferocity.

And he'd been reckless enough to let his fevered gaze drift to the vein that throbbed so enticingly in the side of her vulnerable throat.

Christ.

He'd nearly lost control—something he never allowed to happen. Not once in twenty years had he even been tempted. His guard was always up, his will impenetrable.

Even then, he'd made a habit of avoiding women like Melena, females with the Breedmate mark. To drink from one of her kind would tie him to her singularly, irrevocably. He would always crave her. He would always feel her in his blood, in the root of his soul...unless death severed the bond, as it did when he lost Ellie.

Why the thought didn't freeze his thirst or shrivel his desire for Melena, he didn't want to know. And he sure as hell wasn't going to sit there pondering that fact as she gaped at him in mute terror.

"Damn it." He pulled out of her on a roar. As difficult as it was to deny himself the feel of her silken grip on his shaft—as much as he wanted to have her now, still, again and again—he needed the separation more.

What he needed was to put as much distance as possible between her soft, inviting body and the blood hunger that was suddenly twisting him in vicious knots.

He got off the bed to collect his clothes.

"What are you doing?" Melena asked from behind him. When he began to dress, he heard her slide across the sheets. "Talk to me, please."

He couldn't form words, let alone push them out of his mouth. He still wanted her too much, and he feared that if he let himself cave to that need now, he might not be able to rein it back in. He zipped up his pants, ignoring the persistent bulge of his uncooperative arousal. His hands moved hastily, aggressively, as he donned his shirt, then bent to retrieve his boots.

He had plenty of human females he could call upon to slake his needs. A pity he didn't think to do that before he made the mistake of putting himself alone in the company of a Breedmate as tempting as Melena.

And what a feeble fucking rationalization that was.

Nothing would satisfy him more than to dismiss his near-mistake as something that might have occurred with any female sporting the teardrop-and-crescent-moon birthmark. Far more troubling to realize that it was *this* woman who tempted him like no other.

Melena Walsh would continue to tempt him for as long as she remained in his care, under his dubious protection.

He didn't know how a woman who'd come into his life so unexpectedly—not to mention temporarily—was making him hungry for things that would come with a very permanent price.

"You're just going to walk away then?" She stood beside the bed, watching him prepare to make his escape. For a long moment, she said nothing more, her silence ripe with hurt and confusion, almost too much for him to bear. "You're not even going to acknowledge what almost happened just now?"

That he was only an instant away from taking her vein between his teeth? Or that every particle of his being was so ravenous for a taste of her Breedmate blood, there was a chance he might still act on the powerful impulse?

The memory of her blood scent hadn't left him since he'd first caught a trace of it back in the cave. He knew what she would taste like: caramel and dark, ripe cherries. On top of the other decadent sweetness that still lingered on his tongue from his carnal exploration of her body.

Lazaro cursed roundly, a nasty profanity spoken in a language only the eldest of the Breed like him would comprehend.

"No, Melena, I'm not going to acknowledge it." He caught her gaze, knowing how cold his own must look through her eyes. Yet even as he glowered, furious with his own lack of control, his traitorous body had lost none of its interest in her. "And yes, I am going to walk away, and what happened here will not happen again."

She stared at him. "I think we both know better than that. You still want me, Lazaro. I don't need to read your aura to see that."

"This was a mistake," he snarled through teeth and fangs. "I damned well won't complicate it any more by letting it become something both of us will regret forever."

He turned and walked out the door.

Before his shaky resolve could break completely.

CHAPTER 8

True to his word, he didn't return.

She had showered and dressed, even eaten a fresh meal that Jehan had brought up to her sometime after Lazaro had gone. That was hours ago, according to the old grandfather clock in the hallway. It was well into the evening before she'd finally given up waiting, wondering...God, pitifully hoping, that he would come back and at least talk to her after the incredible passion they'd shared.

Her psychic gift prevented her from sulking over doubts about Lazaro's intentions. It wasn't that he didn't want her tonight. He'd left because he wanted her too much.

But that didn't change the fact that he was quite obviously avoiding her.

She'd since begun pacing the residential suites in the clothing he bought for her, feeling like a prisoner in a beautiful, unlocked cage. Although she had the entire fourth floor to explore, decency kept her from snooping too avidly through Lazaro's home. Not that she'd find anything very personal in his quarters, she'd realized fairly quickly.

Each room was consummately appointed with elegant furnishings and a variety of fine things. Sophisticated pieces, tasteful antiques, a wealth of heirloom Oriental rugs—the kind of things she might expect someone who'd lived as long as him would appreciate.

But there was nothing personal in Lazaro's home. Nothing modern.

There were no photographs on the bureaus or sofa tables or walls. No mementoes scattered about in any of the meticulously kept rooms. There was nothing to remind him of the past century, let alone the past twenty years.

He lived here in a carefully curated, elegant isolation.

Her conversation with Jehan and Savage came back to her now. The fact that Lazaro had never fully gotten over the deaths of his mate and family. That he blamed himself for not being able to save them. And so he'd joined the Order and exiled himself to this place.

If he hadn't found room in his heart for anything or anyone in the past two decades, how could she hope he might let her in after just a couple of days?

She had half a mind to confront him about the way he was living his life. Maybe it wasn't her place to call him on it. Maybe she'd be better off leaving well enough alone and simply wait to return home to the States, where she had her own life to manage.

A life that no longer included her father, she thought, swamped with a fresh wave of grief to think that Lazaro's entry into her life came at the loss of someone else she loved. But even before losing her father last night, even before the loss of her dear mother years before, Melena realized that her life was missing something vital.

She had a life that, if she were truly being honest with herself, wasn't so much different from the cage Lazaro had built around himself here in Rome.

She had a nice apartment of her own at her father's Darkhaven in Baltimore. She had friends. She had lovers when she wanted them. She had colleagues at her father's office and in the GNC. She had her Breed brother, Derek. She had a full life and plenty of companionship whenever she needed it.

And yet, deep down, she was so lonely.

She saw that same emptiness in Lazaro. Maybe he saw it in her too. Maybe that's why when their gazes had locked in the midst of their release tonight, the connection had felt so real. So nakedly, startlingly real.

How could he expect her to ignore that as if it hadn't happened? She couldn't.

And she wouldn't, not without a fight.

Whatever was building so swiftly—powerfully—between them had a chance of growing into something extraordinary. She felt that with a certainty in her bones, in her blood. And she knew she wasn't alone in that feeling.

So, like it or not, Lazaro Archer was simply going to have to talk to her. He might be accustomed to blustering and bossing his way around everyone else in his life, but she wouldn't stand for it.

Steeling herself for a battle she wasn't sure she could win, Melena left the suite on the fourth floor and headed downstairs to the mansion's main level. It was quiet down there, so she continued on, toward the connected command center of the estate.

She didn't get far.

From out of nowhere, a massive wall of muscle materialized to block her path.

It wasn't Lazaro. Not Savage or Jehan either.

She looked up and found herself gaping into the cold, hard face of the one warrior she hadn't yet met. His shaved head and jagged scar made him look even more lethal than the dark stare he held her in now.

He didn't speak. Didn't seem inclined to make even the remotest effort to put her at ease.

Melena lifted her chin in defiance. "I'm looking for Lazaro."

"He's not here." God, that voice was coarse gravel. "And you shouldn't be down here either, female."

As he spoke, Savage and Jehan came out of a nearby chamber in the corridor. Sav hissed. "Trygg, for fuck's sake. Go easy on her. Save the venom for tonight's patrol."

When the scarred vampire didn't so much as twitch in acknowledgment, Jehan stepped forward, placing himself between Melena and the warrior who bristled with a feral darkness.

Jehan squared off against his comrade, gently guiding Melena behind him. "I'm only going to say it once. Back. The. Fuck. Down."

The one called Trygg had an aura that verged on feral. The menacing haze sent a shiver up Melena's spine. She saw pain there too, buried deep, but it was a dangerous pain, as sharp as razorblades.

For a long moment, Trygg didn't move. Neither did Jehan. It wasn't clear which warrior would be the first to spill the other's blood, but there was no mistaking that cool, calm, and cultured Jehan was every bit as lethal as his barely leashed brother-in-arms.

Perhaps more so. Jehan's aura burned with a steady, unyielding resolve. He would be unstoppable in all things he set out to do. Honorable to his last breath.

Trygg seemed to know this about his teammate. He seemed to respect it. With a slow exhale, the terrifying Breed male let his shoulders relax a degree. His jaw pulsed, but he did as his comrades demanded, easing back on his heels with a quiet rumble in his throat.

Then he turned and walked away, stalking down the far length of the corridor.

"You okay?" Sav asked.

Melena nodded. "Is his problem just me, or does he despise all women?"

Sav gave her a sardonic look. "It's not just you. And it's a long, ugly story. If you have a week or five to spare, maybe I'd tell you."

No, she didn't have that kind of time. And the fact that tomorrow Lazaro would be taking her back to the States put a pang of regret in her breast. She wanted to stay a bit longer with Savage and Jehan.

She wanted to get to know them: Savage and his easy charm and gorgeous smile. Jehan, with his intriguing past and enigmatic personality. She wanted to know what obligation awaited him in Morocco, and why was he trying to outrun it. Against her own sense of logic or self-preservation, Melena also wanted to stay long enough to understand what had inspired Trygg's terrifying animosity toward women.

And Lazaro...

Would there ever be enough time in this life to unravel all of his torment and secrets and dark, hidden thoughts? Would he even allow her that, if by some miracle they did have more time? All those rooms of his upstairs, missing memories...she wanted to help him fill them back up again.

She wanted to be the one to save him this time.

"Come on," Sav said. "You really shouldn't be down here in the operations compound. Lazaro will have our balls if—"

The warrior's words cut short as a gust of cold, dark air seemed to blow in from the far end of the corridor. He was there. Melena waited to hear Lazaro growl his fury at the men, or demand to know what she was doing back in the Order's domain after he prohibited her from distracting his team.

But he didn't growl or demand anything. He just stared at her in silence, his sapphire gaze trained on her alone.

Intense. Penetrating. Focused on her with searingly sensual regard.

She trembled a little under that potent gaze, not from anything resembling fear. Seeing him there, looking at her as though no one and nothing else existed but the two of them, it was all she could do to keep from launching herself at him from down the corridor and flying into his arms.

But Melena held back. And now she noticed that there was something different about him tonight. Something different in the relaxed state of his *glyphs*, in his schooled expression.

"You were gone for a long time," she murmured. And then she did start to approach him, though not with the jubilation she felt just a moment ago. This was something heavier. Something that stung as the realization began to dawn on her. "You've fed. You went out to find a blood Host. A woman?"

He didn't deny it.

Damn him, he just stood there, watching impassively as she slowed to a stop in front of him. The array of skin markings on his arms under his rolled-back sleeves were calm, satiated. "Did you fuck her too, Lazaro?"

Behind her, Melena heard Jehan quietly clear his throat. There was brief movement in the corridor at her back, followed by the polite closing of a door as the two warriors made a hasty exit.

"Did you?" she repeated, now that it was just she and Lazaro in the passageway.

He swore, roundly, fiercely under his breath. "Don't be ridiculous."

She scoffed. "You know what's ridiculous? Sitting around waiting for you to return. Hoping that I didn't somehow push you away tonight. But how can I push you away when I never had you in the first place?"

She swept past him on a wounded, furious cry. She didn't know if he followed. In that moment, she didn't care.

But he had followed her. She had only made it to the main floor of the mansion's residential wing when Lazaro halted her by grasping her hand. "Melena—"

"You know what else is ridiculous?" she fumed at him. "Hoping you'd come back and tell me that you realize there's something serious going on between us too." She glanced away, giving a shake of her head. "It's ridiculous to expect that a man who's been living his life like a ghost for twenty years could ever admit that he actually feels something again."

Wrenching out of his light hold, she ran for the stairs. She heard him stalking up behind her, but he didn't stop her now. Her breath was heaving by the time she found herself in the center of Lazaro's palatial living room suite.

"I don't want another blood bond, Melena. I won't risk it." His deep voice sounded brittle at her back. "So, whatever you think is happening here between us, it has no future."

"Whatever I think?" She turned to face him. It stung that he wanted to diminish what they'd shared, but she didn't believe him. She could see that he cared. But he was also determined to push her away. He truly intended to spend the rest of his life alone, punishing himself for something he couldn't control. "I know about your family, Lazaro. I know you blame yourself for not being there to save Ellie and the rest of your Darkhaven."

He glared at her furiously, as if she had violated some boundary simply in speaking of the incident. "They trusted me to keep them safe. I failed them."

"You weren't there. That's all. And that's a completely different thing."

"No, not to me. And if you know so much about it, then you should also understand why I left to find a blood Host tonight. After making love with you, if I'd stayed..." He exhaled sharply. "The ifs don't matter. I don't want another Breedmate shackled to me and reliant on me for protection, for her sustenance. For her life. I won't do that to someone again. I prefer to keep my appetites restricted to human females."

Melena scoffed. "Safe women you can fuck and feed from without the risk of feeling anything."

He stared, unflinching at her jab. "It is simpler that way, yes."

"Women who leave you free to walk away and wallow in your guilt and self-flagellation."

His full lips had compressed in a flat line as she spoke, his expression hardening now. "That's right, Melena. That's exactly the kind of woman I prefer. Simple. Safe. Forgettable. What I don't want is what nearly happened between us today. I'm not going to sacrifice two decades of resolve on a couple of days of passion."

And she didn't want to hear him say that. No more than she wanted to acknowledge the regret she saw in his dark gaze, or the grim determination that emanated from the stormy color of his aura. "How fortunate for you and your martyred honor that I'll be out of your life tomorrow."

She pivoted away from him on a burst of hot anger and bitter pride. She didn't even make it two steps.

Lazaro was suddenly in front of her. And he was fuming. He seized her shoulders, blocking her path with the muscled wall of his body and the power of his sudden fury.

Amber sparks crackled in the midnight-blue pools of his eyes as his gaze clashed and locked with hers. "The fact that you'll soon be out of my life is fortunate for you too, Melena." He drew in a breath and more fire leapt into his irises, reducing his pupils to thinning, inhuman slits. "You should be thanking me for my restraint thus far, not stomping off to pout like a petulant child."

"Let go of me." He didn't. If anything, his grip only went firmer. His face was so close to hers now, the bones of his high, angled cheeks sharpening with the emergence of his fangs. She refused to shrink under the full blast of his Gen One fury. "You call it restraint, the fact that you deny yourself the things you really want? Do you honestly think your guilt is ever going to release you if you only keep feeding it with your self-imposed isolation and pointless, hollow honor?"

A snarl curled up from his throat. It escaped through bared teeth and fangs. "You're far too young to lecture me on life and death or guilt and honor. You don't have any idea what you're talking about."

"Don't I?" she challenged hotly. And maybe a bit recklessly too, but she was so pissed off at him now, she couldn't stop. "Twenty years of licking your wounds, hiding from life? Pretending you don't need anything or anybody? One of us is acting like a sulking child, but it sure as hell isn't me."

A low, thunderous growl. That was all the warning she had. Then Lazaro's mouth came down hard on hers. His kiss was ruthless, punishing. Spiked with raw fury and violent need.

Melena felt his fangs press against her lips, against her tongue when she opened her mouth to his invading kiss. He was holding nothing back now. She felt that hard intent roll through him with the fierce drumming of his heart against her breasts. She felt it in the steely demand of his cock when he brought his arm around her back and hauled her into a brutal embrace, crushing her abdomen into the immense ridge of his arousal.

She felt the wall come up against her spine and realized dazedly that he had moved her there using the power of his Breed genetics to propel them both across the floor in an instant. Lazaro fucked her mouth with his tongue, grazed her lips with the deadly points of his fangs. His big body caged her, allowing her no room to escape, even if she tried.

"Now tell me what you know about my restraint, Melena." His voice had dropped to a timbre so low, so dangerously dark, everything reasonable and sane in her trembled with a dreadful anticipation. His merciless gaze bore into her, daring her to flinch as he bent his head toward her vulnerable throat. "Tell me about my hollow honor."

She couldn't speak. All of her senses were drawn taut, coiled to the point of breaking. His breath rushed hot and fevered across her neck, into the sensitive shell of her ear. Her pulse was racing, electricity coursing through her veins everywhere Lazaro touched her. He reached up, ran his fingertips over the scarlet teardrop-and-crescent-moon mark at the base of her throat.

"Tell me you're not afraid that I'll take your sweet, frantic carotid in my teeth right now and do exactly what I've been dying to do since I first saw you on that boat last night."

She was afraid. And for all her desire for him—despite her sense that she had been waiting all her life for him and had never realized it until now—Lazaro's fangs nestled so dangerously near her throat put an arrow of true panic in her blood.

If he pierced her vein, just one sip of her Breedmate blood would create an exclusive, unbreakable bond. He would be tied to her for the rest of his days—or until her death, should that come sooner.

One sip and he would crave no one else.

He would always feel Melena in his blood, even if they were apart. Even if miles or entire countries separated them.

One sip and there would be no other Breedmate for him, even if he drank from another woman with the mark after his connection was formed with Melena.

And if she drank from him in exchange, their bond would be a complete circle. Sustaining. Eternal. Unbreakable, except by death.

Melena held her breath, suddenly understanding the full impact of what she was inviting. Lazaro Archer, one of the eldest, most formidable

Gen One Breed males in existence, his body pressed against her from breast to ankle, his enormous fangs bared and poised over her carotid.

And he wanted *her.*

Every muscled inch of him was coiled with power, all of it at the razor's edge of breaking. Desire burned in his eyes—desire for her body and for the vein that throbbed so madly near his mouth. Heat and rigid strength pulsed where his pelvis ground so demandingly into her abdomen.

He was feral and wild and nearly unhinged...and she had never known anything hotter in her life.

"Damn you for making me want you," he muttered thickly. His searing breath skated across her electrified skin like a lick of flame. "Damn you for making me want this..."

She heard his brief inhalation. Felt his head descend, his lips and tongue sealing over her skin. Then she felt Lazaro's bite.

Sharp.

Deep.

Irrevocable.

CHAPTER 9

The first hot rush of Melena's blood over his tongue slammed into him
like a freight train. Warm, rich, potent. And laced with the sweetest trace
of caramel and dark, ripe cherries—her Breedmate blood scent, a
fragrance that had tempted him from the moment he'd first encountered
it. Now that scent would call him as surely as a divining rod seeking a
spring of cool, pure water.

He would feel her in his blood, everything she experienced most
intensely would now echo in his veins. Her joy, her sorrow, her fears.
Her hungers. Melena owned him now.

The bond he'd just activated inside him was unbreakable. She had
been a distraction to his mind, will, and body before; now she would be
his lifelong addiction.

And although better than a thousand years' of logic strove to
persuade him that Melena's blood was a shackle he shouldn't want and
damned well didn't need, the part of him that was purely male,
elementally Breed, roared with the one word Lazaro never thought he
would utter again: *Mine.*

He had known this feeling before. But what he had with Melena
now was all the more intense for how desperately he'd tried to resist it.
He groaned with possessive pleasure, knocked off his axis with a force
that staggered him.

Amazed him.

Holy hell, it humbled him.

He drank more, starving for her. Twenty years of feeding from human blood Hosts went up in flames as he drew greedily from Melena's tender vein. Her blood surged into his body, nourishing his cells as it wrapped silken bonds around his soul.

She was his. Even if his mind and will were reluctant to accept that fact, his body knew it with a ferocity he could hardly contain now. And where his desire for her had been consuming nearly from the moment he first laid eyes on her two nights ago, now it was a raging inferno that demanded its own satisfaction.

He wanted her savagely.

Needed her with a fury that left him shaking.

He realized in that moment that it wasn't only the blood bond that lashed her to him. Melena would have owned him even if he hadn't given in to his thirst for her tonight.

As unwelcome as that thought was—as unnerving as he found it, to think that she had obliterated his long-standing, iron resolve—it was a truth Lazaro could not deny.

And right now, he could not get enough of her.

* * * *

Oh, God, she was lost to this man.

She'd never known what it would be like to have a Breed male drink from her. Like so much where he was concerned, Melena hadn't been prepared.

With her head dropped back and Lazaro suckling with long, hard tugs at her carotid, she dissolved into a state of pure, boneless bliss. She held him as he drank from her, cushioning his big body as he thrust against her where they stood.

Her veins were on fire. The core of her had gone molten as well. Each demanding pull at her throat sent arrows of pleasure and need shooting through every cell of her being.

When Lazaro suddenly stopped suckling her and swept his tongue over the wounds he'd made, Melena groaned in protest. "I need you naked now," he muttered thickly against her throat. "I can't wait much longer."

Neither could she. "Yes," she gasped, her hands still clutching at him as he began to sink down before her into a crouch. He made quick work of her slacks and panties, baring her to him with the clothing pooled at her feet. On a low growl, he moved in and kissed each hipbone, then descended farther, burying his face between her thighs. "Oh, God..."

His tongue cleaved her folds, hot and wet and hungry. In long, knee-weakening strokes, he lapped and suckled, then kissed and nipped, wringing a moan from her as he drew her clit into his mouth and teased it toward a frenzy. She felt his teeth graze her sensitive flesh, felt the sharp tips of his fangs getting larger as he feasted on her with ruthless abandon.

She was quivering with hard need, on the verge of orgasm already, as he slowly kissed his way back up her body. With a deep, rolling growl, he stripped off her sweater and bra, then tossed them aside to gaze on her nakedness with burning amber eyes. Her blood stained his sensual lips a duskier hue, making his diamond-white fangs stand out in stark contrast.

He had never looked more dangerous or inhuman...nor more preternaturally beautiful.

"Lazaro," she sighed, her voice feathery, as unsteady as her legs. That sigh became a moan as he lavished her breasts and nipples with his hands and mouth, tongue and teeth.

He muttered her name in a fevered, animal-like rasp that sent her blood surging with even greater pleasure and arousal. He needed her now, as much as she needed him. On a curse he released her nipple and drew back to shuck his pants and shirt. He stood before her like an otherworldly god.

Magnificent. Terrifying. And hers.

Melena reached down between their bodies to grasp the jutting length of his cock. His shaft more than filled her hand, thick and warm and pulsing with strength. He purred deep in the back of his throat as she stroked him, then seized her mouth in a wild kiss. She could taste herself on his tongue, her blood and juices an erotic sweetness that only made her burn even more for him. She stroked him harder, craved him with a desperate ache that demanded to be filled.

"I can feel your need in your blood, Melena," he rasped against her lips. "It's alive in me now. So fucking intense. Everything you feel this strongly, I will feel too." He flexed his hips, his shaft surging even more powerfully within the tight circle of her fingers. "I need to be inside you. Put me there."

She obeyed, guiding him into the slick cleft of her body. He drove home on a savage groan, the fierce thrust making her cry out in pleasure. He gave her more, slamming in hard and urgently, his lack of restraint sending her own control spiraling away. She clawed at him as he fucked her against the wall, orgasm roaring up on her in a shocking wave of sensation.

She came fast and hard, convulsing in tremors that racked her from head to toe. As she shattered around him, Lazaro's tempo became a storm. He crashed into her with abandon, his immense body taut and shaking, so deliciously wild. He cursed against the side of her neck as his own release roared up on him. She felt him go rigid, driving deeper with every stroke, until a wordless shout tore out of him and he released.

Melena registered the hot blast of his orgasm, a heat she felt in her core and in every tingling particle of her being. She was drained and completed all at once, awash in a pleasure that rocked her to her soul.

But Lazaro wasn't finished with her yet, apparently.

Instead of pulling out, he guided her legs up around him, lifting her against him, their bodies still joined and vibrating with the aftershocks of release. He brought her into the bedroom, placed her beneath him on the big bed.

Then he began to drive her mad with desire and pleasure all over again.

* * * *

The temptation to stay with her in his bed had been all but irresistible, but after hours of making love to Melena, Lazaro finally let her sleep. No easy thing, for how much he still craved her. His desire for her soft curves and addicting heat was rivaled only by his newer thirst for her.

He didn't want to think about how strong those urges were, now that he'd indulged so recklessly—selfishly—in both.

He didn't want to think about how right it felt to lie next to her, inside of her, to hear her soft cries of pleasure or the quiet puffs of her breath as she slept so sweetly—trustingly—in his arms.

He didn't want to think about any of that when reality waited for them in D.C. in just a few short hours.

Lazaro slipped away from Melena's side to shower and get dressed, the predawn morning a prickle in his ancient Breed veins as he headed down to the command center to meet with his team. The warriors were just coming in from the night's patrol.

Trygg said nothing as he approached with the others from the far end of the corridor. The brutal warrior merely strode into the team's meeting room for the mission review. Jehan and Sav both slowed as their path met Lazaro's in the passageway. They greeted him with measured nods and sober, suspicious gazes.

"How did it go out there?" Lazaro asked them. "Any rumblings on the street about the explosion on Turati's yacht?"

Jehan answered first. "Nothing that we found. It was just a typical night in the Eternal City. A couple of club brawls to break up before they got too bloody and created a bigger problem. Handful of Breed youths feeding past curfew near the train station."

"No unusual activity at all?"

Sav glanced down, trying to suppress a grin. "Seemed like the only unusual activity going on last night was in here."

Lazaro glared, but he couldn't take offense at the truth.

"Is everything all right, Commander?" Jehan asked, ever the diplomatic professional, despite being one of the most dangerous warriors Lazaro had ever seen. "The situation with Melena seemed...difficult."

Now, it was only more difficult. Not to mention complicated. If she had cause to despise him last night after he'd seduced her then fled to find a blood Host, she had every reason in the world to loathe him for what he did a few hours ago.

And for what he had yet to do, after he saw her safely home to the States.

"Melena Walsh's welfare is no one's concern here but mine," he said, eager to shut down the topic of discussion, even though it weighed heavily on him. "The Order has difficulties of its own to worry about. For instance, does it bother anyone else that no one is stepping forward to claim responsibility for the assassinations of Turati and Byron Walsh the other night? The attack smacks of Opus Nostrum, yet the group hasn't formally declared it was their doing."

"Maybe they're waiting for the right time to own up to it," Savage suggested.

Jehan grunted, not quite convinced, if the shrewd look in his sky-blue eyes was any indication. "If it is Opus, maybe it wasn't a sanctioned attack. Maybe it was an over-zealous member looking to make a name for himself among his comrades. Or maybe it was done for more personal reasons than that. Turati was a high-profile businessman with political connections as well. He could've had any number of enemies. The same could be said of Walsh."

Lazaro gave a grim nod. The warrior could be right about any of those scenarios. And the only thing more troubling than Opus making such a bold move was the thought of a renegade agent operating from his own agenda.

Walking into the meeting room with Sav and Jehan, Lazaro couldn't help but relive the shock and horror of the rocket's destruction. And the fact that Melena might have been part of the carnage? That she had been mere seconds away from complete obliteration along with the others on that yacht?

Christ. What had shaken him that night—what had outraged him as a man and as the one entrusted with the security of those dead men— now put a cold knot of dread in his chest.

It put real, marrow-chilling fear in his bones.

Now more than ever, he needed to ensure she would be kept far out of harm's reach. And as bitter as the taste was on his tongue, he knew that anyone in the Order's orbit, or in that of the ever-expanding number of enemies seeking to incite true war between man and Breed, would always be at risk.

Like Ellie had been.

Like their sons and the dozen other family members living in Lazaro's Darkhaven who were killed on his watch.

He couldn't bear to have anything happen to Melena. She'd been through enough pain and loss already.

And so had he.

As Lazaro took his seat at the head of the conference table in the room with his men, Trygg palmed a slip of paper and slid it toward him. "What's this?"

Trygg nodded his shaved head at the note he'd scrawled. "Located her brother, like you asked." Lazaro glanced at the Baltimore, Maryland, address. "Derek Walsh is on a plane out of London as we speak. Booked the flight yesterday, after his father's death aboard Turati's yacht made international headlines."

Lazaro nodded gravely. He would've rather Melena's brother—Byron Walsh's only blood kin—had heard the news another way, but there was no fixing that now. At least her brother would be there for her. She would be home again, with family and familiar things. God knew, she had needed someplace soft to fall these past days, Lazaro thought grimly. And she hadn't exactly found that with him.

No, she'd found tears and anger and hurt.

She'd found a man ill-prepared to give her what she needed, what an extraordinary, tender-hearted woman like Melena deserved in life...and in love.

Instead of offering her comfort during her most vulnerable state, he'd growled and snapped at her. When he wasn't busy seducing her, that is.

When he wasn't selfishly slaking all of his needs on her as if he would ever be worthy of her heart or her blood.

He had no business giving in to those urges when war was still brewing all around him. So long as there were enemies killing innocents, his duty was, and always would be, to the Order. How could he have let himself slip so egregiously when it came to Melena? How could he be letting himself fall in love when he knew all too well how easily it could be ripped from his arms at any moment?

Love...

Fuck. Of all the rash impulses he had been unable to resist when it came to Melena, that would be the most foolish of them all.

Loving her would be even more selfish than the blood bond he had no right to claim and no intention of completing.

CHAPTER 10

Lazaro was gone when she woke up that morning.

He had stayed away most of the day, vanished to his command center until the time came for Melena and him to leave for the flight to D.C. that afternoon. Even on board the Order's private jet, Lazaro had remained distant, his comm unit to his ear most of the time, or his attention rooted to his work and his computer. She would have called him preoccupied, but his smoky aura had conveyed a deliberate resistance.

Hours later and thousands of miles away from everything they'd shared in Rome, Melena had sat beside him in the debriefing with Lucan Thorne and a few other members of the Order at the Washington, D.C., headquarters, feeling almost as though she were seated next to a polite, detached stranger. He'd introduced her graciously, almost formally, giving no one cause to suspect she was anything more to him than a civilian temporarily placed in his safekeeping following the attack on Turati's yacht.

He was careful not to touch her, even though heat crackled between them at the slightest brush of contact. He was careful not to let his gaze linger too long, even though his indigo eyes smoldered with awareness every time he glanced her way. He was coolly, determinedly remote.

It had made her want to scream.

She still felt that swamping urge, having since been removed from the meeting to accompany some of the Order's women in the living room of the headquarters' elegant mansion while the warriors continued their discussion in private.

"Are you sure you wouldn't like something to drink or eat, Melena?" Lucan Thorne's auburn-haired Breedmate, Gabrielle, offered a warm smile as she indicated a side table laid out with plates of finger sandwiches and tea cakes. Aromatic Darjeeling and chamomile steeped in their pots next to an elegant white china service.

Although her appetite wasn't there, everything looked and smelled delicious, and Melena was reluctant to reject the woman's kindness. "Thank you, I think I will have a little something."

She walked over from the sofa, joined by Gabrielle and two other women of the Order.

All of the Breedmates present tonight at the headquarters had been nothing but kind and welcoming. They were a family. That much was clear. And in the short time she'd been sitting with them, they'd each done their best to make Melena feel at home among friends as well.

Melena had been exhausted from her session with Lucan and the other warriors, to say nothing of the dread she felt every time she looked at Lazaro. Being around other women had helped dissolve some of that anxiety, even if it might only be for a little while.

She couldn't help watching the hallway outside, waiting for some indication that the meeting had broken so she and Lazaro could finally go somewhere to speak privately. So she could get rid of the awful feeling she had that he was somehow already gone.

Gabrielle handed her a small plate, collecting Melena from her dark thoughts. "If you'd like something more substantial, Savannah made a big pot of jambalaya earlier today. You really can't go wrong with any of her amazing cooking."

"I do have my numerous and varied talents," Savannah said, her doe-brown eyes dancing at the compliment. The beautiful, mocha-skinned Breedmate was bonded to Gideon, another of the warriors present tonight. Where her big blond-haired mate had an intense, slightly mad genius quality about him, Savannah exuded tranquility and smooth confidence.

As Melena put a few cucumber sandwiches and peach tarts on her plate, she found it next to impossible to keep from staring at the third woman in the room with them—the one mated to the warrior named Brock. Jenna looked like neither of her Breedmate companions. In fact, Melena didn't think she was a Breedmate at all, though she definitely wasn't fully human either.

Tall and athletic, Jenna wore her brown hair cropped close to her scalp. She was pretty, yet formidable in some indefinable way, and when she leaned across the sideboard to pour a cup of tea, Melena noticed an intricate pattern of skin markings at her nape. Skin markings that looked remarkably, impossibly, similar to...

"Are those tribal tattoos, or—"

"Not tattoos." Jenna's hazel eyes were smiling, but there was a note of seriousness in her voice. She turned to provide a better look. The array fanned out to cover the back of Jenna's neck, disappearing beneath the collar of her shirt. The arcs and swirls tracked upward too, well into her hairline and up the back of her skull. From the looks of it, they continued down Jenna's spine and onto her shoulders as well.

"They're *dermaglyphs*." Melena frowned, astonished and confused. Females born Breed had been unheard of for millennia. They might never have come into existence if not for the genetic experimentations conducted in Dragos's labs in the decades before he was killed by the Order. Even then, there were only a handful of women known to bear the *glyphs* and blood appetites of the Breed.

Melena found herself staring harder now, watching Jenna pile her plate with a healthy assortment of sweets and sandwiches. "You can eat all of that?"

Jenna grinned. "I'll probably come back for seconds."

"I'm sorry," Melena blurted, immediately feeling stupid and rude for letting her curiosity overrule her manners. "I just thought..."

"You thought I was Breed?" Jenna popped a tiny pastry in her mouth and gave a shake of her head. "Not quite. But I haven't been fully human for a long time either. I guess as long as Brock loves me, it doesn't matter where I end up. Together we can handle anything—and we have."

Her two friends nodded in agreement, and Melena smiled even though the sentiment was bittersweet for her. She'd believed she and Lazaro were heading toward something special like that too. Her father's death was still a raw ache in her heart, and would be for a very long time. The attack she'd narrowly survived still held her in a cold grasp.

But Lazaro had helped her through.

He'd been her rock, her comfort, whether he wanted to accept that role or not. And ever since they'd left Rome, she felt that support slipping away. No, she felt pretty damned certain that he wasn't slipping—he was running away. Cutting her off with his forbidding silence and maddening stoicism.

When she finally heard his deep voice approaching with Lucan and the others, Melena's heart started pounding in a heavy, expectant tempo. She didn't know whether to be relieved or terrified when he strode to the threshold of the drawing room and those penetrating dark blue eyes found her, locking on with the intensity that would probably always kindle an instant heat in her blood.

"Melena. May I have a word with you." Not a question, not an invitation. A sober demand.

She rose and walked to meet him as the rest of the group fell into easy conversation behind them. Lazaro led her down the hall to another formal parlor. He carefully closed the door, keeping his back to her for longer than she would have liked.

Melena didn't have to see his impassive face to know he was about to crush her heart when he finally turned around to look at her. His aura was a dark cloud, the shuttered gunmetal gray from before.

Before the first time he'd touched her, kissed her.

Before he'd shown her such incredible passion and tenderness when he made love to her. And when he bit her vein and took her blood into his body, into his soul.

All of those moments seemed to evaporate as she looked at him now. They became nothing under the regretful look in his ageless eyes.

But the moments they had weren't nothing. He'd felt everything she had. He wanted her. He cared for her. He cared maybe even as much as she did for him. She could see that diamond-bright truth breaking through the muddy resistance of his aura.

Everything they'd shared in Rome had meant something powerful and extraordinary to him too. But it wasn't enough.

"Why?" she murmured, her throat dry as ash.

He didn't pretend not to understand. "I told you from the beginning, Melena. I wasn't looking for this. I don't have a place for this in my life."

"For *this*," she said. "You mean, for me. For us."

He gave a somber nod. "For everything you deserve. For everything I can't give you."

"I don't recall asking you for anything, Lazaro. I didn't even ask for your heart."

"No, but you have it," he admitted quietly. "I think you owned a piece of my heart from the night I first dragged you out of that frozen pond in Boston."

"Then why?" Damn him, but those gentle words hurt all the more when she knew she was about to lose him. "Why are you pulling away from me now? Why are you acting as if I don't mean anything to you?"

He held her gaze, his own haunted and filled with remorse. "Because it isn't fair to you, letting you think I could ever be any kind of mate worthy of you."

She couldn't help herself. She scoffed brittly. "A shame you didn't arrive at that realization before you drank my blood."

"I told you I wasn't looking for a bond, Melena." His tone was tender but firm. As resolute as his aura. "I knew I couldn't give you that promise."

"No. Because you prefer simple arrangements. No entanglements or complications. No one to tempt you into throwing away twenty years of resolve on a couple of days of passion. Isn't that what you said?"

He said nothing for a long moment, staring at her grimly. "I'd resisted the temptation for a very long time, Melena. And it was easy. Until I found you."

Maybe she should have been moved by the confession. Maybe, if he hadn't been standing there giving her all of his reasons for why he was intent on breaking her heart. Instead, she thought back on everything they'd said to each other in heated anger and passion last night.

It was true, he had tried to resist her. He'd tried to push her away before he lost his damnable restraint. She hadn't helped, but she wasn't the one pretending she could walk away from what they had—from what they might be able to build together as a couple.

Lazaro had tried to warn her that he wasn't a hero come to save the day.

He tried to warn her that she might not be safe in his arms.

And she'd ignored him every time.

Yet for all his rigid honor and long-lived control, he hadn't been able to stop himself from claiming her.

He'd pierced her vein, swallowed her blood...created a bond that no other woman would ever be able to break for as long as Melena drew breath.

And wasn't that a convenient benefit of his colossal slip of self-discipline?

"Did you use me, Lazaro?"

His ebony brows crashed together. "Use you? Christ, no. Melena, you can't possibly think that—"

"Two decades of denial gone after just two days," she reminded him. "And now, with my blood living inside you, you'll never be tempted by another Breedmate. You have no ability to bond with anyone else as long as I live, so when you walk away from me now, you're free. Free as you've never been all this time. Congratulations. I'm so pleased I could permanently scratch that annoying itch for you."

He moved so fast she couldn't track him. One moment he was several feet away at the closed door of the room, the next he was crowding her with his big body, his hands clamped around her biceps. His eyes flashed with furious amber.

"You are not an itch I needed to scratch." His voice rumbled, low and deep and hard with outrage. "Damn it, Melena. Don't say that. Don't ever believe that."

"Then what are we doing? You've been shutting me out since we left Rome. If you care for me—and I know you do, I can see it, I can feel it—then why are you pulling away?"

"Because I can't do this again. You know loss, Melena, but you don't know what it is to lose a mate. I don't ever want to know that pain again. And with you—" He blew out a harsh curse. "I've seen you nearly die twice. I don't want to know what that would feel like now that your blood lives inside me. And I don't want to be the reason you're not safe. My life is committed to the Order now. It's a dangerous life. I won't put you in the crossfire."

"Don't you think that's something I should decide for myself?"

He stared at her for a long time, silent but unswaying. "I'll see you home safely to Baltimore tonight. Your brother should already be there as well."

"You've talked to Derek? When?" Despite the fact that her heart was breaking, it perked at the mention of her brother. "Where is he? How is he? Does he know I'm okay?"

Lazaro shook his head soberly. "There was no time to contact him before we arrived. Trygg found him on a flight coming in from London tonight."

"I need to see him," she murmured. "Derek needs to know that I'm alive."

"Yes," Lazaro agreed. "We can leave as soon as you're ready."

"Then what?" she asked cautiously. "What about you?"

"Then I'll be returning to Rome."

"When?" she asked, although her dread already knew that answer.

"I leave tonight. Arrangements have already been made. The Order's jet is refueling and waiting for me to return a few hours from now."

"So soon." She exhaled sharply. "I imagine you must be eager to unload your burden and get on with your life."

"Don't think this is easy for me," he said, frowning as he brought his hand up to stroke her cheek. "It would be easier to stay, or to bring you back with me to the command center in Rome. It would be the easiest thing in the world to fall in love with you, Melena."

She swallowed hard, trapped in his bleak, tormented eyes. Afraid to believe he might love her already. Afraid he never would.

He let his hand fall away. "It's become far too easy to imagine you at my side, as my mate. But those are things I can't give you. I can't ask you to risk your life by coming into my world. People die around me. I can't allow myself to be responsible for anyone else's life—your life. Don't you understand?"

"Yes, I think I finally do." The realization settled on her with clarity now, and not a little rage. "You're not doing this out of concern for me at all. You're doing it because you're afraid. I thought you were being noble by denying yourself another blood bond all this time. I thought it was honor that made you refuse to let another woman into your heart— and I think I loved you even more because of that. But I was wrong, wasn't I? You're pushing me away now because you're scared. You're running away from something that could probably be pretty fucking amazing because you're terrified of feeling any kind of pain again. The only person you're concerned about taking care of is yourself."

He didn't deny it. He didn't try to defend or justify anything she said. He let out a slow exhalation. His jaw was set and rigid, his aura uncompromising. "Whenever you're ready, I'll take you home to your family's Darkhaven."

"No, don't bother. You're not responsible for me, remember? I'll find my own way home." She tried to walk past him and he grabbed her arm, misery smoldering beneath the resolve in his dark blue eyes. "Let me go. That's what you want, so I'm giving it to you."

"Melena..."

She wrenched out of his loose grasp. "Good-bye, Lazaro."

This time, he didn't stop her. He stood unmoving, unspeaking, as she stepped around him and walked out the door.

CHAPTER 11

An hour later, Melena sat woodenly in the passenger seat of the Order's SUV as it rolled up to her family's Darkhaven in Baltimore. The big brownstone should have been a welcome sight in so many ways, yet all she felt was sorrow when she looked at it through the tinted glass of the vehicle's window.

Sorrow that she'd never hear her father's voice inside the house again. Sorrow for the pain her brother must be feeling as he walked into the empty home, believing he'd lost not only his father but Melena as well. She didn't want to imagine Derek's anguish, being the sole blood kin of Byron and Frances Walsh, both gone now.

And yes, Melena felt sorrow for herself too. Because instead of facing all of these heartaches with Lazaro's strong arms around her and his love to hold her up if she crumbled, she would be doing it alone.

"I'm ready," she murmured, more to herself than the Breed male behind the wheel.

Lucan and Gabrielle's son, Darion, put the vehicle in park and turned a sympathetic look on her. "I'll walk you inside, Miss Walsh."

"No." She shook her head, warmed by the kind offer. Darion was as gentlemanly as he was attractive. "Thank you, but that's not necessary. My brother won't be expecting me, and I don't imagine it will be easy for him when I walk in the door and he sees that I'm alive. I'd rather do this on my own."

"Okay." Darion frowned, but gave her a nod. The dark-haired Breed male's aura was golden and kind, steadfast with the strength of a born leader. "But I'm gonna wait here until you've gone inside."

She reached over to touch his large hand. "Thank you."

Melena climbed out of the vehicle and headed up the walkway toward the front door. It was unlocked, the soft light in the vestibule a warm, welcoming beacon. She stepped inside and pivoted to wave good-bye to Darion. As the black SUV rolled away, she took a steeling breath and closed the door behind her.

She was home.

She was back on safe, familiar ground. And yet, as she walked quietly through the house, she felt like a stranger to the place. Like a ghost drifting through a life that no longer quite fit anymore.

She drifted past the front rooms and grand central staircase, unsure if she should call to Derek or wait and let him adjust to seeing her once she found him.

She didn't have long to wonder. She heard her brother talking farther down the hallway. In her father's study. Derek was on a call with someone, the low rumble of his voice drawing Melena with a relief and a comfort she definitely needed right now.

"Yes, sir, the shipment is en route and everything is in order. That's right, I saw to it personally."

Melena paused at the open doorway. Derek stood with his back to her, dressed in loose sweatpants, his brown hair still wet from a recent shower. He wasn't wearing a shirt, and although the sight of her Breed brother's *glyphs* were no surprise to her, something did make her breath catch abruptly in her throat.

Derek now sported a number of tattoos on his broad back and shoulders. Unusual-looking stars, crossed swords, some kind of black beetle—a scarab, she realized, confused by the body art that hadn't been there the last time she saw her brother. He must have gotten the tattoos after he'd moved overseas a year ago.

"It should be in your hands tomorrow, Mr. Rior—" Derek's voice dried up.

He realized he wasn't alone now. Disconnecting the call without a word of excuse, he smoothly slipped the phone into his pants pocket.

When he pivoted around, his face was slack with shock...with stark disbelief.

"Melena. My God." He frowned, gave a vague shake of his head. But he didn't rush over to embrace her. He didn't react the way she would have expected at all from a sibling who loved her, worried for her. "I don't understand. The news reports said there were no survivors. I thought you were..."

"Dead," she replied, only understanding in that instant why her brother seemed less than relieved to see her.

He hadn't expected to see her again at all.

His sickening aura told the truth. It hovered around him, oily with corruption. Foul with deceit.

"It was you, Derek." She could hardly form the words, could hardly reconcile what her senses were telling her. "You were the faceless, hidden betrayer he feared. Oh, my God...it was you who arranged for our father's death."

* * * *

Lazaro boarded the Order's private jet in a hellish mood.

He hadn't expected the conversation to go well with Melena, but damn if he anticipated the kind of pain that had lodged itself in his chest from the moment she stormed away from him. That ache was still there, cold and gnawing, creating a vacuum behind his sternum that he didn't imagine would ever be filled.

She was gone.

He'd made certain of that—for her, he wanted to reassure himself. But Melena's words still echoed in his mind. Her condemning, all-too-accurate accusation.

He was a coward.

As the jet began to taxi toward the runway, Lazaro couldn't dismiss the feeling that he was walking away from the best thing that had happened to him in a very long time.

And why?

Because of exactly what Melena said. He was afraid. Afraid to his marrow that he might let himself fall in love with her and risk cutting his heart open again should anything happen to her.

The truth was, he was already falling. Letting her go cut him open, and as he rubbed at the empty ache in his chest, he realized only then what a fucking idiot he was.

Pushing Melena away had been the most cowardly act of his long life.

He'd lived more than a thousand years. He had loved a woman deeply, fearlessly, for several centuries before he lost her. He knew what real love felt like. He knew himself well enough to understand that time, for him, was immaterial. Time could last forever, or it could be gone in the blink of an eye.

He loved Melena. And whether it had happened in a matter of days, or over the span of a hundred years, it was all the same to him. He wanted her beside him. Starting right now, if she would have it in her heart to forgive him.

On a snarl, he punched the call button next to his seat.

"Yes, sir?"

"Turn it around."

The pilot went silent for a moment. "Sir, we're next on the runway to taxi and—"

"Turn this goddamned plane around. Now." On second thought, he couldn't wait that long. He unbuckled his seat belt and stood up. "Never mind. I'm getting off right here."

"But, sir—"

He unlocked the hatch and leapt down from the fuselage onto the dark tarmac. Then he was running. Heading for the Order fleet vehicle he'd parked in the private hangar when he'd arrived.

It was just as he neared the black sedan that his senses suddenly seized up, gripped by something powerful and horrifying. His veins lit up with a piercing dread.

Not his emotions.

Melena's.

He could feel her terror rising in his blood through his bond to her.

Holy hell.

She was in danger.

She was in fear for her very life.

CHAPTER 12

Melena tried to run.

She wasn't even halfway into the hall before Derek yanked her off her feet. His hand wound tight in her hair. Pain raked her scalp as he hauled her face backward to meet his furious sneer.

"You're supposed to be dead, sister dear," he hissed against her cheek. "You and Father both in one fell swoop. I've been planning it since he confided in me about his meeting with Turati."

"You killed him, you bastard!" Melena could hardly contain her contempt or her fear. "You killed more than a dozen innocent people that night, Derek. My God, did you hate us that much or are you simply out of your mind?"

"Arranging for that rocket strike was the sanest thing I've ever done. Killing Father and Turati? Doing it while they were secreted away for a covert meeting to broker their precious fucking peace? Let's just say it won me all the respect I deserve with the people who really matter."

Melena's heart sank even further. "Opus Nostrum."

He chuckled. "I was a mere lieutenant for this past year. They barely knew my name. Now I've got a direct line to the inner circle. I'll be a part of that circle soon. This was my proof of allegiance, my demonstration of worth." Derek's eyes flashed with vicious intent as she fought against his ruthless, unyielding hold. "As for you, Melena, I couldn't very well let you see me after I joined the organization. Your irritating gift would've sniffed me out right away."

"You plotted to kill me all this time?" she asked, hating that his duplicity hurt her so deeply.

Derek shrugged, his crackling amber eyes roaming over her terrified, miserable face with a cold disregard. "At first, I thought I could just avoid you. But then Father confided in me that he'd been having premonitions of a betrayal, and I knew it was only a matter of time before one or both of you discovered my alliance with Opus Nostrum. When he later told me about the meeting and the fact that you'd be accompanying him, I knew it was my chance to act."

Bile rose in her throat as he spoke. "You're a cold-blooded murderer, Derek. You're a sick, backstabbing fuck!"

"Careful, little sister. I'm the only thing standing between you and your grave." He snagged a cord from the table lamp on the desk, sending the thing crashing to the floor. Then he quickly bound her wrists behind her back. "Don't rush me to put you in it."

With that, he wrenched her into a more punishing hold and shoved her forward. He guided her out of their father's study and down the opposite end of the hallway. Melena had no choice but to shuffle ahead of him, panicking when she realized he was taking her outside.

He walked her toward their father's GNC-issued silver SUV parked in the drive.

"What are you doing, Derek?"

He opened the back door. Shoved her into the farthest seat.

"Where are you taking me?" she demanded, hysteria bubbling up as he calmly climbed behind the wheel. "If you're going to kill me, then just do it, damn you!"

"I'm not going to kill you, Melena." His cold eyes met her gaze in the rearview mirror. "I'm going to take you to my comrades in the organization. They're not nice people, I'm afraid. You're going to wish you died in that fucking explosion."

He started the engine. Then he backed away from the Darkhaven and started speeding for the highway.

* * * *

Lazaro gunned the black sedan through the late-night traffic on the highway, speeding like a bat out of hell for Baltimore. He didn't know what had Melena so terrified, but her fear was visceral. And it was eating him alive from the inside.

"Hang on, baby," he muttered as he dodged one lagging car and nearly sideswiped another. "Ah, God, Melena...know that I'm coming for you."

He was just about to veer toward the exit he needed when all of his instincts lit up like fireworks.

She was somewhere close—right now.

Possibly on the same stretch of highway, by the way his veins were clanging with alarm bells.

He scanned both sides of the divided lanes, a chaos of headlights and commuting vehicles. She might as well be a needle in a goddamned haystack.

And then—holy shit.

His Breed senses pulled his attention toward a light-colored SUV that had just merged on to the opposite side of the highway. The vehicle was speeding almost as fast as he'd been. In a big fucking hurry to get somewhere.

Melena.

She was inside the silver SUV. He knew it with total, marrow-chilling certainty.

And whoever had her was going to have bleeding hell to pay if she'd been harmed in any way.

Lazaro yanked the steering wheel and sent the sedan roaring into the median. Grass and mud flew in all directions as he tore across the divider and launched his car into the traffic on the other side. He floored the pedal, tearing up the pavement as he tried to catch the bumper of the vehicle that held his woman.

Flashing his lights, laying on the horn, he tried to get the attention of the vehicle bearing GNC diplomatic plates. It belonged to Byron Walsh, but Lazaro wasn't certain who the Breed male was behind the wheel. But then, as he ran up alongside it briefly, he caught a glimpse of the driver. A cold, sickening recognition set in.

Son of a bitch.

Derek Walsh.

And judging from the vampire's murderous glower, he had no intention of giving up Melena without a fight. The SUV lurched into a more reckless speed. It careened behind a semitrailer, dodging between a car of teens and a commuter bus. Lazaro could only follow, negotiating the traffic and keeping his focus trained on his quarry.

Walsh drove erratically for several miles with Lazaro chewing up his bumper. More than once, there was the opportunity to ram the bastard and send the SUV rolling, or to draw one of his semiautomatics and blast a hole in the Breed male's skull...but not with Melena inside. Not when Lazaro's heart was tied to her and every breath in his body was devoted to keeping her safe.

He hissed when Walsh narrowly avoided a collision with a car drifting into his lane. And when another near-miss snapped off the SUV's passenger side mirror, Lazaro shouted a furious curse. He saw a break up ahead—a chance to get in front of Walsh and force him into the median. Lazaro buried the gas pedal and flew past.

But Walsh saw the maneuver coming.

Instead of letting himself catch up to Lazaro, he hung a hard right and gunned it for an upcoming exit.

An exit that was under construction, littered with barrels and an obstacle course of concrete barriers.

Walsh was going too fast, too frantically.

Lazaro stomped on his brake and was whipping around to give chase again when the SUV clipped one of the barriers and went airborne, rolling into a hard crash.

All the breath seemed to suck out of Lazaro's lungs in that instant. The entire world seemed to stop breathing. Dust went up in the darkness, the haze illuminated by the beams of passing vehicles on the road.

Then, a spark of flame.

"No," Lazaro moaned, his blood screaming for Melena. "Goddamn it, no!"

He threw his vehicle in park on the shoulder and hit the ground running.

Even with his preternatural speed, he'd barely gotten within arm's reach of the wreck before the ruptured gas tank ignited. A blinding wall of flames shot skyward, heat blasting his face.

"*Melena, no!*"

* * * *

She couldn't breathe.

Heat all around her. Splitting pain in her skull, ringing in her ears. She opened her eyes and saw a churning, thickening cloud of gray smoke. And flames.

Oh, God. Fire everywhere.

Melena tried to move, but her arms wouldn't work. Her wrists were tied. She remembered now, awareness coming back to her. Derek had bound her. He'd driven away with her.

He and his Opus Nostrum comrades were going to kill her.

"No," she gasped, choking on smoke and heat. "Oh, my God...no!"

She started kicking, screaming, trying frantically to get free of the restraints. She couldn't loosen them. And something was crushing her in the back of the SUV. She looked up and saw the floor. Beneath her, the roof of her father's GNC vehicle.

The smoke was rolling in front of her eyes, burning them. She couldn't keep her lids open. Hurt to see, to breathe...

"Melena." The deep voice penetrated the fire and sooty air that surrounded her. She wanted to reach for it—for him—but she was trapped, unable to move. "Melena, I'm going to get you out of here, sweetheart. You stay with me, damn it!"

There was a great, groaning howl as the vehicle rocked where it had fallen. A gust of cool air, followed by a rush of hot, intensifying flame.

"I'm coming in to get you," Lazaro said.

She couldn't see him, but she felt him climbing inside the inferno. Crawling all the way to the back, where she lay broken and half-conscious.

And then she felt his strong hands make contact with her.

"Ah, Christ," he hissed, and she knew what he saw couldn't be good.

Another metallic roar filled the air, then the crushing weight that had pinned her down was lifted. Tenderly, Lazaro took hold of her. Started pulling her free of the wreckage.

"I've got you now, Melena. I've got you."

She didn't let the first sob go until she felt the warmth of his chest against her cheek. She buried her face in that comforting strength, breathed in the scent of him even as her throat screamed with pain from the smoke that choked her lungs.

And then he scooped her up in his arms and he was running. Away from the smoke. Away from the heat and the fire and the horror.

Cool night air enveloped her, filled her nose as she braved a cleansing breath. And circled around her were Lazaro's strong arms, holding her close, keeping her safe—carrying her away from certain death.

He set her down in the crisp, moist grass, while behind them came a jarring roll of thunder as a plume of fire and smoke shot up into the moonlit sky. Horns blared out on the highway. Tires screeched as traffic came to a halt at the scene of the accident.

But all Melena knew was the haggard, terrified face of the man she loved, staring down at her as he held her in a careful embrace. He tore off the lamp cord that bound her wrists and tossed it aside on a vicious snarl. When he reached down to smooth a hank of limp hair from her face, his fingers trembled.

Melena tried to speak but couldn't push sound through her lips. Her body ached everywhere, some of the pains searing, others a dull, relentless throb.

Lazaro's dark eyes were sober in his handsome face. His beautiful, sensual mouth was a flattened, grim line. "You're going to be all right, you hear me? I'm not letting you go."

She wanted to argue that he already had. That her heart was still breaking from the thought of him pushing her out of his life. Out of his heart.

He stared down at her, misery swimming in his gaze. "I'm not going to lose you, Melena."

On a curse, he brought his wrist up to his mouth and bit into his own flesh. No hesitation. No asking for permission before he put the punctures to her parted lips. "Drink."

She tried to shake her head. This wasn't the way she wanted him, coming back to save her when he had been determined to leave her. Whether he did this out of some noble sense of obligation or guilt, or simply under the power of his bond to her, she didn't want it. Not like this.

She wanted to reject the gift of his blood, of his bond, but the instant the wet, spicy warmth came in contact with her parched tongue, she greedily drank him in.

And oh, it was incredible.

Lazaro's Gen One blood flowed down her throat like pure light. She felt it strengthening her body, feeding her cells. Mending her injuries.

He tipped his head back on a strangled moan as she swallowed more of his eternal gift, his fangs gleaming, his broad shoulders and immense body silhouetted by the flames he'd walked through to save her.

It was the last thing Melena saw before a bone-deep exhaustion rose up to claim her.

CHAPTER 13

He had lived for more than a thousand years, long enough that few things still held the power to amaze him. The sight of Melena finally opening her eyes to look at him, after lying in bed unconscious for two days, was one of those rare pleasures for Lazaro Archer.

The worst of her injuries had healed. Her burns were gone. She was alive, and he'd never seen anything more welcome in all his life.

He smiled at her and gently stroked his thumb over the back of her hand as he held it. "Hello, beautiful."

"Where are we?" she asked, her voice thready.

"Still in D.C. I brought you here after the accident. I've been waiting for you to wake up so I could ask you something."

"My brother," she murmured.

Lazaro shook his head. "I'm sorry, Melena."

"He was part of Opus Nostrum," she said quietly. "He arranged for the attack on Turati and my father to prove something to his superiors. He was trying to win their recognition. And he was afraid if I ever saw him again, I'd know all of his secrets."

Lazaro and the Order had already surmised that Derek Walsh likely had ties to Opus, but hearing Melena confirm it made his blood seethe with renewed rage. "If he'd survived the accident the other night, I swear, I would've killed the bastard myself."

"He seemed so different. He'd only been away for a year, but he wasn't my brother anymore. And he had strange tattoos I've never seen before. Symbols of some kind, and a black scarab on his back."

"A scarab?" Lazaro thought back to conversations he'd had with Lucan and the other warriors. Reports out of London about human bodies in the morgue bearing the same kind of unusual tattoo.

"Does it mean something?" she asked, worry creasing her brow.

"It might," Lazaro said, seeing no reason to shield her from his world. But he would bring her into that part of his life slowly, after they returned to Rome. If she would be willing, that is. "We need to talk about what's happening with us, Melena. About our bond."

She turned her head on the pillow, looking away from him. "You shouldn't have done it. You didn't need to come back to save me."

"Yes, Melena, I did." He reached out, catching her chin on the tips of his fingers. He brought her gaze back to him. "Do you think I could've left, knowing that you were in danger? I feel you in my blood now."

"I'm not your obligation, Lazaro. I won't be your burden or a regret you'll carry around forever."

"No, you won't," he agreed solemnly. "But will you be my mate?"

She stared at him for a long moment. Then slowly, she shook her head. "No. No, I can't do that. You're only saying it because your honor compels you to."

He swore a harsh curse. "Melena, listen to me. See me. I know you can read my intent, so open your eyes and hear me out. I love you. I want you in my life, by my side. Forever, if you'll have me."

"What about everything you said before? You didn't want another mate under your protection. You didn't want that responsibility ever again."

He blew out a bitter laugh. "And as you so accurately pointed out for me, I was being a coward and an idiot."

"I don't think I said you were an idiot," she murmured, looking up at him from under her long lashes.

"Well, I was. And as soon as I realized that, I came after you."

"Because you were worried about me. You knew I was in danger and your blood wouldn't let you stay away without trying to help me."

"No, Melena. Because I love you." He stroked her cheek. "And because I realized the only thing worse than loving you and dreading that I might know the pain of losing you in the future, was the idea of losing you now. Before we've even begun to know what we can have together."

He leaned over her on the bed and kissed her tenderly, deeply, with all the love in his ageless heart. "I love you, Melena."

"And I love you," she whispered. She held his gaze, her own so open-hearted and trusting, it took all of his control to keep from crushing her in a fierce embrace. "You've saved my life three times now. If I'm going to be your mate, that means you're going to have to let me save you sometimes too."

"Oh, love," he murmured. "Don't you know? You already have."

Stroke of Midnight

Acknowledgments

I am thrilled to be part of the 1001 Dark Nights collection for a second time with this novella in my Midnight Breed vampire romance series. My thanks to the awesome and endlessly creative Liz Berry, MJ Rose, Jillian Stein, and everyone else working behind the scenes at Evil Eye Concepts to make the project a success. Big hugs to my fellow 1001 Dark Nights authors as well. Every year, the lineup gets more impressive and the depth of talent more amazing. I'm grateful for your support and honored to call so many of you my friends.

And I have to send out lots of love and heartfelt thanks to my readers. I can't tell you what it means to me that you continue to embrace my characters and my work. I hope you have fun reading this new Midnight Breed adventure, and I hope you enjoy all the rest still to come!

With love,

Lara Adrian

CHAPTER 1

Screams shot up from one of the many narrow, cobbled alleyways in the heart of Rome's quaint old Trastevere ward. The shrieks of mortal terror pierced the night as effectively as a blade.

Or, rather, a pair of razor-sharp fangs.

Like the ones on the gang of lethal predators who'd shredded the throat of a human civilian in a dance club across the city only minutes ago.

Shit. Jehan swung an urgent look over his shoulder to the two other Breed warriors currently on foot behind him. "They're getting away."

He and his teammates from the Order's Rome command center had been in pursuit of the four blood-thirsty Rogues since their patrol had been alerted to the killing at the club. They had contained the situation before any of the other humans had realized what was going on, but their mission wouldn't be over until they ashed the feral members of their own race.

"Split up," he told his men. "Damn it, we can't lose them! Close in from all sides."

His comrade and good friend, Savage, grinned and gave a nod of his blond head before veering right to take one of the other winding alleys on Jehan's command. The other warrior, a hulking, shaved-head menace called Trygg, made no acknowledgment to his team leader before vanishing into the darkness like a wraith to carry out the order.

Jehan sped like an arrow through the tight artery of the ancient street ahead of him, dodging slow-moving compact cars and taxis who were getting nowhere fast in the district that was clogged with tourists and club-hoppers even as the hour crept close to midnight.

The public out and about tonight was a mix of human and Breed civilians, something that would have been unheard of just twenty years ago, before the Breed's existence had been revealed to mankind.

Now, in cities around the world, the two populations lived together openly. They worked together. Governed together. But their hard-won peace was fragile. All it might take was one horrific killing—like the one earlier tonight—to set off a global panic.

While every Breed warrior of the Order had pledged his blood and breath to prevent that from happening, others among mankind and the Breed were secretly—and not-so-secretly—instigating war.

Tonight's Rogue attack had the stamp of conspiracy all over it. And it wasn't the first. During the past few nights there had been a handful of others, in Rome and elsewhere in Europe. While it wasn't unusual for one of Jehan's kind to become irreversibly addicted to blood, the spate of recent slayings in all-too-public places by Rogues torqued up on some kind of Bloodlust-inducing narcotic had fingers pointing to the terror group called Opus Nostrum.

Just a few days ago, the Order had scored a staggering hit on Opus, taking out its newest leader, who'd been headquartered in Ireland. The cabal was hobbled for now, but its hidden members were many and their machinations seemed to know no bounds. They and all who served them had to be stopped, or the consequences were certain to be catastrophic.

Jehan was a blur of motion as he leapt over the hood of a standing taxi to vault himself up onto the tiled rooftops above the thick congestion on the streets.

His heavy black patrol boots made no sound as he traveled with preternatural stealth and speed over the uneven terrain of the buildings. He jumped from one rooftop to the next, following his instincts—and the trace, metallic scent of fresh blood that floated up on the night breeze as the Rogue attempted to escape his pursuers.

He lived for this kind of action. The adrenaline rush. The thrill of the chase. The conviction that came from doing something with real purpose, something that would have true and lasting impact on his world.

A far cry from the posh wealth and useless decadence he'd been born into with his family in Morocco.

That old life was still trying to call him back, even though he hadn't stepped foot on his homeland's soil for more than a decade.

It had been twelve months and a day since he'd received the message from his father. Jehan knew what that meant, and he couldn't pretend he hadn't heard every tick of the damned countdown clock in the time since.

With a growl, he pushed aside reminders of the obligation he'd been pointedly ignoring. Right now, his focus was better spent on the more urgent mission in front of him.

Down below in a twisting alleyway, Jehan spied one of the fleeing Rogues. Fingers gripping the handle of one of his titanium blades, he drew the weapon and let it fly. Direct hit. The dagger nailed the Rogue in the center of his spine, dropping him in his tracks.

Ordinarily, it took more than that to disable one of the Breed, but the titanium was toxic to vampires who'd gone Rogue, and as corrosive as acid to their diseased bodies. In minutes or less, the corpse would be nothing but ashes in the street.

Jehan didn't wait to see the disintegration happen. As he continued his dash across the rooftops, he spotted Trygg gaining ground on one of the remaining Rogues. The big warrior took the escaping vampire down in a flash of movement. The Rogue howled, then abruptly fell silent when Trygg severed its head with a slice of his blade.

Two down. Two to go.

Make that one left to go. Jehan's acute hearing picked up sounds of a brief struggle as Savage caught up to his quarry on a different stretch of cobblestones and delivered a killing strike of titanium.

Jehan leapt to another roof, racing deeper into the ancient district of the city. His battle instincts heightened as he homed in on the last of the fleeing Rogues. The vampire made a crucial mistake, turning into an alleyway with no exit. A literal dead end.

Jehan sailed off the edge of the rooftop and dropped to the cobbled street behind the Rogue, cutting off any hope of his escape. An instant later, Savage emerged from out of the shadows, just as the feral vampire spun around and realized he had nowhere left to run.

The big male faced the two Order warriors. His fangs dripped with blood and sticky saliva. His transformed eyes glowed bright amber, the pupils fixed and narrowed to thin vertical slits in the center of all that fiery light. His jaw hung open as he roared, insane with Bloodlust and ready to attack.

Jehan didn't allow him the chance.

He threw his dagger without mercy or warning. The titanium blade glinted in the moonlight as the weapon sliced through the distance and struck its mark, burying to the hilt in the center of the Rogue's chest.

The vampire roared in agony, then collapsed in a heap on the cobbles as the poisonous metal began to devour him.

When the process had finished, Jehan strode over to retrieve his weapon from the ashes.

Savage blew out a low curse behind him. "Four Breed males gone Rogue in the same city on the same night? No one's seen those kind of numbers in the past twenty years."

Jehan nodded. He'd been a youth at that time, but more than old enough to remember firsthand. "Let's hope we never see bloodshed again like we did back then, Sav."

And all the more reason to take Opus Nostrum out at the root. For Jehan, a Breed male who'd spent a lot of his privileged life in pursuit of one pleasure or another, he couldn't think of any higher calling than his place among the Order.

He cleaned his dagger and sheathed it on the weapons belt of his black patrol fatigues. "Come on," he said to Savage. "I saw Trygg ash one of these four a few blocks back. Let's go find him and make sure we don't have any witnesses in need of a mind-scrub before we report back to Commander Archer at headquarters."

They pivoted to leave the alley together—only to find they were no longer alone there.

Another Breed male stood at the mouth of the narrow passage. Dark-eyed, with a trimmed black beard around the grim line of his mouth, the vampire was dressed in a black silk tunic over loose black pants tucked into gleaming black leather boots that rose nearly to his knees.

The only color he wore was a striped sash of vibrant, saffron-and-cerulean silk tied loosely around his waist. Family colors. Formal colors, reserved for the solemnest of old traditions.

Jehan couldn't bite back his low, uttered curse.

Beside him in the alleyway, Savage moved his fingers toward his array of weapons.

"It's all right." Jehan stayed his comrade's hand with a pointed shake of his head. "Naveen is my father's emissary."

In response, the dark-haired male inclined his head. "Greetings, Prince

Jehan, noble eldest son of Rahim, the just and honorable king of the Mafakhir tribe."

The courtly bow that followed set Jehan's teeth and fangs on edge almost as much as his official address. From within the folds of his tunic, Naveen withdrew a sealed piece of parchment. The royal messenger held it out to Jehan in sober, expectant silence.

A stamped, red wax seal rode the back of the official missive...just like the one Jehan had received in this same manner a year ago.

A year and a day ago, he mentally amended.

For a moment, Jehan just stood there, unmoving.

But he knew Naveen had been sent with specific orders to deliver the sealed message, and it would dishonor the male deeply if he failed in that mission.

Jehan stepped forward and took the stiff, folded parchment from Naveen's outstretched hand. As soon as it was in Jehan's possession, the royal messenger pivoted and strode back into the darkness without another word.

In the silence that followed, Savage gaped. "What the fuck was that all about?"

"Family business. It's not important." Jehan slipped the document into the waistband of his pants without opening it.

"It sure as hell looked important to that guy." When Jehan started walking out of the alley, Sav matched his clipped pace. "What is it? Some kind of royal subpoena?"

Jehan grunted. "Something like that."

"Aren't you going to read it?"

Jehan shrugged. "There's no need. I know what it says."

Sav arched a blond brow. "Yeah, but I don't."

To satisfy his friend's curiosity, Jehan retrieved the sealed message and passed it over to him. "Go ahead."

Sav broke the seal and unfolded the parchment, reading as he and Jehan turned down another narrow street. "It says someone died. A mated couple, killed together in a plane crash a year ago."

Jehan nodded grimly, already well aware of the couple's tragic demise. News of their deaths had been the reason for the first official notice he'd received from his father.

Savage read on. "This says the couple—a Breed male from the Mafakhir tribe and a Breedmate from another tribe, the Sanhaja, had been blood-bonded as part of a peace pact between the families."

Jehan grunted in acknowledgment. The pact had been in place for centuries, the result of an unfortunate chain of events that had spawned a bloody conflict between his family and their closest neighbors, the Sanhajas. After enough blood had been spilled on both sides, a truce was finally declared. A truce that was cemented with blood spilled by another means.

An eternal bond, shared between a male from Jehan's line and a Breedmate from the rival tribe.

So long as the two families were bound together by blood, there had been peace. The pact had never been broken. The couple who perished in the plane crash had been the sole link between the families in the modern age. With their deaths, the pact was in limbo until a new couple came together to revive the bond.

Savage had apparently just gotten to the part of the message Jehan had been dreading for the past twelve months. "It says here that in accordance with the terms of that pact, if the blood bond is severed and no other couple elects to carry it forward within the term of a year and a day, then the eldest unmated son of the eldest Breed male of the Mafakhir tribe and the unmated Breedmate nearest the age of thirty from the Sanhaja tribe shall..."

Sav's long stride began to slow, then it stopped altogether. He swiveled his head in Jehan's direction. "Holy shit. Are you kidding me? You're being drafted to go home to Morocco and take a mate?"

A scowl furrowed deep into his brow at the very thought. "According to ritual, I am."

His comrade let out a bark of a laugh. "Well, shit. Congratulations, Your Highness. This is one lottery I'm happy as hell I won't be winning."

Jehan grumbled a curse in reply. Although he didn't find much humor in the situation, his friend seemed annoyingly amused.

Sav was still chuckling as they resumed their march up the alleyway. "When is this joyous occasion supposed to take place?"

"Tomorrow," Jehan muttered.

There was a period of handfasting with the female in question, but the details of the whole process were murky. In truth, he'd never paid much attention to the fine print of the pact because he hadn't imagined there would be a need to know.

He didn't really expect he needed to understand it now either, as he had no intention of participating in the antiquated exercise. But like it or not, he respected his father too much to disgrace him or the family by refusing to respond to their summons.

So it seemed he had little choice but to return to the family Darkhaven in Morocco and deliver his regrets in person.

He could only hope his father might respect his prodigal eldest son enough to free him from this ridiculous obligation and the unwanted shackle that awaited him at the end of it.

CHAPTER 2

Eighteen hours later and fresh off his flight to Casablanca, Jehan sat in the passenger seat of his younger brother's glossy black Lamborghini as it sped toward the Mafakhir family Darkhaven about an hour outside the city.

"Father didn't think you'd come." Marcel glanced at Jehan briefly, his forearm slung casually over the steering wheel as the sleek Aventador ate up the moonlit stretch of highway, prowling past other vehicles as if they were standing still. "I have to admit, I wasn't sure you'd actually show up either. Only Mother seemed confident you wouldn't just tear up the message and send it back home with Naveen as confetti."

"I didn't realize that was an option."

"Very funny," Marcel replied with another sidelong look.

Jehan turned his attention to the darkened desert landscape outside the window. He'd been questioning his sanity in answering the family summons even before he'd left Rome.

His Order team commander, Lazaro Archer, hadn't been enthused to hear about the obligation either, especially when things were heating up against Opus Nostrum and a hundred other pressing concerns. Jehan had assured Lazaro that the unplanned leave was merely a formality and that he'd be back on patrol as quickly as possible—without the burden of an unwanted Breedmate in tow.

Marcel maneuvered around a small convoy of humanitarian supply trucks, no doubt on their way to one of the many remote villages or refugee camps that had existed in this part of the world for centuries. Once the road opened up, he buried the gas pedal again.

If only they were heading away from the family compound at breakneck speed, rather than toward it.

"Mother's had the entire Darkhaven buzzing with plans and arrangements ever since you called last night." Marcel spoke over the deep snarl of the engine. "I can't remember the last time I've seen her so excited."

Jehan groaned. "I'm here, but that doesn't mean I intend to go through with any of this."

"What?" Jehan looked over and found his only sibling's face slack with incredulity. His light blue eyes, so like Jehan's own—a color inherited from their French beauty of a mother—were wide under Marcel's tousled crown of brown waves. "You have to go through with it. There's no blood bond between the Mafakhirs and the Sanhajas anymore. Not since our cousin and his Breedmate died a year ago."

When Jehan didn't immediately acknowledge the severity of the problem, his brother frowned. "If a year and a day should pass without a natural mating occurring between the families, the terms of the pact specifically state—"

"I know what they state. I also know those terms were written up during a very different time. We don't live in the Middle Ages anymore." *And thank fuck for that,* he mentally amended. "The pact is a relic that needs to be retired. Hopefully it won't take too much convincing to make our father understand that."

Marcel went quiet as they veered off the highway and set a course for the rambling stretch of desert acreage that comprised their family's Darkhaven property. In a few short minutes, they turned onto the private road.

The family lands were lush and expansive. Thick clusters of palm trees spiked black against the night sky, small oases amid the vast spread of dark, silken sand. Up ahead was the iron gate and tall brick perimeter wall that secured the massive compound where Jehan had grown up.

Even before they approached the luxurious Darkhaven, his feet twitched inside his boots with the urge to run.

While they paused outside the gate and waited to be admitted inside, Marcel pivoted in his seat toward Jehan. His youthful, twenty-four-year-old face was solemn. "The pact has never been broken. You know that, right? Not once in all of the six-and-a-half centuries it's been in place. It's not a relic. It's tradition. That kind of thing may not be sacred to you, but it is to our parents. It's sacred to the Sanhajas too."

His brother was so earnest, maybe there was another way to dodge this bullet. "If you feel that strongly about it, why don't you pick up the torch instead? Take my place and I can turn around right now and go back to my work with the Order."

"Ohh, no." He vigorously shook his head. "Even if I wanted to—which I don't—without another mated couple occurring naturally between our families, the pact calls for the eldest son of the eldest male of our line. That means you. Besides, there are worse fates. Seraphina Sanhaja is a gorgeous woman."

Seraphina. It was the first time he'd heard the name of his intended. A silken, exotic name. Just the sound of it made Jehan's blood course a bit hotter in his veins. He dismissed the sensation with a sharp sigh as he stared at his brother. He couldn't deny that a part of him was intrigued to know more. "You've seen her?"

Marcel nodded. "She and her sister, Leila, are both stunning."

Not surprising, considering they were Breedmates. Although they didn't have the vampiric traits of Jehan's kind, the half-human, half-Atlantean females called Breedmates were flawless beauties without exception. His Paris-born mother was testament to that. As was Lazaro Archer's flame-haired Breedmate back in Rome, Melena.

"So, what's wrong with her, then?" Jehan murmured. "Let me guess. She's a miserable, bickering shrew? Or is it worse, a meek little mouse who's afraid of her own shadow?"

"She's neither." Marcel grinned as he eased the Lamborghini through the opened gates. "She's lovely, Jehan. You'll see for yourself soon enough."

"Not if I have anything to say about that." Crossing his arms, he sat back in the buttery soft leather seat. "I have a return flight to Rome tomorrow. I figure that gives me plenty of time to convey my regrets to our parents and get the hell out of here."

"You can't do that. Everything is already in motion. I told you, arrangements were made right after you called."

Jehan cursed under his breath. "If I'd realized our parents would charge forward without asking me, I could've saved everyone the effort. I should've told them over the phone that I wasn't interested in any of this and stayed put in Rome. Unfortunately, it's too late for that now. Whatever arrangements have been made will need to be canceled."

"I don't think you understand, brother." Marcel slowed the car as they rolled onto the half-moon drive of the Darkhaven's impressive arched entrance. "The handfast begins tomorrow. Which means the families assemble for the official meet-and-greet tonight. There will be formal introductions, followed by the traditional garden walk at midnight, and the turning of the hourglass to mark the celebratory commencement and the start of the handfast period."

Jehan's unfamiliarity with the process must have been as apparent as his disinterest. Marcel frowned at him. "You don't have any idea what I'm talking about, do you? For fuck's sake, the pact's been in place for centuries, but you never took the time to study the terms?"

"I've been busy."

Marcel's lips quirked at the droll reply, but it was clear that he took the pact seriously. Apparently everyone did, aside from Jehan.

For an instant, he felt a pang of loss for his absence all these years. It had been his choice to leave, his choice to make his own way in the world instead of being satisfied with the privileged, if stifling, one he'd been handed at birth. He'd yearned more for adventure than tradition, and supposed he always would.

"So, this handfast entails what, exactly?"

"A period of eight nights, spent together in seclusion. No visitors, no communication with the outside world in any form. Just the two of you, alone at the oasis retreat on the border of our lands and the Sanhajas'."

"In other words, imprisonment for a week and a day with a female who may or may not be a willing party to this whole forced seduction ritual. Followed by what—a public blood bond encouraged at sword point?"

"Forced seduction? Public blood bond?" Marcel gaped at him as if he'd lost his mind. "The handfast is all about consent, Jehan. Touch Seraphina against her wishes and her family has the right to take your head. Drink her blood without her permission and no one would balk if the Sanhajas took out their revenge on the entire Mafakhir tribe. This is serious shit."

Not to mention, archaic. Even though he had no plans to touch Seraphina Sanhaja or any other female who wasn't of his own choosing, Jehan's curiosity was piqued. "I thought the whole point of the pact was to seal the peace between our two families with a blood bond."

"It is," Marcel said. "But only if the handfast is successful."

"Meaning?"

"There has to be a mutual agreement. There has to be love. If there's no desire to bond as a mated couple at the end of the handfast, the couple is free to go their separate ways and the pact then moves on to the next pair in line."

"So, there's an out clause?" Jehan's brows rose in surprise. "That's the best news I've heard all night."

His brother released a frustrated-sounding breath. "I don't know why I'm bothering to explain any of this to you. The terms will be spelled out in detail at the ceremony tomorrow night."

The ceremony Jehan had no intention of attending.

Marcel parked in front of the opulent estate and killed the engine. The Aventador's scissor doors lifted upward and the two Breed males climbed out.

As they began to ascend the wide, polished stone steps leading to the Darkhaven's entrance, Jehan asked, "Who's the next pair in line after Seraphina and me?"

"That would be the Breedmate next nearest the age of thirty in the Sanhaja family, and the unmated eldest son of the second-eldest Breed male in our line. You remember our cousin, Fariq."

Jehan mentally recoiled. "Fariq, who prided himself on his collection of dead insects and snakes as a boy?"

Marcel chuckled. "He's not nicknamed Renfield for nothing."

And Jehan couldn't help but feel guilty that his refusal of the pact would mean some unfortunate Breedmate would eventually have to spend eight nights alone with the repulsive male.

But he didn't feel guilty enough to let the farce continue. He had to halt the whole thing before it went any further.

"Father's waiting for you in his study," Marcel told him as they reached the top. "Everyone else is in the main salon, where the formal introductions will be made."

Alarm shot through him at that last announcement. Jehan grabbed his brother's muscled arm. "Everyone else?"

"Mother and the Sanhajas. And Seraphina, of course."

Ah, fuck. If he thought this was bad enough before he stepped off the plane tonight, the situation had just nose-dived into a disaster zone. "They're here right now? All of them?"

"That's what I've been telling you. Everything is already in motion and ready to begin. We were only waiting for you to arrive, brother."

CHAPTER 3

The sound of deep male voices carried from the foyer. Until that moment, the small gathering inside the Darkhaven's elegant salon had been engaged in pleasant chatter about the weather and a dozen other light subjects. But at the low rumble of muffled conversation somewhere outside the gilded walls, a palpable spike of anticipation pierced the atmosphere in the room.

"Ah, my sons have finally arrived." Beautiful and poised, Simone Mafakhir smiled from her seat on a silk divan, her sky blue eyes lit with excitement. "I know Jehan will be delighted to meet you, Seraphina."

Sera's mouth was suddenly too dry to speak, but she gave a polite nod and returned the brunette Breedmate's warm smile.

"Seraphina's talked of little else all day," her mother said, giving Sera's hand a pat from her seat beside her on a velvet sofa opposite Simone. "She's been full of curiosity about Jehan ever since she arrived back home this morning."

On the other side of Sera, her blonde, twenty-two-year-old sister, Leila, barely stifled a giggle.

It was true. Sera had been full of questions since she'd been called home by her parents. She still didn't know much about Jehan, other than the fact that he'd flown in tonight from Rome, where he'd been living for many years. And that he'd come because he had been summoned to fulfill his role in the ancient handfasting pact that had existed between their families for half a dozen centuries.

The same as she had.

That is, if she managed to make it through the evening without bolting for the nearest escape.

She pressed the back of her hand to her forehead, which had gone suddenly clammy. Her heart was racing, and her lungs felt as if they were suddenly caught in a vise.

She stood up, not quite steady on the high heels she wasn't accustomed to wearing. The flouncy, blush-pink dress she'd borrowed from Leila on her sister's insistence swayed around her knees as she wobbled, lightheaded and fighting the wave of nausea that rose up on her.

"Would it be possible to, um...freshen up for a moment?"

"Yes, of course," Simone replied. "There's a powder room just down the hall."

Her parents both looked at her in genuine concern. "Are you all right, darling?" her mother asked.

"Yes." Sera gave them a weak nod that only made her wooziness worse. "I'm fine, really."

She just needed to get the hell out of there before she passed out or threw up.

Leila stood and grabbed her elbow. "I'll go with you."

They hurried out of the room together, Sera practically leaving her sister in her wake. Once safely enclosed in the large powder room, Sera sagged against the back of the door.

"What on earth is wrong with you?" Leila whispered.

Sera swallowed back a building scream. "I can't do this. I thought maybe I could—for our parents, since it's obviously so important to them—but I can't. I mean, this whole situation...the pact, the handfasting? It's insane, right? I never should have agreed to any of this."

It was all happening too quickly. Yesterday morning, an e-mail from her parents had reached her at the remote outpost where she'd been working. The message had been short and cryptic, telling her that she was needed at home immediately.

Terrified with concern, she'd dropped everything and raced back— only to learn that the emergency requiring her presence was a musty old agreement that would send her away with a complete stranger. A Breed male who may not understand or care that her carotid wasn't up for grabs, regardless of what the pact between their families might imply.

Oh, God. Her stomach started to spin again. She pressed her hand to her abdomen and took a steadying breath.

She paced the cramped powder room, her voice beginning to rise. "I need to get out of here. I can't do this, Leila. I must've been out of my mind for even considering coming here tonight."

Her sister stared at her patiently, her soft green eyes sympathetic as she let Sera vent. "You're just nervous. I would be too. But I don't think you're crazy for being here. And I don't think the agreement between our families is insane, either." She swept a blonde tendril behind her ear and shrugged. "It's endured all these years for a reason. Actually, I think it's kind of romantic."

"Romantic?" Sera scoffed. "What's romantic about a truce struck after years of bloodshed resulting from the kidnap of a virgin Breedmate from our tribe by a barbarian Breed male from theirs six-hundred years ago?"

Leila let out a sigh. "Things were different back then. And it's romantic because they fell in love."

Sera arched her brows in challenge. "Tragic, because despite their blood bond, they both died in the end and set off a long, violent war."

Sera knew the whole, tragic story as well as her sister did. It was practically legend in the Sanhaja family. And if she was being honest, there was a part of her that ached for that long-dead couple and their doomed love.

But it didn't change the fact that centuries later, here she was, standing in a locked bathroom in a borrowed dress and high-heeled sandals, while just down the hall, a Breed male she'd never even met before was expecting her to go away with him for eight long nights—all in their parents' shared hopes that they might come back madly in love and bound by blood for eternity.

Ridiculous.

Sera shook her head. "It might've been true centuries ago that the best way to guarantee peace was to turn an enemy into family," she conceded. "But that was then and this is now. There hasn't been conflict between the Mafakhirs and our family for decades."

Leila tilted her head. "And how do you know that's not because the pact was in place all that time? Since it first began, there's never been a time when there wasn't at least one mated pair between our families. Until now. What if the pact really is the only thing keeping the peace? It's never been broken or tested, Sera. Do you really want to be the first one to try?"

For a moment, hearing her sister's emphatic reply, Seraphina almost bought into the whole myth. At twenty-seven, she was a practical, independent woman who knew her own mind as well as her own worth, but there was a small part of her—maybe a part of every woman—who still wanted to believe in fairy tales and romance stories.

She wanted to believe in eternal love and happy endings, but that's not what awaited her on the other side of the powder room door.

"The pact isn't magic. And the handfast isn't romantic. It's all a bunch of silly, outdated nonsense."

"Well, call it what you will," Leila murmured. "I think it's charming."

"I doubt you'd be so enthusiastic if you were the one being yanked out of your world and all the things that matter to you, only to be dropped into some strange male's lap as his captive plaything." Sera considered her dreamy-eyed younger sister. "Or maybe you would."

Leila laughed and shook her head. "The handfast is only for a week. And you won't be dropped into anyone's lap or held against your will. You're meant to get to know each other away from the distractions of the outside world. That's all. Handfasting at the oasis retreat is symbolic more than anything else. Besides, I can think of worse things than spending a week in beautiful surroundings, getting to know a handsome Breed male. One who also happens to be a prince."

Sera scoffed. "A prince in name only. The old tribes of this region aren't any more royal than you or me." Which they weren't. Adopted by Omar and Amina Sanhaja as infants from orphanages for the indigent, there was no chance of that. Sera cocked a curious look on her sister. "How do you know Jehan's handsome? I thought you've never met him."

"I haven't. But being Breed, he's sure to have his mother's chestnut brown hair and incredible blue eyes. The same as his brother, Marcel."

Sara rolled her eyes. "Well, I don't care what he looks like and I don't care about his pedigree either. I'm not looking for a mate, and if I was, I certainly wouldn't be going about it this way."

Yet despite all of that—despite her unwillingness to be part of some antiquated agreement that had long outlived its expiration date as far as she was concerned—she knew she couldn't walk away from her obligation to her family.

Honoring the pact was important to her parents, which made it important to her as well.

And there was another, more selfish reason she had finally conceded to come.

Several hundred thousand reasons. The amount of her trust fund, which her father had agreed to release to her early. She would have it all at the end of the week—after her handfast with Jehan Mafakhir was over.

Sera needed that money.

As much as her father loved her, he knew she wouldn't be able to turn away from what he had offered. Not when there was so much she could do with that kind of gift.

That didn't mean she had to like it.

Nor did it mean she had to like Jehan Mafakhir.

In fact, she was determined to avoid him as much as possible for the duration of their confinement together. If she was lucky, maybe they wouldn't even need to speak to each other.

Miserable with the whole idea, she exhaled a slow, defeated sigh. "It's only for eight nights, right?"

Leila nodded, then her eyes went wide at the sound of measured footsteps and deep voices in the hallway. Putting a finger to her lips, she cracked open the door and peered out. She reported to Sera in a hushed whisper. "Jehan just walked into the salon with his father and Marcel. You can't leave him waiting. We have to get out of here right now!"

The bubble of anxiety Sera had been fighting suddenly spiked into hot panic. "So soon? I thought I'd have a few more minutes before—"

"Now, Sera! Let's go!" Grabbing her by the arm, Leila opened the door and ushered her outside. As they moved toward the salon, Leila leaned in close to whisper next to Sera's ear. "And I was right, by the way. He's beyond handsome."

CHAPTER 4

Jehan wasn't sure what had presented the most convincing argument for his consenting to take part in the handfasting: his brother's earnest persuasion on the ride to the Darkhaven, or his father's stoic greeting and his resulting obvious, if unspoken, expectation that his eldest son would shirk his obligation to the family.

If he'd been met with furious demands that he must pick up the mantle of responsibility concerning the pact with the Sanhajas, it would have been the easiest thing for Jehan to pivot on his heels and hoof his way back to Casablanca to catch the earliest flight back to Rome.

But his father hadn't blown up or slammed his fists into his desk when Jehan arrived in his study a few minutes ago to explain that he wanted no part in the duty waiting for him in the salon. Rahim Mafakhir had listened in thoughtful silence. Then he'd simply stood up and walked toward the door of his study without a word.

Not that he'd needed to speak. His lack of reaction spoke volumes.

He'd been anticipating Jehan's refusal.

He'd been fully prepared for his prodigal son to let him and the rest of the family down.

And as much as Jehan had wanted to pretend he was okay with that, the fact was, it had stung.

It had been at that precise moment—his father's strong hand wrapped around the doorknob, his stern face grim with disappointment—that Jehan had blurted out words he was certain he'd live to regret.

"I'll do it," he'd said. "Eight nights with the Sanhaja female, as the pact requires. Nothing more. Then, after the handfast is over and my duty is fulfilled, I'll go back to Rome and the pact can move on to the next of our kin in line to heed the call."

Now, as Jehan entered the salon with his father and Marcel, he felt a small spark of hope.

She wasn't there. Only his mother and an anxious-looking couple he assumed was Omar and Amina Sanhaja. No sign of the unmated Breedmate he was supposed to formally meet tonight.

Holy shit. Dare he hope the Sanhajas' daughter had called a stop to this farce?

"Here we are!" An exuberant voice sounded brightly from behind him, killing his hope before it had a chance to fully catch fire.

The voice belonged to a leggy blonde with a megawatt smile and pretty, pale green eyes. Attractive. Certainly cheerful and energetic. As far as temporary housemates went, Marcel was right—there were worse sentences he could endure.

The blonde paused to glance behind her, and that was when Jehan realized his error.

"Come on, Seraphina!" She grabbed the hand of a tall, curvy brunette who'd hesitated momentarily just outside the threshold. "Don't be shy. Everyone's waiting for you."

The blonde was lovely, as Marcel had assured him. But her reserved, darker-haired sister was something far more than that.

Blessed with the figure of a goddess and the face of an angel, when she appeared in the doorway, Jehan could barely keep from gaping. He glanced briefly to his brother and met Marcel's *I-told-you-so* grin.

Damn.

Seraphina Sanhaja was, in a word, extraordinary.

Framed by a mane of cascading brown curls, a pair of long-lashed eyes the color of rich sandalwood flecked with gold lifted to meet Jehan's arrested gaze. Her face was heart-shaped and delicate, an exotic artistry of fine bones and smooth, sun-kissed olive skin that glowed with rising pink color as she stared at him.

How this stunning woman had managed to get past the age of twenty without some other Breed male locking her into a blood bond, Jehan couldn't even imagine.

His pulse stirred at the sight of her, sending heat into his veins. Even though he wasn't in the market for a mate, as a hot-blooded Breed male, it was impossible to deny his body's intense reaction to the female. He drew in a slow breath, his acute senses taking in the cinnamon-sweet scent of her and the subtle uptick of her heartbeat as he held her in his unblinking gaze.

For a moment, he was sorry he didn't have any use for tribal laws or ancient pacts that would put Seraphina Sanhaja in his company—better yet, in his bed—for the next eight nights.

Her sister tugged her forward on a light giggle. "Isn't this exciting?"

Where Leila crackled with unbridled enthusiasm, Seraphina was nearly impossible to read. Her lush lips pursed a bit as she made a silent study of him, her expression carefully schooled, inscrutable.

Standing before him, she was reticent and aloof.

Assessing and...*unimpressed?*

Jehan's brows lifted. He didn't want to admit the jab his ego took at her apparent lack of interest in him. With his thick, shoulder-length dark hair, tawny skin and light blue eyes, he'd never been at a loss for female attention.

Oh, hell. What did he care if she didn't like what she saw? The week ahead was going to pass a hell of a lot faster if he didn't have to spend it with a blushing, eyelash-batting Breedmate who couldn't wait to surrender her carotid to him.

Jehan stared her down ruthlessly as the formal introductions were made.

He was still trying to figure her out after what seemed like endless polite, if awkward conversation in the salon. Their parents made pleasant small talk together. Marcel and Leila fell into easy chatter about books and music and current events, both of them clearly striving to bring Jehan and Seraphina into the discussion.

It wasn't working.

Jehan's thoughts were back with his team in Rome. When he'd spoken earlier tonight with Lazaro Archer, he'd learned that rumors were circulating about Opus Nostrum moving weapons across Europe and possibly into Africa.

Even though he was only going to be delayed from his missions with the Order for a week, he already itched to be suited up in his patrol gear and weapons, not stuffed into the white button-down, dark trousers, and gleaming black dress shoes he'd worn from the airport.

As for Seraphina, Jehan got the feeling she was only seconds away from making a break for the nearest exit.

The otherwise cool and collected female jumped when the clock struck twelve. Smiled wanly as her mother erupted into excited applause.

"It's time!" Amina Sanhaja crowed from across the room. "Go on now, you two. Go on!"

As their families began to urge them out of the salon together, Jehan slanted a questioning look on Seraphina.

"The midnight garden stroll," she murmured under her breath, the first thing she'd said to him directly all night. She stared at him as if annoyed that she needed to explain. "It's part of the tradition."

Ah, right. Marcel had mentioned something about that in the car when Jehan was only half-listening. He'd much rather watch Seraphina's mouth explaining it to him again.

She softly cleared her throat. "At midnight, we're supposed to walk together privately to mark the turning of the hourglass and the beginning of our—"

"Sentence?" he prompted wryly.

Surprise arched her fine brows.

Jehan smirked and gestured for her to walk ahead of him. "Please, after you."

With their parents and siblings crowding the salon doorway behind them, he and Seraphina left the room and headed down the hallway, toward a pair of arched glass doors leading out to the moonlit gardens behind the Darkhaven estate.

The night was cool and crisp in the desert, and infinitely dark. Above them stars glittered and a half-moon glowed milky white against an endless black velvet sky.

It might have been romantic, if the woman walking alongside him didn't take each delicate step as if she was being led to the gallows. She glanced behind them for about the sixth time in as many minutes.

"Are they still there?" Jehan asked.

"Yes," she said. "All of them are standing in front of the glass, watching us."

He could fix that. "Come with me."

Taking her elbow in a loose hold, he ducked off the main garden path with her to one of the many winding paths that crisscrossed the manicured topiary and flowering, fragrant hedges.

The sweet perfume of jasmine and roses laced the night air, but it was another scent—cinnamon and something far more exotic—that made him inhale a bit deeper as he brought Seraphina to a more private section of the gardens.

She hung back a few paces, following him almost hitchingly in her strappy high heels. When he glanced over his shoulder, he found her pretty face pinched in a frown. Then she stopped completely and shook her head. "This is far enough."

"Relax, Seraphina. I'm not going to push you into the hibiscus and ravish you."

Her eyes widened for a second, but then her frown narrowed into an affronted scowl. "That's not why I stopped. These shoes...they're killing my feet."

Jehan walked back to her. Eyeing the tall spikes, he exhaled a low curse. "I don't doubt they're killing you. In the right hands, those things could be deadly weapons."

She smiled—a genuine, heart-stopping smile that was there and gone in an instant.

"Hold on to my shoulder."

Her fingers came to rest on him, generating a swift, unexpected electricity in his veins. Jehan tried to ignore the feel of her touch as he reached down and lifted her left foot into his hands. He unfastened the pretty, but impractical, shoe and slipped it off.

Her satisfied sigh as he freed her bare foot went through him even more powerfully than her touch. Gritting his teeth to discourage his fangs from punching out of his gums in heated response, Jehan made quick work of her other shoe, then stepped away from her.

"Better?" His voice had thickened. Along with another part of his anatomy.

"Much better." She was looking at him cautiously as she took the pair of sandals from where they dangled off his fingertips. "Thank you."

"My pleasure." And it was. More than he might have wanted to admit. He cocked his head at her. "How old are you, Seraphina?"

"Excuse me?"

He immediately felt rude for asking, but there was a part of him that wanted to know. Needed to know. "We're supposed to be getting to know each other, aren't we?"

The reminder seemed to calm some of her indignation. "I'm twenty-seven. Why do you want to know?"

"I just wonder why you aren't already mated and blood-bonded. You were raised in a Darkhaven, so you must know many Breed males. If any of the ones I know ever saw you, there'd be at least a hundred of them beating a path to your door."

She stared at him for a moment in uncertain silence, then shrugged. "Maybe I prefer human men."

Shit. He hadn't even considered that. "Do you?"

"To be honest, I haven't given the idea of a blood bond a lot of thought. My life is full and I keep busy enough with other things."

She started walking away from him, her bare feet moving softly, fluidly, along the bricked path. And he couldn't help noticing she hadn't really answered his question.

He strode up next to her. "What kind of things have kept you so busy that you're still unmated and nearing the ripe old age of thirty?"

She scoffed, but there was humor in her tone. "Important things."

"Such as?"

"I volunteer at some of the border camps, taking care of people who've been displaced by wars and other disasters. I guess you could say it's been something of a calling for me."

Well, he hadn't been expecting that. Granted, she didn't seem the type to flutter around in fancy dresses and high-heeled sandals all day, but he also wouldn't have imagined a stunning woman like her spending her time covered in dust and sweat. Or putting herself in harm's way in those turbulent areas that had never known peace, even before the wars between the humans and the Breed.

"What about you, Jehan?"

"What about me?"

"For starters, how old are you?"

"Thirty-three."

She glanced at him. "Younger than I expected. But then it's impossible to guess a Breed male's age. It's always seemed unfair to me that your kind never looks older than thirty, even the Gen Ones who've been around for centuries."

Jehan lifted his shoulder. "A small consolation for the fact that we can never put our faces in the sunlight. Unlike your kind."

"Hm. I guess that's true." She tilted her head at him. "What exactly do you do in Rome?"

"I'm part of the Order. Captain of my unit," he added, not sure why he felt the need to impress her with his elevated rank.

She stopped dead in her tracks again, and something told him it didn't have anything to do with sore feet. A chill rolled off her as Jehan pivoted to look at her. She barked out a brittle laugh and shook her head. "No wonder they didn't tell me anything about you."

"Who?"

"My parents." Her arms crossed rigidly over her chest. "If they'd mentioned you were part of that brutal organization, there's no way in hell I would've agreed to any of this. No matter what leverage they used to try to convince me."

Jehan's suspicions rankled along with his pride. "You have a problem with the Order?"

"I have a problem with cold-blooded killers."

Was she serious? "My brethren and I are not—"

She didn't let him finish. "I've devoted myself—everything I am—to saving lives. You're in the business of taking them." When he exhaled a tight curse and shook his head, she gave him a sharp look. "How many people have you killed?"

"Me personally, or—"

"I think that answers my question." She moved past him and started walking away at a swift clip.

He caught up in a handful of strides. "There's nothing cold-blooded about what the Order does. Are we brutal sometimes? Only when there's no other choice. But we call it justice. We're protectors, not killers."

"Semantics."

"No, it's reality, Seraphina." When she didn't slow her pace, he reached out and caught her arm. She flinched at the contact. He wondered if it was purely out of indignation or the fact that even though a chill had expanded between them, the heat of attraction still sparked to life the instant they touched. Her pulse fluttered at the base of her elegant throat, her heart pounding so hard and fast he could feel it through his fingertips.

His entire body responded to that frantic drumming, his veins heating, his fangs prickling as they elongated behind his closed lips. His cock responded just as hungrily, pressing in demand against the zipper of his trousers.

She pulled out of his grasp. "I can't do this. You need to know that I have no interest in any kind of handfast, and I'm not looking for a blood bond. Especially with you."

Jehan drew back. "You don't want to be part of this because you just found out I belong to the Order?"

Her lush lips compressed into a flat line. "I never wanted to be part of it."

"That makes two of us."

"What?" She gaped at him.

He shook his head. "I only agreed out of obligation. Because I feel I owe it to my family to uphold their traditions, even if they don't mesh with mine."

Her breath rushed out of her. "Oh, thank God!"

She didn't hold back her relief. She sounded like a death row inmate suddenly granted a full pardon, and his pride took another ding to hear the depth of her alleviation. "So, what do we do now, Seraphina? Go back inside and tell them we're calling the whole thing off?"

"You mean, break the pact? We can't do that." She glanced down at the bricks at her feet. "I can't do that."

"Maybe it's time someone did."

He studied her under the thin light of the moon and stars overhead. Everything Breed in him was urging him to touch her—to lift her chin and sweep the loose tendrils of her curly brown hair away from her eyes, if only so he could see their unusual shade again. But he kept his hands to himself, fisting them at his sides when the desire to reach out nearly overrode his good sense.

"You strike me as a forward-thinking, intelligent woman. You don't actually believe the pact holds any kind of sway over the peace between our families anymore, do you?"

"No, I don't. But it's important to my parents, and that makes it important to me. But..." Finally, she lifted her head to meet his gaze. "There's another reason I agreed to the handfasting. I have a trust fund. A sizable one. It's not due to release to me until my thirtieth birthday, but my father's promised it to me early. At the end of the handfast."

"Ah." Jehan lifted his chin. He hadn't taken her for the type to be motivated by money, but he supposed there were worse things. "So, you're here on bribery, and I'm here out of some pointless obligation to prove to my father that I'm not his greatest disappointment."

"That's why you're here?"

Her voice was quiet, almost sympathetic. The soft look in her eyes threatened to unravel his thin control.

He gave a dismissive wave of his hand. "It doesn't matter why either of us are here. Apparently, we both just need to get through the next eight nights so we can get on with our real lives."

She nodded. "How are we going to do that?"

Looking at her standing so close to him in the cool night air, her beautiful face and tempting curves making his mouth water and his blood streak hot through his veins, Jehan wasn't sure how the hell he was going to survive a week of seclusion with her. Not without putting his hands or fangs—or any other part of his anatomy—within arm's reach of her.

One thing was certain. They would have to set some clear boundaries. Rigid boundaries that couldn't be crossed.

And rules.

Jehan let his gaze travel the length of her, desire hammering through every cell in his body.

Oh, yeah. To survive the next week alone with this female, he was going to need *a lot* of boundaries and rules.

CHAPTER 5

She should have said no.

She should have trusted her good sense and left Jehan standing in the middle of the midnight garden alone last night, not helped him set down terms of their own for the ritual neither of them wanted to be part of.

Instead, that next evening, she found herself seated beside him at the head of a long banquet room in her parents' Darkhaven in front of a combined hundred members of their two families who had assembled to celebrate their send-off and the start of the handfast's first night.

In less than an hour, she and Jehan would be delivered to the private oasis retreat and left to fend for themselves until officials from both tribes came to retrieve them at the end of the eight nights. Until then, she would be trapped with him in close quarters. Intimate quarters.

Oh, God. She must be out of her damn mind.

Sera reached for her wine glass and drained it in one gulp.

"Pace yourself," Jehan drawled from beside her. "If you get too tipsy, I'd hate to have to carry you out of here tonight."

"Like hell you will." She smiled and spoke under her breath, doing her best to pretend he wasn't the last male she'd ever choose to spend time with. "And we have a deal, remember? One that specifically states no touching. I expect you to honor that."

A chuckle emanated from him, so deep it was almost a growl. "Don't worry, I have no intention of touching you."

She placed her empty glass back on the table. "Good. Then don't even joke about it."

"Trust me, Seraphina, you'll know when I'm joking."

She made the mistake of looking at him and found him smirking as he leaned back in his chair. But there wasn't any humor in his light blue eyes. Only a dark promise that made her pulse skitter through her veins.

According to tradition, he was dressed in a white linen tunic and loose pants. A long, striped sash bearing his blue-and-gold family colors was tied around his trim waist. He looked decadent and confident, sprawled against the back of his seat. As arrogant as a prince accustomed to having the world bend to his whim, even if his title was as musty as the pact that bound her to him tonight.

As for Sera, she had been clothed according to tradition too. Wrapped and knotted into yards of diaphanous red silk that somehow formed a body-skimming gown, she was also dripping in beads and bangles. Painted henna patterns swirled in delicate flourishes and arcs over the backs of her hands and up her limbs.

The dress constricted her breathing and the decorations on her skin made her feel like an offering headed for the altar.

Jehan's searing gaze beside her wasn't helping.

Even though they'd agreed to avoid each other as much as possible for the next week, Sera couldn't forget the heat that had ignited between them in the garden. Or in the moment they'd first made eye contact in the Darkhaven's salon.

He was attractive; she couldn't begin to deny that. With his luxurious chestnut hair and impossibly blue eyes, he was heart-stoppingly gorgeous. The fact that his massive, muscular body and powerful presence seemed to suck all the air out of the room only made the handsome Breed male even more magnetic.

The V-neck of his linen tunic was cut several inches down his powerful chest, baring a lot of tawny skin and smooth muscle, and the edges of his Breed *dermaglyphs*. The color-infused skin markings indicated the vampire's mood, and right now, the neutral hues of Jehan's *glyphs* told her that he'd recently fed.

Not surprising. It was customary for a Breed male about to enter the handfast to slake his blood thirst on a willing human Host before the week began. This to ensure that he didn't drink from his Breedmate companion and bond to her out of physical need instead of love.

A vision of Jehan drinking from the throat of another woman sprang into Sera's mind uninvited. His dark head nestled into the curve of a tender neck. His sensual mouth fastened to smooth, pale skin as his sharp fangs penetrated a pounding vein and he began to drink his fill.

Would he gentle a woman with coaxing words and soothing caresses when he took her carotid between his teeth? Or would he spring on her like the predator he was, dominating her with speed and force and white-hot power?

Some troubling part of her she didn't recognize stirred with the need to know.

Sera groaned. She squirmed in her seat as her pulse thudded faster and erotic warmth bloomed between her thighs.

She wanted to cross her legs to relieve the unwelcome ache, but the skirts of her ceremonial dress were too restricting. Elsewhere in the banquet room, her father was reciting the traditional terms of the handfast. She only half-listened, too distracted by Jehan's presence beside her and the heat of his gaze on her as she fidgeted and shifted in her chair.

It suddenly occurred to her that the room had gone strangely quiet. Expectantly quiet.

All eyes in the room were fixed on her, and her father was no longer speaking.

Jehan stood up and pointedly cleared his throat. "It's time for us to go, Seraphina."

"Oh." She rose to her feet, eager to escape the weight of everyone's gazes. Plus, she couldn't wait to put some much-needed distance between herself and Jehan.

But he wasn't moving. Why wasn't he moving?

"Don't forget the kiss!" someone shouted cheerfully from among the gathering. "It's tradition to seal the pact with a kiss!"

Leila. *Damn that girl.*

Sera shot a narrowed glare at her exuberant sibling but her grin showed no remorse.

"Kiss her!" she shouted again.

And then across the room, Marcel called for the kiss too. Someone else picked up the chant, then another. Before long, the entire place was applauding and thundering with the command. "Kiss her! Kiss her! Kiss her!"

Sera turned a miserable look on Jehan. "We don't really have t—"

Before she could finish, he moved closer and his mouth slanted over hers in a blast of heat. His lips caressed hers, impossibly soft, achingly sensual. His hands held her face, and yes, they were gentle. His kiss was too, but beneath its tenderness was a possessiveness—a raw power—that rocked her.

He mastered her mouth in an instant, and every brush of his lips had her aching to be claimed by him.

Her thoughts scattered. Her knees went a little boneless.

Even worse, the coil of warmth that had gathered between her thighs a few moments ago blazed molten and wild now.

Sera raised her hands to grip his shoulders, if only to keep from sagging against him in front of a hundred onlookers. All the reassurances of their private agreement to spend the next week in separate corners flew away like leaves on the wind as Jehan kissed her. She couldn't help it. She moaned against his mouth, her pulse quickening, hammering even louder than the cheers of the gathering around them.

Jehan released her abruptly. His blue eyes glittered with sparks of amber heat, their transformation making his desire all too clear. He ran his tongue over his wet lips and she saw the points of his fangs, now gleaming in his mouth like razor-sharp diamonds. His breath rasped out of him, rough and raw.

"Let's go," he growled for her ears only. "The sooner we get this damned farce over with, the better."

Then he took her by the hand and stalked away from the table with her in tow.

CHAPTER 6

Jehan's body was still rock hard and vibrating with lust more than an hour after he and Seraphina were delivered to the oasis retreat.

Holy hell. That kiss...

As short-lived and chaste as it had been, it had gripped him in a way that staggered him.

He hadn't been able to deny how attracted he was to Seraphina from the instant he laid eyes on her. Now he knew she wanted him too. Her response to their kiss had left no question about that. The color that had rushed up her throat and into her cheeks couldn't be blamed on anything else, nor could her soft little moans. He'd felt her desire for him. He'd breathed in the sweet scent of her arousal, felt it drumming in her blood.

His own blood had answered, and now that his mouth had sampled a taste of Seraphina's kiss, everything primal and male in him—everything Breed—pounded with a dark, dangerous need for more.

Somehow, he'd managed to rein it in back at the Darkhaven celebration.

Now, he just had to make sure to keep his desire in check for the duration of their confinement at the private villa.

Eight nights, that's all, he reassured himself.

One hundred and ninety-two hours, give or take the few that had already passed tonight.

Which meant somewhere around eleven thousand minutes. All of them to be spent in too-close quarters with a woman who lit up every nerve ending in his body like a flame set to dry tinder.

Yeah, the math wasn't helping.

Everything they might need had been provided for by their families. Clothing, toiletries, a fully stocked kitchen for Seraphina. They would want for nothing from the outside world, and no one would interrupt their time together until the handfasting had ended.

They'd divvied up the place as soon as they'd been dropped off, negotiating territory and establishing boundaries where neither of them would cross. It only seemed right to give her the privacy of the massive bedroom. As for Jehan, he would inhabit the general living quarters, and use the big nest of cushions in the main room as his bed for the next week.

With Seraphina settling into the sole bedroom suite on her own, Jehan prowled the open space of the villa like a caged cat, taking stock of the unfamiliar surroundings. He strode across richly dyed rugs spread over terra cotta tiled floors. Above his head, the high, domed ceiling glowed with soft golden lights that glinted off a mosaic of gem-colored glass embedded into the white stucco plaster.

Down the wing of the hallway opposite the bedroom where Seraphina had sequestered herself was a traditional bathing room with a steaming, spring-fed pool surrounded by silk-draped columns and fat pillar candles.

In the adjacent, open-concept chamber, more beds of cushions and pillows were arranged around the room, some steeped in shadows, others strategically placed in front of tall, ornately framed mirrors. Erotic statuary and tables holding bottles of perfumed oils and incense jars completed the pleasure den.

Jehan frowned, shaking his head. The handfast agreement may forbid a male from forcing himself on the Breedmate sent with him to this place, but every room in the villa was obviously designed with sex and seduction in mind.

And try as he might to resist imagining Seraphina reclined on those cushions or stepping naked out of the steam-clouded baths, his mind refused to obey.

Eight nights.

He would be lucky to make it through this first one without losing his mind or tearing down the bedroom door she was currently hiding behind on the other side of the villa.

He needed fresh air. What he really needed was a hundred-foot wall between him and his unwanted roommate. A length of sturdy chain wouldn't hurt either.

Jehan walked back out to the main living area and headed for the French doors leading out to an oasis patio in back. As he crossed the room, he heard Seraphina hiss a curse from inside the bedroom.

He paused, listened. Told himself to keep walking in the opposite direction.

She swore again and he detoured for the passage leading to the bedroom.

"Are you all right in there?"

"Yes. Everything's fine." Her reply was quick, dismissively so.

He stood outside the closed door and heard her grumble in frustration. "I'm coming in."

"No. Wait—"

She stood in the center of the big room, tangled in the complicated yards of red silk that comprised her dress from the celebration. When he chuckled, she glowered. "It's not funny, you arrogant ass."

"Really?" He didn't even try to curb his grin. "Looks pretty funny from where I'm standing."

She huffed, narrowing a glare on him. "If you're going to stand there laughing at me, you might as well help."

He held up his hands. "No touching, remember? How can I help without breaking that part of our deal?" Of course, they'd also said no kissing, but that rule was already shot all to hell, even before they'd arrived tonight. "Ask me nicely and maybe I'll consider bending the rules."

Her shoulders sagged in defeat, but the baring of her straight, white teeth hardly looked submissive. "Jehan, will you please help me?"

He didn't want to admit how enticing his name sounded on her pretty lips. Especially when it involved asking him to assist in undressing her. His blood agreed, licking through his veins in eager anticipation as he stalked across the bedroom to where she stood.

She raised her right hand and gathered her long cascade of bead-strewn, soft brown curls off her neck as she presented her back to him. "There must be a dozen tiny knots holding this dress together. And I can't figure out where the ends of the long wrappings begin either."

Jehan stood behind her for a long moment, just looking. Just drinking in the sight of her graceful nape and elegant spine. She was blessed with hourglass curves and long, lean legs. The ceremonial dress hugged every inch of her in all the right places. Including the rounded swells of her beautiful ass.

How was it that his mouth could water, yet feel desert dry at the same time?

His gums prickled as his fangs swelled against his tongue. Another part of him was swelling too, pressing in carnal demand against the loose white linen of his pants. Heat rose in his blood and in his vision, swamping his irises with amber fire.

He reached out and began to loosen the first of the intricate knots.

There were eight of them, not a dozen. Each one was a test of his dexterity as well as his self-control. One by one, the fastenings fell away, baring Seraphina's naked back to his fevered gaze, inch by torturous inch.

Somewhere along the way, his lungs had stopped working. Desire raked him, sharp talons stealing his breath as he freed the last of the tiny knots and the scarlet silk slackened in his fingers.

Seraphina didn't seem to be breathing either. She stood unmoving, her mane of long hair still held aloft in her hand. Warmth poured off her skin, and he knew she had to feel his heat reaching out to her too.

Her heartbeat ticked frantically in the side of her neck, drawing his blazing eyes. The urge to stroke that tender pulse point—to touch and taste every enticing inch of her—nearly overwhelmed him.

Clamping his molars together, he fought to keep a grip on those urges. When he finally found his voice, it came out in a gravelly rasp. "There you go. All finished."

Seraphina paused, letting her hair fall. She turned a glance over her shoulder at him. "The wrappings too?"

Shit. He scowled and began a quick search for one of the ends of the lengths of silk. He tugged it loose and began to unwind it from around her bodice and waist. The damn thing was too long to pull free.

He swore and shook his head. "You'll have to turn with it."

"Like this?" She obeyed, pivoting in front of him. He nodded, then pulled the silk taut, letting the tail of it collect on the floor as she slowly spun before him. Around and around and around, her springy brown curls dancing as she turned, the beads threaded through the strands twinkling under the soft lights of the bedroom.

He couldn't take his eyes off her.

In some primitive part of his brain, he was the conquering desert warlord and she was his mesmerizing captive. His irresistible, stolen prize. He watched her spin, watched the ribbon of scarlet silk unwind, revealing more and more of the beautiful woman wrapped inside.

He wanted to keep undressing her.

When he looked at Seraphina, when he breathed in her cinnamon-sweet scent and felt the warmth of her skin with each dizzying turn she took in front of him... Damn him, but being near her like this, there was *so much* he wanted.

The drumming beat of her pulse vibrated in the small space between their bodies, and it made his own blood throb in answer. It made him hunger in a way he'd never fully known.

It made him want to burn the pact between their families and take her right here and now, willing or not.

Claim her.

Possess her in every way.

Make her his.

Dangerous thinking.

And a temptation he wasn't at all certain he would be able to resist.

Not for this one night, let alone seven more.

CHAPTER 7

She didn't know the exact moment when the air between them changed from simply hot and playful to something darker. Something so fierce and powerful, it made all of her nerve endings stand at full attention.

Jehan wanted her.

She'd have to be an idiot not to realize that.

She wanted him too.

And she was too smart to think for one second that he hadn't picked up on her staggering awareness of him as a man. As a dangerously seductive Breed male who could have her carotid caught in his teeth just as swiftly as he could have her legs parted beneath the driving pound of his muscular body.

Sera swallowed hard, her breath and heart racing as she slowed to a stop before him.

She glanced down, to where she was tethered to his strong hands by the unraveled length of red silk.

Although she was covered where it counted, there wasn't much of her dress left. Most of it lay on the floor at her feet; yards of scarlet pooled in the scant space between her body and Jehan's.

She licked her lips as she struggled for words. She should tell him to go, but everything female in her yearned for him to stay. She was no trembling virgin, no stranger to sex. But never with a Breed male. And the electricity that crackled to life between Jehan and her was something she'd never felt before.

It was arresting.

Consuming.

Terrifying in its intensity.

Yet it wasn't fear of him she felt when she held his piercing light blue eyes. It was fear of herself and of the way he made her feel. Fear of the things he made her want.

"Jehan, I..." She shook her head, unsure what she meant to say to him. Leave?

Stay?

Forget the fact that neither one of them had come to this place willingly, nor intended to walk away from the archaic tradition with a blood-bonded mate?

But that's not what this moment was about.

What she saw in Jehan's amber-swamped gaze right now didn't have anything to do with their romantic surroundings or the expectation and hopes of their families. The things she was feeling had nothing to do with any of that either.

It was desire, pure and simple.

Immediate and intense.

Her body throbbed with it, longing pounding furiously in her breast and stirring a molten heat in the center of her. She drew a shallow breath— then held it tight as Jehan reached out to caress her cheek. His warm fingers felt hard and strong against her face, but he stroked her with such tenderness, she couldn't hold back the soft moan that spilled past her lips.

She stood rooted in place while her thoughts and emotions spiraled with rising anticipation.

The cool air of the room made her exposed skin feel even tighter. Her nipples ached behind the gauzy ribbons of silk that barely covered them. Goose bumps rose on her naked shoulders and arms with each second she endured under Jehan's hot, unwavering stare.

His fingers drifted away from her face slowly, then skated in a scorching trail down the side of her neck and onto the line of her left shoulder. She felt him trace the small red birthmark that rode her bicep— her Breedmate mark. His fingertips caressed the teardrop-and-crescent-moon symbol that signified she was something other than simply human.

That mark also meant that if she drank his blood, she would be bound to him and only him, for as long as either of them lived.

As if in answer to his touch, her veins vibrated with a primal quickening, pulse points throbbing in response to each tender stroke.

"You are...so incredibly beautiful." His deep voice was a growl of sound, tangling through his teeth and fangs. "But we made a deal,

Seraphina."

She knew they had a deal. No looking. No touching. No physical contact of any kind. They had set clear boundaries and established separate corners where they could cohabitate for the week without having to spend any awkward time together. When the handfast was over, they would simply say their good-byes and return to their normal lives.

So why was she wishing so desperately that Jehan would pull her into his arms?

Why was she longing to feel the press of his muscled, hard body against her?

Why was the coil of smoldering need within her winding tighter, all of her nerve endings on fire and eager for more of his touch?

Eager for his kiss and everything that was certain to follow...

But he didn't kiss her.

A snarl curled up from the back of his throat. An animal sound. An otherworldly sound.

One of denial.

He shook his head, sending the thick waves of his dark hair swaying where they brushed his broad shoulders. His hand dropped away, down to his side. On a slow exhale, he stepped back, creating a cold vacuum of space between them.

He stooped to pick up the pool of red silk from the floor. He was retreating, yet when his gaze lifted to hers, his eyes still blazed with fiery desire, so hot it seared her. His fangs still glittered razor-sharp and hungered behind his lips.

He wanted her. It was written in his fierce expression and in the arousal that made itself obvious when she glanced down at the sizable bulge tenting his loose linen pants.

And he knew that she wanted him just as badly.

She could see that knowledge gleaming in his arrogant, knowing stare.

Damn him. He knew very well, and he was enjoying her torment!

He placed the mound of silk into her hands, a grin tugging at the corner of his mouth. "Goodnight, Seraphina."

He pivoted back toward the door. Then he strode out of the room without so much as a backward glance, leaving her to stare after him, half-dressed, fuming, and determined to avoid the infuriating ass for the duration of her confinement with him.

CHAPTER 8

For the next two days, he hardly saw Seraphina.

She spent her evenings behind the closed door of the massive bedroom suite, pointedly ignoring his existence. During the daytime, she slipped outside to the villa's sunbaked patio for hours on end, safely out of his reach and about as far away from his company as she could get.

She was pissed off, punishing him with frosty silence and deliberate avoidance.

Exactly as he'd intended when he'd left her high and dry—and as sexually frustrated as he was—that first night.

Better to earn her contempt than test his control under the desire-drenched heat of her gaze again. Her absence was a reprieve he welcomed. Better that than trying to withstand the temptation of her enticing curves and infinitely soft skin, now that he knew the pleasure of both.

Fuck. He'd only touched her for a few moments and the feel of her was branded into his fingertips. Her warmth and cinnamon-sugar scent was seared into his senses.

Even though she was out of sight now—rummaging quietly in the kitchen, by the sound of it—all he had to do was close his eyes and there she was in his mind. Standing in front of him in nothing but a few scraps of scarlet silk, her parted lips and heavy-lidded eyes inviting him to touch her. To take her.

No, pleading for him to do so.

But he'd shown her, right?

Pretending he was the one in control, denying both of them the pleasure they both wanted because he'd been too swamped with need to trust he could control himself. Now she was going to great lengths to ignore him, no doubt cursing him as a cold bastard. Meanwhile, he was walking around the villa like a caged animal with a semipermanent case of blue balls.

Damn.

He wasn't only a bastard. He was an idiot.

On a curse, he raked a hand through his hair and got up from the large floor cushion where he'd been unsuccessfully attempting to doze. It was just about sundown and he was twitchy with the need to be moving, to be doing something useful. Hell, he'd settle for doing anything at all.

He'd never been good at inactivity and the boredom of his exile was driving him insane.

More than once, he'd thought about slipping out in the middle of the night to run off some of his tension. Or say fuck the handfast and hoof it all the way to Casablanca and take the earliest flight to Rome.

With his Breed genetics, he could make it to the city in about as many hours as it would take to drive it. Maybe sooner.

Tempting.

But he couldn't leave Seraphina by herself out here. And as much as he wanted to get back to work going after Opus with his teammates at the Order, he wasn't about to abandon his honor or his family's by violating the terms of the pact.

If she could endure the week together and adhere to the ridiculous restrictions imposed on them by the ancient agreement—in addition to their own set of rules—then so could he.

And he supposed he really owed her an apology for the way he acted the other night.

Padding silently on his bare feet, Jehan strode toward the kitchen where he'd heard her a minute ago. She had her back to him, seated on an overstuffed sofa in the adjacent dining nook.

With her knees drawn up and her head bent down to study whatever she held in her hands, she didn't even notice him stealing up behind her from the kitchen. At first, he thought she'd taken one of the many books from the villa's library. But then he realized the small object was something else.

A phone.

In direct violation of the "no communication with the outside world" terms of the handfast.

The sneaky little rebel.

He opened his mouth to call her out on the breach, but then his acute sight caught the last few lines of a text message thread filling the display. Some guy named Karsten was asking her where she was and why she'd left him without saying where she'd gone. He was worried, he said. He needed her. Said he wasn't any good without her.

For reasons he didn't want to examine, the idea that Seraphina had another man waiting for her somewhere—that she wouldn't even mention that fact to him at any point when they talked—sent a streak of anger through Jehan's veins.

That she would look at him so wantonly the other night when this other male—what the fuck kind of name was Karsten, anyway?—obviously cared about her, needed her, made Jehan wonder if he'd read her wrong from the start.

Of course, she'd already confessed to him that she only agreed to participate in the handfast to collect a handsome payout at the end. So, why should it surprise him to realize she was already spoken for?

"You're breaking the rules." His voice was low and even, betraying none of the heat that was running through his veins.

She startled so sharply, the phone practically leapt out of her fingers. She scrambled to keep it and whirled around on the sofa to gape at him in horror.

"Jehan! I didn't hear you come in the room."

"You don't say." He gestured to the phone now clutched tight to her breast. "How'd you get that in here?"

She had the decency to look at least a little contrite. "I made Leila smuggle it in with the clothing she packed for me. She didn't want to, but I insisted. How was I supposed to go an entire week completely cut off from everything?"

"And *everyone*?" Jehan prompted. "Who's Karsten?"

Her face blanched. No need for her to ask him if he saw her texts. Her guilty look said it all. "He's my partner."

"Partner?" He practically snarled the word.

"My coworker. Karsten volunteers with me at the border camps."

Some of Jehan's irritation cooled at the explanation. "For a coworker, he sounds very eager to have you back. He's no good without you?"

Her expression relaxed into one of mild dismissal. "Karsten is...a bit dramatic. Right now, he's concerned about a food and medical supply shipment that's being held up at a checkpoint near Marrakesh. Normally I make sure things clear without delays, but unfortunately this shipment didn't come in until after my parents called me home."

"What happens if the shipment doesn't get cleared?"

She crossed her arms over her breasts. "The food will rot and the medicine will spoil. It happens all too often."

"And this Karsten is unable to retrieve the supplies without you?" Jehan couldn't mask his judgment of the other man. If necessary food and medicine were sitting somewhere waiting to be delivered, he'd make damn sure it got where it needed to go.

Seraphina slipped off the sofa and walked to the marble-topped island where Jehan stood. "A lot of times, when things are delayed like this, my father's name helps loosen them up. Sometimes, it's a matter of finding the right palm to grease."

Jehan nodded. Corruption in local governments was nothing new. That Seraphina seemed comfortable navigating those tangled webs was impressive. She kept impressing him, and he wasn't sure he should like it as much as he did. "What do you think will free up this shipment of supplies?"

She shrugged faintly. "Does it matter? Karsten hasn't been able to get them on his own so far, and by the time our week is out here, it'll be too late. Food and medicine doesn't last long in the desert."

No, he supposed it didn't.

But maybe there was some way to fix the situation.

"You say you know the checkpoint where the supplies are being held up?"

"It's on the outskirts of Marrakesh. A lot of our materials pass through that same one."

Jehan considered. "That's only a few hours away from here by car."

"What are you saying?" She frowned. "Jehan, what are you thinking?"

"Let me borrow your phone."

She handed it over, still staring at him in question. Jehan entered his brother's number and waited for him to pick up. It took several rings, then Marcel's confused voice came over the line in greeting. "Hello?"

Jehan got right to the point. "I have a favor to ask of you."

"Jehan? What the hell are you doing calling me? And where did you get the phone? You know there's supposed to be no technology or outside communication—"

"I know," he bit off impatiently. "Where are you right now?"

"Ah...I'm home, but I'm getting ready to head out for a while. What's going on? Is everything all right with Seraphina?"

"She's fine. We're fine," Jehan assured him. "I need a vehicle. As soon as possible."

Marcel gasped. "What?"

Seraphina's eyes went about as wide as he imagined his brother's had just now.

"It's important, Marcel. You know I wouldn't ask if it wasn't."

"But you can't leave the villa. If you leave Seraphina alone out there, you'll be breaking the pact. Hell, you already are just by making this call to me."

"No one will know I called except you." Jehan glanced at Seraphina and shook his head. "As for breaking the pact by leaving her at the villa without me, not happening. She's coming with me, and we won't be gone long. No one will be the wiser."

"Except, once again, me." Marcel groaned. "I probably don't want to know what any of this is about, do I?"

"Probably not." Jehan smiled.

Marcel exhaled a curse. "Please tell me you don't want my Lambo."

"Actually, I was hoping for one of the Rovers from the Darkhaven fleet. With a full tank of fuel, if you would."

Marcel's deep sigh gusted over the line. "Does Seraphina realize yet what a demanding pain in the ass you can be?"

Jehan met her gaze and grinned. "I imagine she's figuring that out."

Marcel chuckled. "I'll drop it off at sundown."

CHAPTER 9

"Careful with that crate, Aleph. Those glass vials of vaccines are fragile."

Walking across the moonlit sand with her arm around one of the children from the refugee camp and a box of bandages held in her other hand, Sera directed another of the volunteers to the open back of the supply-laden Range Rover. "Massoud, take the large sack of rice to Fatima in the mess tent and ask her where she'd like us to store the rest of the raw grains. Let her know we have some crates of canned meats and boxes of fruit here too."

Behind her at the vehicle, Jehan was busy unloading the crates and boxes and sacks they'd just arrived with from the checkpoint near Marrakesh. Sera couldn't help pausing to watch him work. Dressed in jeans and a loose linen shirt with the sleeves rolled up past his *glyph*-covered forearms, he pitched in like the best of her other workers. Even better, in fact, since he was Breed. His strength and stamina outpaced half a dozen humans put together.

She still couldn't believe what he'd done for her tonight. For a village of displaced people he'd never met and didn't have to care about. All of the indignation and anger she'd felt toward him since their first night at the villa evaporated under her admiration for what he was doing now.

And it wasn't only admiration she felt when she looked at him.

There was attraction, to be sure. White-hot and magnetic.

But something stronger had begun to kindle inside her today. As unsettling as her desire for him was, this new emotion was even more terrifying. She *liked* him.

Jehan had intrigued her from their first introduction, even after she'd learned he made his living as a warrior. Their kiss at the banquet had ignited a need in her that she still hadn't been able to dismiss. And then, when he'd helped her out of her dress that initial night at the villa, she'd wanted him with an intensity that nearly overwhelmed her.

After he'd left her humiliated and awash in frustration, she'd almost been able to convince herself that he was simply an arrogant bastard and an aggravation she would just have to avoid or endure for the rest of their week together.

Now he had to go and do something kind for her like this. Something surprising and selfless.

Frowning, she turned away from him on a groan. "Come on, Yasmin. Let's go see if Fatima has anything good waiting in her kitchen tonight."

As they walked into the center of the camp, a Jeep was arriving from the other end of the makeshift village of tents and meager outbuildings. Yellow headlights bounced in the darkness as the vehicle jostled over the ruts in the dirt road into camp. The Jeep came to a halt several yards up and Karsten Hemmings hopped out of the driver's seat.

"Sera?" He jogged to meet her, a welcoming grin on his ruggedly handsome face. "I was down at the southern camp when I got word the supplies had been released." He gave her a quick kiss on the cheek as he took the box out of her hands. Then he reached down to pat the child's head with a smile. "What's going on? I thought you said you were going to be delayed with your parents for a few more days?"

She shrugged at the reminder of the small lie she'd told him. "I found an opportunity to get away for a little while, so I thought I'd run to Marrakesh and see what I could do about the supplies."

Karsten made a wry sound in his throat as he tossed the box of bandages to a passing camp volunteer. "How much did it cost this time?"

"A few thousand."

After haggling the checkpoint supervisor down as far as she could manage, she'd arranged to have the money wired to the corrupt official's personal account. It simply was the way business was done in her line of work sometimes, but all of the "few thousands" had added up over the years. Her account was nearly tapped dry now—at least until she completed the handfast and her father released her trust.

A group of children ran past and shouted for Yasmin to join them in a game of tag. The promise of treats in the mess tent quickly forgotten, the little girl ran off to join her friends.

"Stay close to camp, all of you!" Karsten called after them, watching them go. Then he cocked his head at Sera. "It's good to see you. When I heard you'd left to go to your family without telling anyone what it was about, I was afraid something was wrong." He glanced down, finally taking in her appearance. "What the hell happened to your clothes?"

Seeing how Leila had outfitted her for a week of lounging and potential romance, before Sera left the villa, she'd raided Jehan's wardrobe for something practical to wear out in the field.

She couldn't show up wearing any of the dresses or peasant skirts her sister had selected, so Sera had appropriated Jehan's white linen tunic from the night of the banquet and a loose-fitting pair of linen pants. With the pant legs rolled up several times, the waist held around her by a makeshift red silk belt, and a pair of her own kid leather flats, her clothing wasn't fashionable, but it was functional.

It also had the added benefit that it carried Jehan's deliciously spicy scent, which had been teasing her senses ever since she slipped the tunic over her head.

She wasn't sure how to explain what she was wearing, but then Karsten no longer seemed interested. His gaze flicked past Sera now, to where Jehan had just unloaded the last of the crates and supplies.

His brow rankled in confusion. "Who's that?"

"A friend," she said, unsure why she should feel awkward calling him that.

"He's Breed." Karsten's eyes came back to her now, wariness flattening his lips as he lowered his voice. "You brought one of them into the camp?"

Even though it had been twenty years and counting since the Breed were outed to mankind, prejudices still lingered. Even in her affable coworker, apparently.

"It's okay. Jehan is, ah...an old friend of my family." She waved her hand in dismissal of his concerns. "Besides, we won't be staying long. We have to get back to the villa tonight."

"The villa?"

Shit. She really didn't want to explain the whole awkward family pact and handfasting scenario to him. For one thing, it was none of Karsten's business—even if she did consider him a friend after they had dated briefly once upon a time. And maybe it was none of his business precisely *because* of the fact they had once dated.

Whatever the reason, she felt strangely protective of the time she'd spent with Jehan. It belonged to them—no one else.

"Once we get everything settled here in the camp, Jehan and I need to return. We're expected to be back as soon as possible." Which was about as close to the truth as she was going to get on that subject.

Karsten shook his head. "Well, you won't be leaving tonight. There's a big dust storm rolling in off the Sahara. It's moving fast, due here in the next hour or less. No way you'll be able to outrun it."

"Oh, no." A knot of anxiety tightened in her chest. "That's awful news."

"What's awful news?"

Jehan's deep voice awakened her nerve endings as sensually as a caress. He'd closed up the Rover and strode up behind her before she even realized it. When she pivoted to face him, she found his arresting blue eyes locked on Karsten.

"You must be Jehan." Instead of extending his hand in greeting, Karsten's fists balled on his hips. "I'm Karsten Hemmings, Sera's partner."

"Coworker." Jehan subtly corrected him. And as far as introductions went, his didn't exactly project friendliness either. His palm came down soft and warm—possessively—on her shoulder. "What's awful news?"

She tried to act as though his lingering touch was no big deal, as if it wasn't waking up every cell in her body and flooding her with heat. "There's a dust storm coming. Karsten says we may have to wait it out here at the camp. I know we need to get back soon, though. Your brother's waiting for us to return the Rover tonight—"

"Sera, if your friend has somewhere he needs to be," Karsten piped in helpfully, "then why don't you wait out the storm here at camp and I can bring you back to your parents' place tomorrow, after it passes?"

"Not happening." Jehan's curt reply allowed no argument. "If Seraphina stays for any reason, so do I."

Although he didn't say it outright, the message was broadcasted loud and clear. He wasn't about to leave her alone with Karsten, storm or no storm.

And if the protective, alpha tone of his voice hadn't sent her heart into a free fall in her breast, she might have found the good sense to be offended by his unprovoked, aggressive reaction to the only other male in her current orbit.

Karsten smiled mildly and lifted a shoulder. "Suit yourself, then. I'm going to start boarding things up ahead of the storm. If you need me, Sera, you know where I am."

She nodded and watched him walk away. Then she wheeled around to face Jehan. "You were very rude to my friend."

"Friend?" He snorted under his breath. "That human thinks he's more than a friend to you." Jehan's sharp blue eyes narrowed. "He was more than that at one time, wasn't he?"

"No." She shook her head. "We went on a few dates, nothing more. I wasn't interested in him."

"But he was interested in you. Still is."

"You sound jealous."

He exhaled harshly through flared nostrils. "Call it observant."

"I called it jealous." She stepped closer to him in the moonlight, weathering the heat that rolled off his big body and flashed from the depths of his smoldering gaze. His jaw was clamped hard, and the dark-stubbled skin that covered it seemed stretched too tightly across his handsome, perturbed face. "Why the hell should it bother you if Karsten is a friend of mine or something more? It's not like you have any claim on me. I could go after him right now and there's really nothing you can say about it."

A low sound rumbled from deep inside of him. "I would hope you don't intend to try me."

"Why? Because of some stupid pact?" Her voice climbed with her frustration. "You don't even believe in it, but yet you want to pretend we have to live by its terms."

"I don't give a fuck about the damned pact, Seraphina."

"That didn't stop you from using it as an excuse to make me feel like an idiot."

Sparks ignited in the shadowed pools of his eyes. "If you really think my walking away from you that night had anything to do with the pact, then you *are* an idiot."

She sucked in a breath, ready to hurl a curse at him, but he didn't give her the chance.

In less than a pace, he closed the distance between them. One strong hand slid into her loose hair and around her nape. The other splayed against her lower spine as he drew her to him and took her mouth in a blazing hot, hungry kiss.

Seraphina moaned as pleasure and need swamped her. Her breasts crushed against the firm, muscled slabs of his chest. Against her belly, his cock was a thick, solid ridge of heat and power and carnal demand. Hunger tore through her, quicksilver and molten. It burned away her anger, obliterated her outrage and frustration. As he deepened their kiss and his tongue breached her parted lips, all she knew was need.

She speared her fingers into his thick, soft waves and clung to him, lost in desire and oblivious of their surroundings. Willing to ignore everything so long as Jehan was holding her like this, kissing her as if he'd been longing for it as much as she had.

He drew back on a snarled curse and looked at her. His eyes snapped with embers, his pupils nothing but vertical slits in the middle of all that fire. His wet lips peeled back off his teeth and fangs as he drew in a deep breath, scenting her like the predatory being he truly was.

For a moment, she thought he was about to pick her up and carry her off to some secluded corner of the camp as if he owned her. She wouldn't have fought him. God, not even close.

But as they stood there, Sera felt a subtle sting start to needle her cheeks and forehead. Her eyes started to burn, then the next breath she took carried the grit of fine sand to the back of her throat.

The storm.

It was arriving even sooner than Karsten had warned.

She didn't have to tell Jehan. Pulling her close, he tucked her head against his chest and rushed with her toward the nearest outbuilding as the night began to fill with a roiling swell of yellow dust.

CHAPTER 10

By the time they reached the aluminum-roofed storage building several yards ahead, the biting wind had picked up with a howl. Sand churned across the camp, blowing as thick as a blizzard.

His body still charged with arousal, Jehan held Seraphina against him as he threw open the rickety wooden door. "Inside, quickly."

She no sooner entered the shelter than a muffled cry somewhere amid the storm drew both of them to full alert. The voice was small, distant. Unmistakably terrified.

"Yasmin." Seraphina's face blanched with worry. "Oh, God. The little girl who came to greet us when we arrived. She and some other children ran off to play a few minutes ago."

The cry came again, more plaintive now. There was pain in the child's voice too.

Jehan cursed. "Stay here. I'll find her."

Without waiting for her to argue, he dashed back into the night using the speed of his Breed genetics. The little girl's wails were a beacon through the blinding sea of flying sand. Jehan followed her cries to a deep ditch on the far side of the camp. At the bottom of the rugged drop, her small body lay curled in a tight ball.

"Yasmin?"

At the sound of her name, she lifted her head. Agony and terror flooded her tear-filled eyes. The poor child was shaking and sobbing, choking on the airborne sand.

Jehan jumped down into the ditch. Crouching low beside her, he sheltered her with his body as the sandstorm roiled all around them. "Are you hurt?"

Her dark head wobbled in a jerky nod. "My leg hurts. I was trying to hide from my friends, but I fell and they all ran away."

Jehan gingerly examined her. As soon as his palm skated over her left shin and ankle, he felt the hot pain of a compound fracture. The break streaked through his senses like a jagged bolt of lightning. "Come on, sweetheart. Let's get you out of here."

He collected Yasmin into his arms and carried her up from the ditch. At the crest of it, Seraphina was waiting. A heavy blanket covered her from head to toe as a makeshift shield from the storm. She opened her arms as Jehan strode toward her, enveloping him and the child as the three of them made their way across the camp.

"She needs a medic," he informed Seraphina as she murmured quiet reassurances to the scared child. "I felt two fractures in the lower part of the left fibula, and a fairly bad sprain in the ankle."

Seraphina's brows knitted for a second, then she acknowledged with a nod. "The medical building is in the center of camp. This way."

She set their course for one of the glowing yellow lights emanating through the sand and darkness up ahead.

Jehan didn't miss the uncertain glances he drew as he and Seraphina brought the injured child into the small field hospital. Their wariness didn't bother him. Being Breed, he was accustomed to the wide berth most humans tended to give him. And it didn't escape his notice that one of the nurses carrying a cooler with a large red cross on it made an immediate about-face retreat the instant her eyes landed on him—as if her stash of refrigerated red cells might provoke him to attack.

The humans needn't have worried about that. His kind only consumed fresh blood, taken from an open vein.

And right now, the only veins that interested him at all belonged to the beautiful woman standing next to him. Even dressed in his worn shirt and oversized pants, Seraphina stirred everything male in him the same way she stirred the vampire side of his nature.

Just because their kiss had been interrupted by the storm and a distressed child, that didn't mean he'd forgotten any of that fire Seraphina had ignited in him. Now that the little girl was safe and in the care of a doctor, Jehan's attention—all of his focus—was centered on how quickly he could get back to where he and Seraphina had left off.

But he stood by patiently as she made introductions and explained to her fellow volunteers that Jehan was her friend, that he was the one who went out into the storm to locate Yasmin. Seraphina's vouching for him seemed enough to put the humans at ease, since it was clear that everyone at the camp trusted and adored her.

He was beginning to feel likewise.

More than beginning to feel that way, in fact.

After the medic and nurses went back to their work, Seraphina turned to look up at him.

"When you brought Yasmin out of the storm, you said her leg was broken." He nodded, but that didn't seem to satisfy Seraphina's curiosity. "Actually, you said her fibula had two fractures and that her ankle was badly sprained. You were right, Jehan. According to the field medic just a few minutes ago, you were one hundred percent accurate. You told me you *felt* her injuries. You can feel physical injuries?"

He shrugged, barely acknowledging the ability he so seldom used.

"Can you heal them too?"

"No. And now you know my curse," he murmured wryly. "I can inventory someone's wounds, but I can't help them."

She tilted her head at him, warmth sparkling in her eyes. "You helped Yasmin tonight."

Jehan stared at her, unsure how to respond. Seraphina couldn't know how his so-called gift had hobbled him in his life. He'd grown up feeling useless, aimless. It wasn't until he'd found the Order that he realized there were other ways to do something meaningful with his life. That his life had purpose.

She was still studying him, looking gorgeous and far too interested in him as she held his gaze. "The storm's really blowing out there. Do you want to wait it out in here or would you rather go to my place?"

He arched a brow. "Your place?"

"My tent." She smiled, and the warmth of it went straight to his groin. "It's where I stay when I'm here at the camp for any length of time. It's not all that comfortable, but it is private."

Jehan's grin broke slowly across his face. "Miss Sanhaja, are you trying to seduce me?"

She licked her lips, tilting her head as she held his hungry gaze. "I think I might be."

Holy hell. The promise in her voice had his blood racing so hard and fast to his cock, he wasn't sure he'd make it to her tent.

"Lead the way," he drawled thickly, his fangs already punching out of his gums.

He held the blanket aloft over them as they dashed out of the medical building and raced through the blizzard of sand. Seraphina's tent stood toward the far end of the camp. By the time they reached it and found their way past the zipper and ties that secured the shelter's entrance, they were coated in a thin layer of grit. They stumbled inside together hand-in-hand, Seraphina laughing and breathless in the dark.

She left him for a moment, bending to turn on a lantern.

The soft light put a glow on her pinkened cheeks and on the flush of color rising up the smooth column of her throat, making the fine sand that dusted her skin glitter like diamonds. Under the windblown tangle of her long brown curls, her sandalwood-colored eyes were fathomless and filled with desire. Her breath was still racing and shallow, the outline of her breasts teasing him from under the crisp white linen of his shirt.

He'd never seen anything so lovely.

With the storm howling all around them, sand buffeting the tent like rain, Jehan stood speechless, the sight of her like this branding itself into his memory forever.

He couldn't resist reaching out to stroke the velvet of her cheek. And then that wasn't enough either, so he cupped her face in his hands and dragged her into a fierce kiss.

The instant their mouths met, it was as if no time had passed between their fevered kiss before the sandstorm and this electric moment now. Hell, it was as if they were merely picking up where they left off that first night at the villa. All of the hunger he felt for this female, all of the desire...it was right there below the surface, waiting for the chance to reignite.

And he knew that Seraphina felt it too.

On a moan, she melted against him, her lips parting to give his tongue the access it demanded. Heat licked through his veins at the taste of her passion, scorching everything in its path. In an instant, his fangs punched through his gums to fill his mouth. Need hammered in his temples, in his chest. In the aching length of his cock.

He groaned with the intensity of it.

He had to pace himself. Wanted to take this slowly with her, despite his own impatience to have her spread out beneath him as he buried himself inside her.

But Seraphina was merciless. Her wet mouth and gusting breath tore at his resolve. Her soft curves and strong, questing fingers on his shoulders and chest, in his hair, stripped away his already threadbare control.

Sliding his hands under the loose hem of the tunic, he greedily caressed the firm swell of her satin-covered breasts. Seraphina gasped, arching into him as he flicked open the front clasp of her bra and cupped her bare flesh in his palms. Her nipples were tight little buds that pebbled even harder as he rolled and tweaked them between his fingers, hungry to taste them.

He released her, but only so he could take the shirt off and feast on her with his eyes.

He drew the linen over her head and let it fall to the floor of the tent. The red sash holding up her pants came off next. He untied it and watched as the slackened waistband of the linen trousers slid off her hips to pool at her feet.

"So beautiful," he murmured, reaching out to run the backs of his knuckles down her arm, then across the flat plane of her belly. He ventured further, toying with the lacy edge of her delicate panties. "This is what I wanted to do that first night with you, Seraphina. Undress you inch by inch. Pretend I had the right to look at you like this and think I could ever be worthy of having you."

She slowly shook her head. "I don't want you to pretend, Jehan. Tonight, I don't want you to stop. I didn't want you to stop that first night either."

A sound escaped him, something raw and otherworldly. He slid his fingers into the scrap of fabric between her legs, and...holy fuck.

She was almost bare beneath the lace. And wet. So damn wet. Hot, liquid silk bathed his fingertips as he delved into her slick cleft.

She bit her lip, dropping her head back on a sigh. Holding on to him as he stroked her silky folds, she squirmed and shuddered against his touch. "Jehan, don't make me wait. Please, don't make me want like this again."

"No chance of that," he uttered, his voice like gravel in his throat, raw with desire. "Not tonight."

Not ever again, some possessive part of him growled in agreement.

He didn't know where it came from—the bone-deep sense that he belonged with this woman.

That she was *his*.

And that as ridiculous as the ancient pact between their families was, it had somehow delivered him to the one woman he craved more than any other before.

Jehan drew her mouth to his and kissed her again, as reverent as it was claiming. He broke contact only so he could strip out of his shirt and jeans, leaving both at his feet. He wore nothing underneath, and as soon as his cock sprang free, Seraphina's hands found him.

She stroked and caressed him, her fingers so sure and fevered, he nearly came on the spot.

Need twisted tight and hot with every slide of her hands over his stiff shaft, pressure coiling at the base of his spine.

Somehow, he managed to collect himself enough to douse the lantern with his mind. The tent plunged into darkness. Although the sandstorm raged outside, driving everyone in the camp indoors, he wasn't going to share Seraphina or this moment with anyone else.

Pulling her down onto the pallet of blankets and pillows with him, Jehan removed her panties, then smoothed his hand along every beautiful swell and delicately muscled plane on her nude body. The temptation of her sex was too much. The sweet scent of her arousal drenched his senses as he moved over her, parting her thighs until she was opened to him like an exotic flower.

One he couldn't wait to taste.

He lowered his head between her legs, groaning in a mix of agony and ecstasy as his tongue met her nectar-sweet, hot, wet flesh. His fangs were already fully extended, but at the first swallow of Seraphina's juices, the sharp points grew even larger.

The urge to bite—to draw blood and make her his in the most powerful way he knew how—rose up on him without warning.

No.

He tamped the impulse down hard, blindsided by the force of it.

Losing himself to carnal pleasure was one thing. Binding Seraphina to him for eternity was another. And it was a line he wouldn't cross.

He had no room in his life for a mate, and if she woke up in the morning with regrets, he sure as hell didn't want one of them to be irrevocable.

Tonight, he wanted to give her pleasure.

Selfishly, he wanted to give her the kind of pleasure that would ensure that every other male who'd ever touched her was obliterated from her memory.

Tonight, Seraphina was his—not because some ridiculous agreement said she should be, but because she wanted to be.

Because she felt the same undeniable desire that he did.

"Come for me," he rasped against her tender flesh. "I want to hear you, Seraphina."

"Oh God," she gasped in reply, arching up to meet his mouth as he kissed and sucked and teased with his lips and tongue. When she writhed and mewled in rising pleasure, he gave her more, sliding a finger through her juices and into the tight entrance of her body. She cried out as he added another, thrusting in tempo with his tongue's deep strokes.

He glanced up the length of her twisting body. "Open your eyes, beauty. I want to see you come for me."

She obeyed, lifting heavy lids, her gaze drunk with pleasure. "Jehan, please..."

Her hands tangled and fisted in his hair as he coaxed her higher, desperate for her pleasure—for her release—before he would let himself inside.

Ah, fuck. He'd never seen anything as erotic as Seraphina caught at the crest of orgasm. The sexy sounds she made. The unbridled response of her body. The tight, hot vise of her sheath, clamping down around his fingers as he flicked his tongue over her clit and drove her relentlessly toward a shattering release.

She held his gaze in the dark, and when she crashed apart a moment later, it was with his name on her lips.

Jehan couldn't curb his satisfied grin.

He rose over her, pressing her knees to her chest as he guided his cock between the slick folds of her sex. Her eyes were locked on his, her body still flushed and shuddering with the aftershocks of her release. He tested her tight entrance with a small thrust of his hips, groaning as her little muscular walls enveloped the head of his shaft.

He grasped for control and found he had none.

Not where this woman was concerned.

And why that didn't scare the hell out of him, he didn't know.

Right now, with Seraphina wet and ready for him, the question damn well didn't matter.

With a harsh curse, he flexed his pelvis and seated himself to the root.

CHAPTER 11

She gasped Jehan's name as he took her in one deep, breath-stealing thrust.

His wicked mouth and fingers had left her nerve endings vibrating and numb with sensation, her body slick and hot from release. But each rolling push of Jehan's hips stoked her arousal to life once more. His cock stretched her, filled her so completely she could barely accommodate all of his length and girth. She closed her eyes against the staggering ecstasy that built as he moved inside her, his powerful strokes and relentless tempo driving her to the edge of her sanity.

She'd never felt anything as intoxicating as the naked strength of Jehan's magnificent body. That all of his passion—all of his immense control—was concentrated on her pleasure was a drug she could easily become addicted to. Maybe she already was because her hunger for him was only growing more consuming with every hard crash of his body against hers.

Reaching up between them, he drew one of her legs down from where it lay bent against her chest and wrapped it around his waist as he shifted into an even more intense angle. The new position gave her access to his *glyph*-covered pecs and muscled abdomen, which she explored with questing fingers and scoring nails. She lifted her head and watched him pound into her, mesmerized by the violent, erotic beauty of their need.

Jehan made an approving noise in the back of his throat. "Do you like the way we look, Sera? Your legs spread open so wide for me, my cock buried in your heat?"

"Yes." *Oh, God.* Had she thought she was already at the brink of combusting? His dark voice inflamed her even more. She tore her gaze away from their joining only to meet the crackling fire that blazed down at her from his transformed eyes. "Jehan...I didn't know it could be like this. Watching you push inside me like you can't get deep enough. I love seeing us together like this. I love the way we feel."

"Mm," he responded, more growl than reply. "Then let me give you even more."

He set a new pace that destroyed her already slipping control. Another orgasm mounted and twisted inside her, sweeping her into a dizzying spiral of pleasure. She caught her lip between her teeth on a strangled moan as the climax swelled, nearing its breaking point.

Jehan's rhythm showed no mercy. He rode her harder, deeper, his hips pistoning furiously.

She arched beneath him, unable to hold on any longer. Turning her head into her pillow, she let go of a scream as her release broke over her in wave after wave of bliss.

Jehan pumped furiously as she came, then a rough curse ripped out of him. He tensed, his muscles hardening like granite beneath her fingertips as she clung to him. His amber-lit eyes blazed hot, locked on her.

He hissed her name, torment and pleasure etched in his handsome, savage face. Then a roar boiled past his teeth and fangs. His hips thrust viciously, then he plunged deep on a curse as the sudden, scorching flow of his seed erupted inside her.

She'd never felt so sated. So deliciously fucked.

She caressed Jehan as his body relaxed and his orgasm ebbed. But his cock had lost little of its stiffness inside her. And as he murmured rumbling praises for the way she felt, his strong fingers petting her hair and cheeks and breasts, that lingering stiffness had returned to steel again.

She couldn't control her body's response to him, nor could she curb her shaky sigh of pleasure as his shaft swelled to capacity and the walls of her sex clenched to hold him. She moved beneath him, creating a slick friction.

"Holy fuck, Sera." He closed his eyes for a moment, head tipped back on his shoulders as she invited him to take her again. When his gaze came back to hers, the fire that had been there before flared even hotter. "I should've walked away. Now, it's too late. It's too fucking late for both of us."

She nodded, knowing he was right. They should have resisted this heat that lived between them.

They should have refused the handfast and all that came with it.

They both should have realized that giving in to this desire would only spark a greater need.

For Sera, what she felt for Jehan went beyond physical need or even a passing affection. Tonight, she'd seen a new side of him. Not the arrogant Breed male who strode through life as if he owned the world. Not the Order warrior who dealt in ruthless justice and death.

Tonight, at the camp, she'd witnessed a different side of him. Jehan was a kind man, a compassionate man. She'd glimpsed the honor inside him, and now that she had seen those things, she would never be able to regard him in any lesser light.

So, yes. It was much too late for her to walk away from anything that happened between them tonight.

And if she should regret that fact, she never would.

Not when Jehan was looking at her the way he was now, with fever in his eyes and desire riding the furious arcs and swirls of his multicolored *dermaglyphs*. And not when his amazing cock was making her yearn to be taken all over again.

"On your knees this time," he commanded her, his deep voice husky and raw.

Her eyes widened in surprise, but she eagerly scrambled out from under him to obey. He loomed behind her, the heat of his presence scalding her backside. His fingers waded through their combined juices, wringing a desperate mewl from her throat as the wet sounds of his caresses joined the dry howl of the sandstorm still raging outside the tent.

She felt the thick length of his cock between her swollen folds. Then he grasped her hips in his hands and slowly impaled her on him, inch by glorious inch.

They set a less frantic pace now, somehow finding the will to savor the pleasure, making it last as long as they could hold out. After they had both climaxed again, they dropped into a lazy sprawl on her blanket-strewn pallet.

For a long while, there were no words between them. They lay together in the dark, listening to the hiss of swirling sand as the storm continued to sweep through the camp.

Sera was stretched alongside him, one arm resting on his chest. She traced the pattern of *glyphs* that spread over his smooth skin, memorizing the Breed skin markings that were unique to him alone. They were beautiful. And so was he.

"I need to thank you for tonight, Jehan."

He grunted. "No need, trust me." His strong arm tightened around her, bringing her closer against him. "I should be the one thanking you."

She rose up to look at his face. "No, I mean for what you did tonight. For helping me bring the supplies here. For going out into the storm to find Yasmin and make sure she got the care she needed for her injured leg."

He shrugged mildly. "Again, there's no need for thanks. I did what anyone would do."

"Not anyone," she said. "And I never would've expected it from you. I misjudged you when we met, and for that, I also owe you an apology."

He cupped her nape and brought her down to him for a tender kiss. "Maybe we both were too quick to judge. When you told me you only agreed to the handfast to collect the trust from your father, I assumed you were willing to take his bribe because you wanted the money for yourself. And not that it should matter why you wanted it, but it did. Tonight at the checkpoint, I know what you did. I realized what you've been doing all along—using your personal funds to buy clearance for camp supplies."

She frowned. "It's only money. How can I keep it when those supplies mean life or death to the people who depend on me?"

"Your work obviously means a lot to you." There was a soberness in his eyes as he studied her in the darkened tent. "You told me that night we walked in the garden that your work is a calling."

"I did say that, yes." It surprised her that he remembered the offhand remark.

"What did you mean, Seraphina?"

She glanced down at her hand where it rested on his chest. "When I was eighteen, I volunteered one winter at an orphanage about an hour away from our Darkhaven. My parents encouraged it, since I was orphaned as an infant too."

Jehan made an acknowledging sound. "A lot of Breedmates find their way into Breed households as abandoned and orphaned babies or young girls."

She nodded. She and her sister were both adopted by the Sanhajas in such a way. "I was lucky. Someone saw my birthmark and recognized that I was different. There was a place for me because of that. But there were no

Breedmates in the orphanage I went to that year. Only human children. Many of them were refugees whose parents had been killed in wars or died of famine and disease." She curled her fingers into a tight ball. "There was so much pain in that place. I felt it every time I held a crying baby or embraced one of those sweet, terrified kids."

"You felt it," Jehan murmured, understanding fully now. He reached up to take her hand, bringing her knuckles to his lips. "You felt their emotional pain, because, like me, you're an empath."

Every Breedmate, like every Breed male, was born with a unique extrasensory ability. Some were blessings, others were less of a gift. Where Jehan could register physical injuries, hers was the ability to feel emotional pain with a touch.

"I thought I could handle it," she said. "But everything I felt stayed with me. Until my time working at the orphanage that winter, I didn't know how to help. Now I do what I can."

He'd gone quiet as she spoke, and Sera knew he understood. Given his own ability, Jehan probably understood her better than anyone else could.

"You're an incredible woman, Seraphina." He shook his head, his thumb stroking idly over her jawline. "I think I recognized that the minute we met, but I was too busy looking for reasons to dislike you. I wanted to find hidden flaws, since it was obvious I wasn't going to find any on the outside."

His praise warmed her. "I haven't been able to find much fault in you either. And believe me, I tried. I called you a killer when I found out you were a warrior with the Order. That wasn't fair. I know that now. I also thought your biggest personal flaw might be an overblown opinion of your own charms. I think you've proven the point tonight, though. I suppose I have to give credit where it's due."

He chuckled. "If what I just did with you was charming, then just wait until you see my wicked side."

She grinned down at him. "When can I look forward to that?"

"If you're not careful, sooner than you think."

He grabbed her ass and gave it a playful smack. Then he tumbled her onto her back and covered her with his hard, fully aroused body. The crackling embers in his eyes promised he was about to make good on his threat right then and there.

CHAPTER 12

The storm had passed some time ago.

Jehan lay on his back in the dark tent, holding Seraphina as she slept naked and draped over him in a boneless sprawl. He'd been awake for a while, listening to the calm outside and trying to convince himself that he needed to get out of bed.

As much as he hated to disturb her sleep or forfeit the pleasant feel of her resting sated in his arms, he knew he should go out and check their vehicle, make sure it wasn't buried under a mound of sand. With the weather cleared, he was eager to get on the road.

He guessed it to be early morning, probably only two or three hours after midnight. If they didn't delay too long, it was possible they could make it back to the villa before sunrise. Otherwise, it meant spending the day at the camp, waiting until sunset when it was safe for him to make the drive again.

And while he could think of a lot of interesting ways to pass the hours with Seraphina alone in her tent, he wasn't ashamed to admit that he'd rather explore those options in the comfort of the villa.

Which meant getting his ass out of her bed ASAP, so he could expedite that process.

With care not to wake her, he eased himself out from under her and rolled away from the thin mattress on the floor.

Dressing quietly, he then slipped out of the tent to begin the trek toward the place he'd parked the Rover. He was the only one outside so soon after the storm. He hoofed it through the quiet camp, his boots putting fresh tracks on the sand-drifted road that cut through the center of the tents and outbuildings.

The Rover could have been worse. Sand coated the black vehicle and had blown into every crack and crevice. He dug it out and brushed it down as best he could and was just about to start it up when his preternatural hearing picked up the sound of men's voices elsewhere in the dark. Somewhere near the main supply building.

Jehan recognized Karsten Hemmings's dramatic tenor instantly. The other man sounded like one of the helpers who'd assisted in unloading the delivery earlier tonight.

Jehan listened, suspicion prickling his senses. On instinct, he reached into the Rover and retrieved the pair of daggers he'd stored under the driver's seat. Although he had busted Seraphina's pretty ass over the fact she'd brought her phone to the handfast, his breach of the terms by bringing his Order patrol blades was probably the worst of the two offenses.

Right about now, he was damn glad he had the weapons.

Tucking one into his boot and the other into the back waistband of his jeans, he stole around the rear of the tents and outbuildings, his senses trained on the pair of men. Sand sifted with their quick footsteps. Karsten issued orders to his accomplice in a low, urgent whisper.

"Pick up the pace, Massoud! My contact has been waiting on this shit for days. We've got less than an hour to make the drop and collect our money."

What the hell?

Karsten's Jeep was parked at the rear of the outbuilding. The back hatch had been swung open, while Karsten and the other camp worker were apparently loading the vehicle with crates taken out of the main supply.

Jehan crept through the shadows, peering at the contents of the Jeep while both men had gone back inside the building for more. Three crates labeled as canned meat sat in the back of the vehicle. Supplies that he and Seraphina had delivered earlier tonight.

One of the crates had been pried apart, several of the cans inside opened. An odd blue glow emanated from inside the containers.

At first, Jehan wasn't sure what he was seeing.

Not canned meats, that much was certain.

Each container held a palm-sized electronic object comprised of a metal casing and a glass center chamber. Inside the glass was a milky blue substance that glowed like a vial of pure energy.

Like a source of harnessed, weapons-grade ultraviolet light.

Holy shit.

The instant realization dawned on him, Karsten's cohort came around the back of the building. He was empty-handed, but the second his eyes lit on Jehan, he reached for his gun and fired a panicked round. Reacting almost instantly, Jehan let his blade fly, dropping Massoud dead in the sand.

The discharged bullet flew wild into the air. The cracking report of the gunshot echoed, shattering the sleepy calm of the camp. Screams and commotion stirred at once in some of the nearby tents.

Karsten raced out of the supply building. "Massoud, for crissake—"

He drew up short when he came face to face with Jehan holding his comrade's gun.

Jehan bared his fangs. "Doing a little dealing on the side, I see. What's the going rate on UV grenades these days?"

Karsten narrowed his eyes. "More than you could imagine, vampire."

The impulse to blow the human's head off was nearly overwhelming. But caution warned him that this was also Seraphina's longtime coworker. She considered Karsten Hemmings her friend.

As much as Jehan wanted to waste the bastard for profiting off Breed-killing UV arms and using Seraphina's goodwill to front it, that call wasn't his to make. Not like this.

"We both know you're not going to use that gun on me," Karsten taunted. "She'll hate you for it. Of course, if you pull that trigger, you'd better be prepared to die with me."

It was then that Jehan noticed the human held something tight in his fist. The blue glow poured out between his fingers.

"The detonator is already tripped," he confirmed. "The UV blast won't give me more than a sunburn. You, however..."

Jehan ignored the threat. He would deal with the fallout if and when it occurred. Right now, he wanted answers. If he had any chance of getting information to the Order, he needed answers.

"Who's waiting for this shipment, Karsten? Who's paying you for this shit?"

"Oh, come now. I think you know. Every warrior in the Order should know the answer to that question." He chuckled. "Yes, I know you're one of them. I did some checking tonight. Made a few calls. You're part of the Rome unit."

Jehan glowered. "And you're part of Opus Nostrum."

Karsten pursed his lips and gave a faint shake of his head. "Merely a businessman. And a like-minded individual. I despise your entire race of blood-sucking monsters. If Opus wants your kind eradicated and a war to make it happen, I'm only too happy to help send you all to your graves. Or into the light, as the case may be."

"Karsten?" Seraphina emerged out of the darkness, disheveled and confused. "Oh, my God. Jehan, what on earth is going—"

"Seraphina, stay back!"

Jehan's warning came too late. She had already strayed right into the middle of the standoff.

And Karsten seized his chance to let his weapon loose.

The UV grenade went airborne.

Jehan had precious little time to react. He dived under the Jeep as the light exploded all around him. The power of it was immense. Even from beneath the undercarriage of the vehicle, he could feel the searing energy of the solar detonation. It extinguished a moment later, plunging the desert back into darkness.

He was shielded.

He was alive.

But the act of self-preservation had just cost him dearly.

He heard Seraphina cry out, and he knew Karsten Hemmings had her.

The realization tore his heart from his chest. He couldn't let her be harmed. He couldn't lose her.

He never wanted to lose her.

On a roar, Jehan rolled out to his feet to face the bastard. Karsten had a pistol on her, held against the back of her head. And Jehan had dropped his gun somewhere in the sand.

"Let her go."

Karsten sneered. "Let her go so you can have her? She deserves better than you, vampire. Better than anything you can ever give her."

Jehan wasn't going to argue when he was thinking the same thing now, miserable as he drank in the sight of her terrified face and her tender brown eyes pleading for him to help her.

"Let her go, Karsten. If you do, maybe I'll let you live. But only if Seraphina wants me to."

The human chuckled. "No, I don't think so. We're going to leave now. I'm going to make my drop and collect my money. Then Sera and I are going to get out of this godforsaken hellhole and enjoy our spoils." He nestled his open mouth against her cheek, the nose of the gun still pressed against her skull. "You'll see, my love. I can give you everything you need."

She winced and closed her eyes, a miserable sound curling up from her throat.

Jehan couldn't bear another second of her torment. He had to act. He had one chance to end this, but he couldn't do it without her total faith in him.

"Seraphina." He spoke her name softly, reverently. Hoping she could hear how much she meant to him. "Look at me, sweetheart."

Her eyes opened and found his gaze through the dark.

He couldn't say the words out loud without betraying his plan, but he needed her to understand. He needed her to trust him.

Do you trust me, Seraphina?

He said it with his eyes. With his heart.

Trust me, baby. Please...

She gave him a nearly imperceptible nod.

It was enough. It was all the permission he needed.

Moving with every ounce of Breed agility and speed he possessed, Jehan reached around to his back and pulled out the dagger he'd stashed there. He let it fly from his fingertips.

An instant later, Karsten Hemmings dropped to the ground, Jehan's blade protruding from the space between his wide-open eyes.

Jehan ran to Seraphina and pulled her into his arms.

In that moment, nothing else mattered.

Not Karsten Hemmings. Not the Jeep full of UV grenades, or Opus Nostrum.

Not even the Order mattered as he drew Seraphina close and kissed her with all the relief and emotion—all the love—he felt for her.

He stroked her beautiful face and stared down into the soft brown eyes that now owned his heart and his soul. "Come on," he said, drawing her under the protection of his arm. "Let's get out of here."

CHAPTER 13

Sera was still numb with shock and disbelief several hours later, after Jehan had driven them back to the villa.

Karsten's betrayal cut deep. That he had used her to free up the supplies containing his hidden cargo was bad enough. But the idea that greed and hatred had poisoned his humanity so much that he was willing to kill—willing to traffic in weaponry designed for the wholesale slaughter of the Breed—was unthinkable. It was unforgivable.

Countless innocent lives were saved today, now that the UV grenades had been diverted from their buyer and stowed safely inside the villa.

As for Karsten and Massoud, when the other camp workers and residents came upon the scene and heard what the two men had been up to, there had been no shortage of volunteers offering to dispose of their bodies in the desert so that Sera and Jehan could get on the road as quickly as possible to beat the sunrise.

Sera had considered Karsten a friend for years, but there wasn't any part of her that mourned his death today even for a second. If not for Jehan's quick thinking and speed with his blade, she had no doubt that Karsten would have killed her.

He had almost killed Jehan too.

The terror she'd felt at that possibility had nearly gutted her as she'd stood helplessly in Karsten's grasp. Even now, the reality of how close she'd come to losing Jehan left her physically and emotionally shaken.

But he was alive.

Because of his warrior skills, they both were alive.

"Are you all right, Sera?" His deep, caring voice wrapped around her as they stood inside the villa together. "Is there anything I can do for you?"

She shook her head but couldn't keep from moving into the shelter of his arms. This was all she needed. His warmth enveloping her. His strong heartbeat pounding steadily against her ear as she rested her head on his muscled chest. She just needed...him.

"You should call your brother," she murmured. Marcel had left two messages on her phone in the past couple of hours, asking them to contact him as soon as possible. "We should let him know we've returned, at least so he can stop worrying that we're going to break the pact."

Jehan's chest rumbled with a sound of disregard. "I should call the Order too, and tell them what I'll be bringing back to Rome with me in a few nights. But my brother and everyone else can wait. The only thing I'm concerned about right now is you."

He pulled back and looked at her, a dark storm brewing in the pale blue of his eyes. When he lifted her chin and took her mouth in a slow, savoring kiss, it was easy to imagine that what she saw in his gaze—what she felt in his embrace and in his tender kiss—was something deeper than concern or simple affection.

It was easy to imagine it might be love.

"You're trembling, Seraphina." He reached out to caress her face and shoulder. "And you're cold too. Come on. Let me take care of you."

Maybe Leila had been right—that there was some brand of magic at work when it came to the pact between their families. Sera could almost believe it now because with Jehan leading her through the villa, his fingers laced with hers, it was far too easy to imagine that everything they shared since entering the handfast was somehow paving a path toward a future together. A future that might just last an eternity.

She hadn't missed his reference to the life waiting for him at the end of the handfast. She couldn't pretend that her own life wasn't waiting for her too.

But for the next few nights, she wasn't going to let reality intrude.

Jehan brought her into the cavernous bathing room with its towering marble columns and steaming, spring-fed bath the size of a swimming pool. He sat her down on the edge, then crouched down in front of her to remove her shoes. The soft leather flats were caked with sand and spattered with Karsten's dried blood. Jehan hissed a low curse as he set them aside.

When he lifted his head to meet her gaze, there was doubt in his eyes.

"Can you forgive me, Sera?"

"For saving me from Karsten?" She shook her head. "There's nothing to forgive."

"No." His mouth flattened into a grim line. "I mean, for saving myself. For giving him the chance to get a hold of you in the first place."

Oh, God. Is that what he thought? Is that what weighed on his conscience now?

Sera leaned forward to take his tormented, handsome face in her palms. His anguish was palpable. She could feel the dull pain of it through her empathic gift. "Jehan, when I saw that flash of light as Karsten let the grenade go, I knew it would be lethal to you. I thought I was about to watch you die. If you hadn't protected yourself, we both would've been dead today. You saved me."

He studied her for a long moment, as if he wanted to say something more. Then he turned his face into her hand and placed a kiss in its center before drawing out of her loose grasp. "Let's get these clothes off and get you warm."

He stood up, taking her with him. With careful hands, he undressed her, peeling off the rumpled linen tunic and her bra. Then he drew down the loose-fitting pants and her lacy panties beneath. His gaze drank her in slowly, his eyes crackling with amber sparks.

When he finally spoke, his voice was dark and gravelly, rough with desire. "Earlier tonight, when I saw you naked like this for the first time, I said you were beautiful."

She licked her lips. "I remember."

She would never forget anything he said in her tent a few hours ago, nor anything he'd done. Arousal spiraled through her, as much at the reminder as under the intensity of his gaze now.

"I said you were beautiful, Seraphina...but I was wrong." He cupped her cheek in his palm, then slowly let his fingers drift down her shoulder, his thumb pausing to caress the Breedmate mark on her upper arm. "You are exquisite. The loveliest female I have ever, and will ever, lay my unworthy eyes on."

She started to shake her head in protest of his self-deprecation, but his kiss caught her lips before she could speak.

All of her desire for him—all of her tangled emotions—rose up to engulf her. She wanted him.

Loved him so powerfully it staggered her.

Only fear held her confession back.

Fear, and need.

She pulled back, breath heaving. Wordlessly, she unbuttoned his shirt and pushed it off his strong arms. Each swirl and flourish of the *dermaglyphs* that tracked over his powerful chest and muscled abdomen was a temptation to her fingers and her mouth.

She touched and kissed and licked her way down his immense body, finally lowering herself to her knees before him. His lungs rasped with the ragged tempo of his breathing as she unzipped his jeans and slid them down his hard thighs.

His cock bobbed heavily in front of her, the thick shaft and blunt, glistening plum at the crown making her mouth water for a taste. He groaned as she grasped his length in her hands, his muscles tensing, breath hitching, as she stroked him from root to head and back again.

When she leaned forward and wrapped her lips around him, his spine arched and he let out a tight hiss and guttural snarl. She'd never held so much force and power in her hands before, nor in her mouth. She couldn't get enough. And as his body's response quickened, it only made her hungry for more. For all of him.

She glanced up as she sucked him and found his fiery eyes locked on her. His pupils were thin and wild, utterly Breed. His broad mouth was pulled into a grimace, baring his teeth and the enormous length of his fangs.

She moaned, overwhelmed by the preternatural beauty of the male staring down at her. His large palm cupped the back of her head, his long fingers speared into her hair as she took the full depth of him into her mouth at a relentless tempo.

"Seraphina," he uttered hoarsely. "Ah, fuck..."

On a sharp groan, he withdrew from between her lips and scooped her up into his arms as if she weighed nothing at all. He carried her down into the steaming bath, fastening his mouth on hers in an urgent, fevered kiss as he sank to his shoulders in the warm water with her held aloft in his arms.

He tore his mouth away from hers, scowling fiercely. "I'm supposed to be the one taking care of you, if you recall."

She lifted a brow in challenge. "Is that your charming side talking or your wicked one?"

Sparks flared in his hot gaze. "Which do you prefer?"

"I haven't decided yet." Pivoting under the surface of the water, she faced him on his lap and wrapped her legs around his waist. The thick jut of his cock rose tall between them, the crisp hair at its root tickling her sex. She looped her arms over his shoulders and drifted close for a teasing kiss. "Fortunately, we've got all day to figure it out."

His hands gripped her ass and he smirked against her mouth. "All day, and another five nights after that."

"You think it's long enough?" she murmured, her lips still brushing his.

His answering chuckle was purely male and totally wicked. As was the meaningful shift of his hips that positioned his erection at the hot and ready entrance of her body. "Why don't you tell me if it's long enough?"

He lifted her onto him, and her laugh melted into a pleasured sigh as he sheathed every last inch.

CHAPTER 14

When he'd first arrived at the villa, Jehan had imagined what Seraphina might look like unclothed and wreathed in the steam of the bathing room as he made love to her. Now he knew. And none of his fantasies were any match for the true thing.

She met his rhythm stroke for stroke. Arousal arced through him with each rotation of her hips, making his vision bleed red as fire filled his gaze. This woman had ruined him for any other. She destroyed him with a smile, with every moan and gasp, and he hadn't even begun to show her what true pleasure was.

He rocked inside her, balanced on the edge of madness for how incredible they felt together.

Eight nights wasn't enough.

The part of him that was more beast than man snapped at that tether. Eight nights was nothing. And they had already lost three of them.

The part of him that was nearly immortal demanded much more than that. It wanted forever.

Something he couldn't give Seraphina.

Not when forever meant one of them would have to give up the life that waited for them on the other side of the handfast.

Real life—the one that she had devoted herself to, and the opposite one he was equally committed to. Real life, where her selflessness had nearly gotten her killed a few hours ago, and where he was the Order warrior whose work revolved around violence and death. Where cowardly men like Karsten Hemmings served diabolical groups like Opus Nostrum.

He couldn't turn his back on the things that mattered to him any more than he could ask Seraphina to turn her back on hers.

But it was damned tempting to think about forever when they were enveloped within the fantasy of the handfast.

With his arms around her and her legs circling his waist as they moved together, joined beneath the fragrant, steaming water, forever was the only thing on his mind.

Eternity with Seraphina at his side.

As his Breedmate.

Bonded by blood.

The thought sent his gaze to the smooth column of her throat. Her pulse fluttered, beating with a rhythm he could feel echoing in his own veins. His fangs, already elongated from passion, now throbbed with an equally primal need.

A dangerous, selfish need.

One bite and there would be no other woman for him as long as he lived. All it would take was a single taste. Everything Breed in him pounded with the urge to sink his fangs into her flesh and take that binding sip.

Equally strong was his need to bind Seraphina to him by blood as well. If she drank from him, she would belong to no other male. His forever.

He couldn't do that to her.

He wouldn't.

Instead he guided her toward a fevered climax, driving into her body with all the hunger that rode him in his blood. He gave her pleasure, moving relentlessly until she broke apart in his arms on a scream.

Then he pivoted her around and moved in behind her to follow her over the edge.

As he came inside her on a shout, he couldn't dismiss the cold knowledge that the clock on their time together was ticking—so fast he could feel it in his bones.

Eight nights with Seraphina wasn't enough.

But somehow, at the end of it, he was going to have to find the strength to let her go.

CHAPTER 15

Sera woke from a long sleep later that morning feeling drowsy and sated. Sore in all the right places. She couldn't curb the smile that crept over her face as she recalled the hours she'd spent in the bathing room making love with Jehan. Their sex had been exhausting and incredible—which, she was beginning to realize, was the norm where he was concerned.

He was a tireless, wickedly creative lover. When she'd lost count of her orgasms and was sure she couldn't take any more pleasure, he had lifted her from the steaming pool and carried her to one of several nests of plump cushions and silk pillows on the floor for another bone-melting round.

If she'd thought watching their bodies move together in the darkness of her camp tent had been erotic, it had been nothing compared to seeing every carnal nuance of their passion in the candlelit reflection in the bathing room mirrors.

Just the thought of their tangled limbs and questing mouths had her pulse thrumming all over again as she wandered into the villa's kitchen for a light breakfast. Jehan was awake too—if he'd slept at all. His deep voice carried in a low, indistinct murmur from the main living area in the heart of the retreat. He was on her phone apparently. She hoped he had gotten back to Marcel after his brother's repeated messages for them to report in.

Sera made some tea and grabbed a peach from a bowl of fruit on the counter. Her long curls poured loose around her shoulders and over her bare breasts as she padded quietly out of the kitchen in just her panties to join him.

Biting into the ripe peach as she walked, she considered how much sweeter the juice would be if she were licking it off Jehan's muscled body. Or sucking it off the hard length of his cock.

Oh God...she had it bad for this male.

He made her feel more alive than anything in her life ever had. Yes, she lived for her work. It had fulfilled her for a long time, given her purpose. But Jehan gave her pleasure. He gave her yearning and contentment, excitement and peace. He had opened a part of her she hadn't even realized had been closed before.

Most unsettling of all, he made her long for the one thing she'd never imagined she might need. A mate by blood. A bond that could never be broken, not even by time.

As he'd made love to her hours ago, there had been a moment when she almost believed Jehan might want that too.

She wouldn't have refused him.

They'd been drunk with passion, and in the heat of that limitless pleasure, he could have taken all of her—body, heart, soul, and blood. She would have surrendered everything she was. Without even knowing what a future together might look like once the handfast was over and they left the cocoon of the villa.

She would give it all to him now too, clear-headed and sober.

Not at the end of their eight nights, but now.

And as much as it scared her, she had to let him know what he meant to her. Even more terrifying, she had to know if what she'd read in his tormented eyes a few hours ago was anything close to the depth of emotion she felt for him.

If he loved her too, then nothing else mattered. They would find a way to blend their lives and form their future together.

But as she rounded the corner of the corridor and overheard some of his conversation, all of her hopes faltered, then fell away. He wasn't talking to Marcel. She hung back, out of Jehan's sight as he spoke with one of his fellow warriors.

"I appreciate your understanding, Commander. I'm eager to be back in Rome to assemble my team and put the new mission into action. I'll be there as soon as my obligation here is over." He paused to listen to the warrior on the other end, then exhaled a heavy sigh. "No, I haven't made Seraphina aware of my decision. To be honest with you, sir, my mind is made up where she's concerned. I don't intend to give her any room to disagree."

He chuckled as if he and his comrade had just shared a joke. Meanwhile, Sera felt as though she'd been punched in the gut.

He was going back to Rome. Eager to get back to his team there.

As for her, he'd just disregarded her as if she didn't matter to him at all.

Sickness roiled in her stomach, in her heart. She shivered, suddenly self-conscious of her nudity in the center of the romantic villa. Silently, she retreated back to the kitchen and dropped the half-eaten peach in the trash.

What a fool she'd been to let herself think this was anything more than a joke to him. It had been from the start. An obligation he felt compelled to fulfill.

One he just admitted to his commander that he would walk away from as soon as it ended.

Thank God she hadn't let herself look even more idiotic by confessing her feelings for him.

Now she had several more nights of torture to look forward to, knowing that Jehan couldn't wait to be finished with the handfast and leave her behind.

CHAPTER 16

Complaints of a headache had driven Seraphina outside to the sunshine for most of the afternoon. Jehan had tried to persuade her that another vigorous round of orgasms might make her feel better instead, but his attempt at humor—and seduction—had failed miserably.

If he wasn't mistaken, her escape to the daylight on the patio seemed no less deliberate now than it had that first full day they'd spent together at the villa. When she'd gone there in an effort to avoid his company.

Had he done something wrong?

Or had she realized how close he'd been to burying his fangs in her carotid the last time they'd made love and was now determined to steer clear of him?

Whatever it was, it bothered him that she didn't seem interested in talking to him about it.

Roaming around the villa alone while she avoided him outside was maddening. He missed her, and she had only been away from him for a couple of hours.

How empty would his life feel if she was gone from it for good?

That was the question that had ridden him most of the past twelve hours—ever since their escape from the danger at the camp. Now that he'd had Seraphina in his life, in his arms, how would he ever be able to return to his existence without her?

He thought he'd known the answer, but maybe he was mistaken.

As twilight fell outside and she still didn't come inside to face him, Jehan decided he had to know. If she didn't feel the way he did, then he was ready to call off the rest of the handfast and try to save some shred of his sanity, if not his dignity.

He was stalking toward the patio doors when a knock sounded on the villa's front entrance.

Diverted from his mission, Jehan swung around and went over to see who it was.

Marcel stood there in the moonlight, grinning like an idiot.

And beside him—clinging to his arm with an equally besotted smile on her face—was Leila.

"You didn't return my call, brother."

Jehan raked a hand through his mussed hair and blew out an impatient curse. "Yeah. I, ah, was just about to do that."

"Bullshit." Marcel gestured to the Range Rover. "What the hell happened to the Rover? It looks like you drove it through a sand dune."

"Long story," Jehan said. "Suffice it to say things have been somewhat...interesting around here."

"Things have been a bit interesting with me too. With us." Marcel glanced at Leila, and she bit her lower lip as if to stifle the giggle that burst out of her anyway.

Jehan glanced at both of them. "What the hell are you talking about?"

Leila tried to peer around him, into the villa. "Where's Seraphina?"

"She's out on the patio, getting some air. Why are the two of you grinning like you've lost your damn minds?"

"We're in love!" Leila exclaimed.

"And we're blood-bonded," Marcel added.

"What?" Before Jehan could choke out his astonished response, Seraphina did it first. She stood behind him now in a long skirt and curve-hugging tank, a look of utter shock on her face. She crossed her arms. "What do you mean you're in love? How did that happen? And blood-bonded so soon? For God's sake, you only just met each other."

Jehan glanced at her, tempted to point out that they'd only just met too and he was already ruined for anyone else. But her pained expression kept him silent.

Marcel and Leila's excitement left no time for him to reply either. The pair stepped inside, practically vibrating with their news.

"We've been spending a lot of time together the past several days," Leila gushed.

Marcel wagged his brows at her. "And a couple of nights."

"Marcel!" She rolled her eyes, but her cheeks were flooded with bright color. "At first, we thought we only had the handfast in common. We both wanted it to be a success, of course. And honestly, we thought the two of you would make an adorable couple."

Jehan noted a cooler shift in Seraphina's posture as her sister mentioned the handfast. "How can you be sure you're not making a terrible mistake, Leila? You don't know anything about him. No offense, Marcel. You do seem like a good, decent male."

Unlike his brother? Jehan wondered.

Leila stared up at Marcel, warmth beaming from her eyes. "He makes me feel alive, Sera. He makes me laugh. He makes me feel special and beautiful, like I'm the only woman he sees."

Marcel cupped her face in a tender caress. "Because you are."

They kissed, leaving Jehan in awkward silence next to Seraphina. He glanced at her, but she stared rigidly ahead, refusing to meet his gaze.

"Congratulations," she murmured as the jubilant couple finally stopped devouring each other's faces. "I'm happy for you both. I'm sure our families will be happy to hear this news too."

"That's why we're here," Marcel said. "The handfast—"

Leila nodded. "Now that Marcel and I are blood-bonded, there's no need to continue with the handfast. It's over as of right now."

Marcel must have read Jehan's grim expression. He cleared his throat. "That is, unless you *want* to continue...?"

"Don't be ridiculous," Seraphina replied quickly. "Neither one of us wants that. We're both very eager to be done with this obligation and get back to our real lives. Isn't that right, Jehan?"

He scowled, uncertain how to answer. It seemed obvious that continuing the handfast with him wasn't what she wanted. He was impatient to get on with his life outside the villa too, but only if she would be part of it.

She stared at him as he struggled with the urge to tell her how he felt and risk her rejection in front of both their oblivious, elated siblings.

"Sera," he murmured.

But she was already pivoting away from him. "Now that this farce is over, I'll go collect my things."

When she sailed off in a hurry, both Marcel and Leila gaped at him.

"What the hell did you do to her, brother?"

Jehan shook his head. "I don't know." And then, the truth settled over him. Something about what she said. Something about *how* she said it...

She'd heard him today.

His conversation with Lazaro Archer back in Rome.

He cursed under his breath. Then he started to chuckle.

Marcel frowned at him. "She's pissed as hell at you about something and you're laughing?"

"Yeah, I am." Because now he understood her cold-shoulder today. He understood her anger at him now. And he'd never felt more elated about anything in his life.

Rounding up his brother and Leila, Jehan pushed both of them out the door.

"What are you doing?"

"Sending you on your way," he replied. "Don't come back for four more nights. This handfast isn't over until I say it is."

He closed the door on their confused faces, then turned to go after his Breedmate.

CHAPTER 17

Sera folded the red silk gown and placed it on the bed, trying not to let her heart crumble into pieces.

Outside the massive bedroom suite, the villa had gone quiet. As much as she wanted to celebrate Leila and Marcel's newfound love and bond, part of her was aching for everything she thought she might have had with Jehan.

Now that the handfast was over, she didn't even have those few remaining nights left with him.

Which was probably for the best.

Being around him now was its own kind of torture.

He was already making plans without her. Plans he didn't intend to discuss with or allow her any say in.

So why should she mourn the fact that their week together had just been cut short?

"Where do you think you're going?"

She froze at the sound of his voice but forced herself not to turn around. If she did, she was afraid she'd be tempted to run to him. With her heart so heavy in her breast, she was afraid she'd be unable to keep herself from whirling on him with pounding fists and streaming tears. Demanding that he explain how he could look at her so tenderly and make love to her so possessively if he only meant to leave her behind in a few more nights.

Although she didn't hear him move, she felt the heat of his large body at her spine. "I asked where you think you're going, Seraphina."

"Home," she said. "As soon as possible, I hope."

She walked back into the wardrobe to retrieve another of the pretty, feminine dresses that Leila had packed for her. Jehan was waiting when she came out. He had placed her bag on the floor, and now he sat on the edge of the bed, his sky blue eyes holding her in an unwavering stare.

Why did he have to look so intense and imposing, so impossible to ignore?

The sight of him waiting there, his handsome face grim with purpose, made her limping heart start to gallop.

She forced herself to move, walking over to pick up her bag and place it on a nearby chair so she could continue filling it. "Shouldn't you be packing your things too? If we're lucky, we might be able to get out of here in the next hour or so."

"I'm not leaving, Seraphina."

She glanced up at that. She couldn't help herself.

He stood up and walked over to her. "I'm not going anywhere tonight. Neither are you."

"What are you talking about?"

Her breath caught as he closed the space between them. As always, his presence seemed to suck all of the air out of the room. Right now, it was leeching away some of the resolve she wanted to hold on to so desperately.

"You heard it yourself, Jehan. The handfast is over. We've both made good on our obligations to our families, so now we're free to go."

He shook his head, his expression sober. "Eight nights, Sera. That's what we agreed to. I'm holding you to it. I don't give a damn if the pact terms say you can leave me now. I have four nights left with you, and I mean to claim them." He reached out and stroked his fingers down the side of her face. "I mean to claim *you*, Seraphina. As my woman. As my Breedmate."

"What?" Shock and confusion washed over her. "But I heard you on the phone today. You said you were leaving. That you had decided to go back to Rome. You disregarded me to your commander as if I didn't matter at all. I heard you—"

His thumb swept over her lips, stilling them. "What you apparently didn't hear was that I also told Lazaro Archer I had fallen in love with you."

No, she hadn't heard that.

And hearing it now sent spirals of joy and relief twisting through every cell in her body.

"You didn't hear me tell him that I needed to make a place for you in my life. Or that I couldn't leave the handfast without knowing you were mine." He caressed her cheek, eyes smoldering with affection and desire. "My life is with the Order, Sera. I can't give that up."

"I would never ask that of you, Jehan. I understand that you're doing something important, something that you're devoted to. After what we found at the camp, I realize your mission with the Order has probably never been more crucial."

"No, it hasn't," he said. "I can't leave my duty, but I know you can't give up yours either. I'm not going to ask you to leave your life behind to be with me in Rome."

She frowned, grateful that he understood what her work meant to her, yet unsure how their two worlds could mesh as a mated couple.

"That's why I've decided to pull a new team together here in Morocco. After last night, it's obvious that Opus has a strong presence here, so I've been tasked with pursuing those leads here on African soil. I'll work out the details with Commander Archer when I return to Rome at the end of the week."

She couldn't believe what she was hearing. She couldn't believe what he was doing for her. For them both. For the new bond he meant for them to share.

"Jehan, I don't know what to say."

He lifted her chin on the edge of his fingers. "You can start by saying you love me."

"Yes," she whispered. Then she said it again with all the elation in her soaring heart. "I love you."

He drew her close and kissed her, his lips brushing hers with such tenderness she wanted to weep. The next thing she knew, he had her spread beneath him on the bed. As he undressed her, then hurriedly stripped off his own clothing, his *dermaglyphs* pulsed with all the deep colors of his desire. His cock stood erect and enticing, awakening a powerful hunger in her—for his body, and for his blood.

Jehan clearly knew what she was feeling. His own hungers blazed in his transformed eyes and in every formidable inch of his naked flesh.

His fiery gaze scorched her face as he looked at her in utter devotion. And need.

So much need, it rocked her.

He lowered himself between her legs and entered her slowly, as he bent to lick a searing path along her jawline, then her neck. "You're mine, Sera."

"Yes," she gasped, arching into his abrading kiss as his fangs tested the tender flesh of her throat. "For the next four nights, I'm yours however you want me, Jehan."

He glanced up at her, baring those beautiful, sharp tips with his hungry, definitely wicked smile. He gave a slow shake of his head. "Four more nights is only the beginning. Starting now, you're mine forever."

She nodded, too swept up in love and desire to form words.

Emotion overwhelmed her as she watched him bite into his wrist to open his veins for her. "Drink from me," he rasped thickly, bringing the punctures to her parted lips.

Sera fastened her mouth to the wounds and stroked her tongue across the strong tendons of his wrist. His blood called to her, more deeply than she could ever have imagined. She moaned as the first swallow roared through her senses, into her cells. She drank more, reveling in the power of the bond as Jehan's essence—his life—became part of hers.

And all the while she drank, he rocked within her, creating a pleasure so immense she could hardly bear it.

"You're mine, Seraphina." He stared down at her as she fed, as she came on a shattered scream. "Starting tonight, you're only mine."

"Yes."

On a rumble of satisfaction, he drew his wrist to his mouth and sealed the punctures closed with a swipe of his tongue. His blazing eyes were locked on her throat.

Sera brought her arms up around him as he lowered his head to her carotid and licked the fluttering pulse point that beat only for him.

And when her handsome Breed warrior—her eternal love—sank his fangs into her vein and took his first sip, Seraphina smiled.

Because whether she believed in magic or not, tonight she was holding the prince, the fairy tale, and the happily ever after in her arms.

Midnight Untamed

Acknowledgments from the Author

I am so excited to be part of the 1001 Dark Nights collection again with this new novella in my Midnight Breed vampire romance series. Thank you to Liz Berry, MJ Rose, Jillian Stein, and the rest of the creative, marketing, and editorial teams at Evil Eye Concepts for the incredible vision and enthusiasm you bring to each release in the collection. It's a pleasure to be working with all of you!

To my amazing readers, thank you for your continued support and for joining me on yet another adventure within the Midnight Breed story world. I hope you enjoy Savage and Bella's story, and all the rest still to come.

Happy reading!

Love, Lara

CHAPTER 1

The palatial villa two hours outside Rome glittered like a jewel beneath the starlit night sky. Lights glowed from within the sprawling mansion and along the circular drive out front, where half a dozen sleek sports cars were parked on the cobbled stones.

From his vantage point on a tree-studded hill five hundred yards away, Ettore Selvaggio watched as a beautiful red Ferrari rolled up to the villa and took its place between a silver Bugatti Veyron and a blue Pagani Huayra. Add in the pair of Lamborghinis, the Maserati, and another Ferrari, and there was well over ten million dollars' of automotive luxury parked outside Vito Massioni's mansion. Plus a collection of vehicles worth twice that amount stowed inside the massive bays of the reputed drug-dealing Breed male's private garage.

If nothing else, Massioni and his criminal associates had impeccable taste in cars.

"Apparently, selling your soul to Opus Nostrum pays well," he muttered into the wireless mic that linked him to the Order's command center back in Rome. "You getting my visual on this place?"

"Visual acknowledged, Savage."

The deep gravel voice of his comrade, Trygg, was never easy to read, and tonight was no exception. Not that Savage actually expected the menacing warrior to appreciate the fleet of fine Italian machinery belonging to Massioni and his cohorts.

And not that it mattered, anyway.

In a few minutes, the cars, the mansion, and everyone in it would be nothing but ash and smoking rubble.

Damned shame about the cars.

"Status," Trygg prompted over the earpiece as Savage hunkered down to watch the coming fireworks.

"Packages have been delivered and the last party guest just arrived. We're good to go."

"You collected the receipt?"

"Right here in my pocket," he said, tapping the flash drive Trygg referenced.

Twenty minutes before Savage arrived at his observation position on the hill, he'd been inside Massioni's villa on a covert solo mission to download key computer data, then take out the target. According to intel newly obtained by the Order's headquarters in Washington, D.C., Vito Massioni was the European distributor of a dangerous narcotic that turned otherwise law-abiding Breed vampires into blood-obsessed, murderous Rogues.

This new drug with the street name Red Dragon was said to be even more powerful than its predecessor, Crimson, which had cost countless Breed and human lives when it hit the streets twenty years ago. Now, thanks to Massioni and his collusion with the terror group, Opus Nostrum, Rogue outbreaks were on the rise again in the States and across Europe, creating panic among an already anxious human public. As leader of the Order, Lucan Thorne had made it clear that he wanted the problem cut off at the source, and cut off swiftly.

Savage was more than happy to be tapped for the covert assignment. It had been a serendipitous bonus to learn that Massioni had called a private meeting with his lieutenants tonight. So, instead of a data grab and stealth assassination—one of many lethal specialties that had earned Savage his nickname in the Order—the scope of the job had expanded to mass elimination.

To that end, four explosive devices with enough firepower to level an entire city block were now planted around Massioni's villa. All Savage had to do was set them off by remote detonator and Opus would lose yet another key ally. The Order wasn't about to rest until the entire organization was dismantled, the cabal of members at its helm unmasked and destroyed.

Savage lifted his field glasses to his eyes and peered at the mansion. Although his vision as one of the Breed was superhuman, the lenses allowed him to zoom in on the illuminated window of the grand salon where Massioni and his men were gathered.

The seven Breed males evidently had plenty of cause for celebration. They greeted one another with a lot of laughter and back patting, a lot of ingratiating smiles and kowtowing for the dark-haired, hawk-nosed Vito Massioni from his underlings. No doubt the Red Dragon dealer and his cronies had been handsomely rewarded for their part in the spike of Rogue attacks the past few nights. Savage couldn't wait to send them all to their final reward tonight.

"Light it up at your ready," Trygg advised.

Savage smiled behind his binoculars. "With pleasure."

Glancing away from the meeting taking place inside the mansion, he reached to retrieve the remote detonator. Normally he didn't get invested in witnessing a target's demise, but it was hard not to take some satisfaction in crashing Massioni's little party tonight.

He brought the field glasses back up to his face—just in time to see that a woman had entered the room. The petite blonde wore a flashy red dress that clung to her slender body like liquid silk. The neckline plunged low in front, the slit in the skirt slicing high up her leg, baring a lot of creamy thigh with each gliding step she took toward Massioni.

What the fuck?

Savage hadn't realized there was a female in the mansion. Not that he felt much sympathy for anyone who associated with a thug like Massioni. And not that it should stop him from pushing the button on the detonator. But still…

His thumb froze, hovering over the trigger.

"Unidentified female on the premises," he murmured into his mic. "Stand by, base."

"Standing by," Trygg said. Then he made a low, appreciative noise that might as well have been a wolf-whistle, coming from the eternally inscrutable warrior.

Yeah, the female was hot. Savage barely contained his own primal growl at the sight of all those slender curves poured into a column of scarlet silk. He'd long avoided blondes—for personal reasons of his own—but everything male in him responded to the sight of this one like flame to gasoline.

He stared through the lenses, watching as every head in the room turned to look at her as she approached Massioni. As soon as she was close enough, the vampire's beefy arm snaked out to hook her around the waist, pulling her roughly against him as his buddies grinned and chuckled.

More than one of the Breed males gathered in the room wore an expression of unabashed lust as their boss crudely cupped the young woman's breast in front of them all.

A jab of disgust spiked through Savage's blood at Massioni's manhandling of the woman.

"There was no mention of a female in the intel," Trygg said.

"No, there wasn't." Savage's reply was clipped, irritation combined with this unwanted element of surprise. "The report out of D.C. specifically stated that Massioni is unmated, so who the fuck is she?"

"Collateral damage," Trygg replied evenly. "Pop the charges and get the hell out of there."

Savage nodded, knowing that was sound advice.

But his thumb didn't move on the detonator.

Something was starting to bother him about the woman the longer he stared at her. Something that gnawed at the perimeter of his memory.

"I need a closer look."

Without waiting for confirmation from his comrade, he set the detonator down in the soft grass, then tightened the focus on his binoculars. Not on Massioni or his men, but on her. The gorgeous blonde whose heart-shaped face and pixie features seemed strangely, distantly familiar somehow.

Which was impossible, considering this female was clearly Massioni's plaything.

The face that teased at the frayed edges of Savage's mind—and his heart—had no place here. Not with criminals and killers like the ones assembled inside the villa that was wired to blow on his command.

Holy shit.

It couldn't be her.

Trygg's voice sounded in his ear. "You got problems over there?"

Savage couldn't answer that. Not when his veins were filling with adrenaline and a sick feeling of apprehension was starting to take up space behind his sternum.

He brought the woman in closer, his eyes burning from the intensity of his unblinking stare. She was still caught within the cage of Massioni's thick arm, smiling indulgently as the Breed male showed her off like some kind of prize to his leering friends. Showing her off as if the bastard owned her.

Fuck. Don't let that be her.

"Status," Trygg demanded now. "What's going on?"

"I'm not sure. I think the woman is…" He drew in a breath, hoping like hell he was wrong. "Christ, I think I know her."

Trygg's curse scraped across the earpiece. "Bad fucking time for a reunion with one of your many conquests, man. And if the bitch belongs to our target, you don't know her now."

No, he didn't.

Not anymore.

Hell, not for a very long time.

As Savage watched, Massioni finally released the woman from his possessive hold. He said something to his colleagues, a remark that made them all chuckle. Then Massioni gestured at her dismissively. Her placid smile still in place, the beautiful blonde pivoted away from the men.

It wasn't until she turned around that Savage's suspicion was confirmed.

The proof was there on the back of her left shoulder—the scarlet mark of a Breedmate. Only the rarest of women bore the unique birthmark signifying they were something more than mortal.

The small teardrop-and-crescent-moon symbol rode this female's shoulder in the precise spot that Savage dreaded it would.

"Son of a bitch. I don't believe this."

It *was* her.

After all this time—nearly a decade.

Arabella Genova.

Savage snarled as Massioni playfully smacked her ass, sending her on her way. Unfazed, she glided out of the room as elegantly as she'd entered a few moments ago, Savage following her progress with the field glasses held in a grip so tight they should have shattered.

Trygg was right. He didn't know her now.

How the girl he once adored had ended up in the hands of a thug like Vito Massioni, he could only guess.

And it didn't matter.

Savage had a job to do.

That's what he told himself, even as he pulled the binoculars away from his face and hissed a sharp curse into the darkness.

The Bella he'd known as a girl all those years ago was just a memory. This Bella was in the wrong place at the wrong time, and on the dead wrong side of the law.

Collateral damage, just like Trygg said.

Savage knew what he had to do. The Order might never have the chance to get this close to Massioni and his lieutenants again. Everything was in place. The mission was moments away from success. All he had to do was hit the detonator.

He picked it up, staring at the trigger that would erase Massioni and his entire operation from the face of the Earth.

And, now, Bella too.

"Fuck."

Savage raked a hand over his tightly clamped jaw. His pulse was banging in his temples, his heart slamming against his ribs with each heavy beat.

"Status," Trygg said, a note of warning in the warrior's gravel voice. "I don't like what I'm hearing over there, Savage."

He didn't answer. Nothing he said now would put his comrade or anyone else at the command center in Rome at ease.

Savage set aside the binoculars. Then he carefully deactivated the detonator and slipped the remote into his back pocket.

"Stand by, base. I'm going back in."

CHAPTER 2

Arabella held her composure until she had reached her private quarters on the villa's second floor. Once inside, she leaned against the closed door and let her revulsion leak out of her on a shudder. At least she was getting better at the charade. There was a time when she might have had to bite back a scream.

Her skin crawled everywhere Vito had touched her. She could still feel his hard fingers on her body, on her breast. The sting of his offensive smack to her backside burned her dignity even more than it did her ass.

She hated being trotted out in front of his friends as his personal show pony, forced to dress and act as if she belonged to the coarse, criminal Breed male.

Though to be fair, in many ways Massioni did own her. Her life. Her freedom. Her unique Breedmate gift for premonition—the thing that first brought her to his attention three years ago. He owned all of that, no matter how much she despised him.

He might have owned her body, too, if she hadn't found a way to convince him that the price of taking that part of her would cost him the one thing he couldn't afford to lose.

The threat had kept her out of his reach so far, but there were times when she knew he'd been tempted to test her. She only hoped she wouldn't kill him if he tried. Because no matter how clever she wanted to think she was in dealing with him, Vito Massioni always had one final, terrible card to play.

And so long as he held that over her head, she had no choice but to serve him.

She could never escape him, not even in death.

He'd made certain of that.

Arabella knew better than to keep Massioni waiting. He'd sent her away to fetch her scrying bowl while he entertained his boot-licking cronies in the grand salon. They were gloating over a large payout from a shipment of Red Dragon to the States and the United Kingdom—a narcotic that destroyed the minds of their own kind, the Breed, creating blood-addicted monsters from just the smallest dose. They didn't care that their sudden windfall came at the expense of both Breed and human lives. She had learned a long time ago that Vito Massioni's greed knew no bounds.

Nor did his violence.

That her gift had helped him amass his growing fortune, and the power that came with it, made Arabella want to retch.

How often had she thought about giving him a false reading from her scrying bowl?

How many times had she dreaded that her visions would one day prove incorrect?

But she hadn't deceived him, not once.

And, thankfully, her visions had never been wrong.

Either of those failings would come at the cost of innocent lives. Not her own, but the people she cared about most in the world. The only family she had left now.

It was those precious lives she held close in her heart as she walked over to the cabinet across the room and retrieved the hammered gold bowl she would need for her reading downstairs. In reality, her gift would awaken when she peered into any standing pool of liquid, but Massioni insisted she use the ridiculous carnival fortune-teller's style bowl for dramatic effect whenever she performed a public reading.

Cradling the shallow bowl in her palms, she drew the empty vessel out of the cabinet. Her own face stared back at her in the reflection on the polished gold basin—but that wasn't all.

Behind her stood the ominous shape of someone else.

A man.

Tall, immense.

An intruder dressed entirely in black tactical gear.

Bella sucked in a startled breath.

Fear streaked through her, but before her shriek could rip up the back of her throat, a broad palm came up to cover her mouth.

Oh, God.

The bowl slipped out of her grasp, thudding onto the thick rug. Muscular arms caged her from behind, immobilizing her. She staggered on her high-heeled sandals, drawn helplessly against the unmistakable heat of a very strong, very male body.

Not Massioni's. This wasn't any of the other men gathered in the salon with him either, although there was no question that the male trapping her in his unbreakable hold was Breed.

"Don't scream, Bella."

He spoke against her ear, his growled command voiced in a deep baritone that brushed over her jangled senses like a caress.

He knew her name. How? Who the hell was he? Where had he come from?

She struggled and fought to break free, but he didn't let go. He was much too strong, and none of her squirming or resisting was getting her anywhere. All her grunts and cries for help were snuffed by the hand still sealed firmly across her lips.

Trapped, she could only stand there, her breath rushing out of her nose in panicked gusts while terror wrapped around her heart like a vise.

"Be calm. I'm not going to hurt you."

Did he think she was a fool? She didn't believe him for a second, not when she could feel the lethal power radiating off his big body. Whoever this man was, he was beyond dangerous, and she had no doubt that his only business in the villa was death.

She groaned, trying futilely to pull away from him in another burst of desperation. Her heart was speeding, banging against her rib cage as if on the verge of exploding. Yet despite her alarm, her instincts had begun to prickle with some kind of distant recognition.

She knew it was impossible, this strange feeling that this intruder was no stranger at all. Her blood was still racing and cold with terror, but beneath the fear was a growing sense of familiarity.

A name skated across her memory, one she had tried for years to bar from her thoughts and her heart.

No. It couldn't be him.

The beautiful, golden-haired Breed male she had known all those years ago had been a scholar, not a soldier. He would have no business in a place like this, among thugs like the ones gathered downstairs.

Then again, there was a time when she'd have said the same thing about herself.

"I'm going to remove my hand from your mouth now," he murmured.

As he spoke, his breath skimmed warmly against her cheek and along the side of her neck. She shivered from the sensation, astonished to realize how deeply he affected her, even after all this time.

Because, yes, she did know that low, velvet voice.

Just as she knew the scent that enveloped her as she stood immobilized in his arms. Heaven help her, but she had carried the scent of him, the sound of his voice, in a private corner of her heart since she was a teenage girl.

"Don't be afraid, Bella. I didn't come here to harm you. Nod your head if you understand."

She nodded, and his grip on her relaxed. His palm fell away from her lips, leaving a coldness in its wake. Arabella slowly turned around in his slack hold.

"Oh, my God." The words leaked out of her on a disbelieving sigh. "Ettore."

Even though she thought she was prepared to see him again now, her first glimpse of Ettore Selvaggio standing mere inches away from her was a complete shock to her system.

She brought her fingers to her lips, her fear replaced by an overwhelming feeling of incredulity…and confusion.

Although she knew his voice and scent, she barely recognized the hard, disapproving face that stared back at her.

A black knit skullcap covered the loose golden waves that would have framed his lean, angled cheeks and firm, square jaw. While she knew that when he smiled there were dimples on either side of his lush mouth, right now his sculpted lips were held in a grim, unforgiving line. His hazel eyes were intense, his brows lowering as he pinned her in a measuring stare that felt as dangerous and unyielding as his hold on her a moment ago.

"Jesus Christ," he whispered on a sharp exhalation. His expression hardened even more. "It really is you, Arabella. I had to be sure. I didn't want to believe it."

She frowned. He sounded as surprised to see her as she was to be looking at him.

It had been ten years since they last saw each other. Ten years since he crushed her heart and walked away, never to return. Now, here he stood, dressed like a nightmare in black combat gear and staring at her in accusation, as if she were the one to blame.

His gaze seared her, making her feel cold and exposed in the curve-hugging red silk dress Massioni insisted she wear tonight. She knew what she must look like, what Ettore must think.

As much as everything inside her urged her to explain, she had bigger things to worry about than his opinion of her now.

"What the hell do you think you're doing? How did you get in here?" She couldn't hide the shock in her voice, or her dread. If Massioni or any of his guards discovered Ettore inside the villa, they would kill him. And Bella didn't doubt for a second that she would be made to suffer too. "Are you insane? Get out of here now, Ettore. You have no idea how dangerous it is for you to be here."

He gave her a smile that chilled. "I'm not the one in danger. Your lover and his cronies are. I've rigged this place to blow sky-high as soon as I hit the detonator in my pocket."

Oh, God. She swallowed, stricken to hear him admit what she'd already guessed. He was here to kill Vito Massioni.

And she could not let that happen.

Because if Massioni died, he had promised that she and her remaining family would die too.

A muffled rumble of laughter carried from the salon downstairs. Massioni and his guests would be growing restless soon. She'd already been gone too long. She couldn't risk anyone coming to look for her.

No more than she could risk allowing Ettore the chance to carry out what he'd come here tonight to do.

"I'm sorry," she murmured, shaking her head as she took a step away from him. "I'm sorry... Ettore, I have no choice."

Before he could stop her—before he probably even guessed what she was about to do—Bella screamed at the top of her lungs.

CHAPTER 3

There was barely a second of silence between the sound of Bella's scream and the pandemonium that followed.

Male voices shouted from the salon below. Heavy boot falls began to thunder from all directions, while outside, perimeter floodlights blinked on, illuminating the villa and its surrounding grounds in a blinding daylight glow.

Holy shit.

He couldn't believe she'd done it—betrayed his presence to the entire mansion.

Then again, it shouldn't come as much of a surprise. He had certainly earned her scorn. Arabella Genova owed him nothing anymore, not even an explanation for how she'd ended up on the arm—and possibly in the bed—of a criminal scum like Massioni.

No choice, she'd said.

What the hell did she mean by that?

"Bella—" He reached for her, but she jerked out of his grasp, putting several paces between them.

"Get out, Ettore." Her soft brown eyes were desperate beneath her furrowed brows. And outside the closed door of her quarters, it sounded as though several of Massioni's men were already rushing up the stairs to the second floor. She threw an anxious glance over her shoulder at the pounding of approaching feet in the hallway. Her voice was a tight, fearful whisper. "Please, go. Get out of here while you still have a chance!"

Jesus, she was terrified.

And it wasn't directed at him.

What the hell had that bastard done to her?

Savage ground out a curse, feeling precious seconds tick by. He had a mission to carry out tonight—and he would—but not until Bella was safe and secured. Whether or not she intended to cooperate with that plan.

"Come with me." He grabbed for her again, this time snagging her wrist.

"No. Let go of me!" she cried, projecting her voice louder than necessary. For who? Massioni and his goons? "I said stay away from me!"

"Listen to me, damn it." Savage took hold of her shoulders and forced her to meet his gaze. "I'm trying to save you, Bella."

She scoffed brittly. "You can't save me. No one can."

Christ, she really believed that. He knew her too well to think otherwise. He'd always been able to read her emotions in her eyes, in that lovely face that had haunted his dreams for longer than he cared to admit.

When she tried to break loose from his hold, he realized there was only one way he would be able to get her out of the villa without fighting her every step of the way.

She might hate him even more for this, but he had no choice either. He wasn't about to leave her behind.

Laying his palm against her forehead, he tranced her into an immediate and deep sleep.

She no sooner sagged into his arms than the door to her quarters burst open and two armed guards filled the space.

Savage was crouched low, having just guided Bella's limp body to rest on the rug. His weapon was already drawn and ready as the pair of Breed males crashed into the room. He dropped them both with sniper precision, squeezing off two headshots that nailed each guard between the eyes.

There would be more behind them. By the sound of the chaos unraveling all around the villa now, Savage expected he'd have to take on Massioni's entire army of thugs as soon as he stepped out of the room.

Fortunately, he had another plan.

Lifting Bella over his shoulder in a fireman's carry, he dashed to the other side of her suite where a large window overlooked the circular driveway below. A handful of armed guards scurried across the cobbled bricks, some heading into the mansion as backup while others fanned out to patrol the surrounding grounds.

The odds of getting past the security detail down there weren't great, but they were a hell of a lot better than charging into the fray inside the villa.

Lifting the glass with a mental command, he swung his legs over the sill, then dropped to the ground with Bella held securely in his arms.

He threw another psychic order at the nearest vehicle, smiling to himself when the V12 engine of the blue Pagani rumbled to life. The gullwing doors lifted and Savage hurried over to slip Bella into the passenger seat and fasten her in.

One of the perimeter patrol guards spotted him and shouted the alarm to the others. Bullets rang out from all directions. Savage dodged the incoming fire, diving into the driver's seat of the sleek sports car and dropping the doors. Throwing the vehicle into gear, he sped away from the villa just as Massioni and several of his lieutenants came pouring out behind him.

Savage already had the detonator in hand, the safety switched off.

He pushed the trigger on it, watching in the rearview mirror as a sudden fireball ignited and the whole place exploded against the night sky. The percussion made the Pagani jump on the pavement, but he held the wheel and pushed the pedal to the floor.

He couldn't deny his satisfaction at seeing the fiery plume and cloud of black, roiling smoke behind him. He only hoped the explosives did the job as intended. Ordinarily, he'd stick around to make sure his target was neutralized, but not tonight.

Not with precious cargo in tow.

His gaze strayed to Bella. Slumped in her red silk gown on the seat beside him, she slept as peacefully as a kitten, her mind still caught in the web of the trance he'd placed on her. The urge to touch her was too much to resist. Reaching over, he smoothed an errant blonde tendril from her cheek.

Damn, she was even lovelier than he recalled. No longer the coltish Breedmate girl who'd been his best friend's sister. No longer the tomboy teenager who used to delight in racing through the cultivated fields of her family's vineyard, but a twenty-eight-year-old woman with a refined beauty that stirred everything male in him.

Not to mention his blood.

Memories of a night ten years ago came to life in his mind in vivid, erotic detail. Her warm, naked skin against his. Her sweet, breathless cries as he tasted every virgin inch of her beautiful body.

Her trusting, open-hearted gaze as he made love to her for the first—and only—time.

How she must have hated him...after.

He'd despised himself enough for both of them. If he'd been in the least to blame for pushing Bella toward another man—especially one like Vito Massioni—he would never forgive himself.

And if he wanted to pretend he had forgotten her even for a moment during the past decade, seeing her beside him now was as if all that time had simply evaporated.

He didn't know what he was going to do with her now. She sure as fuck hadn't been part of the equation when he'd set out on tonight's mission, but seeing her again had changed everything. Once he had spotted her inside the villa, nothing would have kept him from making sure she was safe.

Not even Bella herself could have stopped him.

So much for a simple operation going according to plan.

Savage forced his gaze away from her and put both hands back on the wheel. His eyes trained on the road, he buried the Pagani's accelerator and headed for the highway that would take them back to Rome.

CHAPTER 4

Bella couldn't wake from the sleep that cocooned her.

Nor did she want to.

Warm fingers stroked the side of her face as she slept, soothing her with a touch that was both sheltering and enticing. So strong. So infinitely gentle.

Ettore's touch.

Her senses knew it, even if her mind struggled to comprehend. His caress felt like a dream, but it was real. As real as he was, seated close enough to her that his scent filled her lungs with each waking breath she drew.

No, this was no dream.

This was something deeper than sleep.

Her head felt thick, as if her mind were cushioned in cotton.

Then she remembered. The shock of seeing Ettore inside Massioni's villa. Her dread at learning what he had come there to do.

She remembered him insisting that she leave with him, go somewhere safe. When she refused, he had reached up to touch her brow…

He'd tranced her!

Outrage speared through her. The sudden jolt of adrenaline and fury helped shake off the loose threads of the fading trance. She opened her eyes and found Ettore glancing at her. His handsome face and solemn hazel eyes held her gaze in the dim light of the vehicle's dashboard.

Beneath her, the low purr of an engine vibrated.

"Are you okay?" he asked, drawing his hand away from her face now.

She instantly missed the warmth, despite the alarm that was flooding her veins.

"What are you doing?" She dragged herself out of her slump in the soft leather seat. On the other side of the passenger window, the nighttime landscape was a blur. Jesus, Ettore was driving like a bat out of hell. She swung an anxious look behind them. "Where's Massioni?"

"Don't worry about him. He was mine to deal with. And I did."

Fresh horror swamped her. "You killed him?"

Ettore looked at her, his expression grim. "I hope so, but there wasn't time to verify that."

Oh, God. No. "Where are we going?"

A frown creased his brow. "I'm taking you to Rome, Bella. You'll be safest at the Order's command center there. My comrades and I will make sure of that."

The Order. As shocked as she was to realize the golden, charming young man she had known all those years ago now made his living dealing in violence and death as a member of that lethal organization, she also knew that no one—not even the Order—could protect her from the worst of Vito Massioni's threats.

For all she knew, it was already too late.

"Let me out of here, Ettore. Let me out right now."

"What do you mean, let you out?" He gaped at her as if she had lost her mind. "Sweetheart, we're going a hundred and twenty miles an hour."

"I have to go back. Please, Ettore!"

Overcome with worry, she fumbled with her seatbelt, unfastening it and tearing it away from her body. She had to get out of the car and go back to beg Massioni's forgiveness.

If he was still alive.

Dear God, don't let him be dead.

Don't let her family be killed because of her failure to protect them.

A sob raked her throat. "Goddammit, I said stop this fucking car!"

He slowed the growling sports car and eased off the empty highway to the shoulder. As soon as the vehicle stopped, she leaped out. She paused only long enough to toss her high heels into the grass, then started running the opposite way on the rough gravel that edged the pavement.

Ettore's curse exploded behind her. "What the hell are you doing?"

He caught up to her instantly, gifted with Breed genetics that made him faster than any other creature on the planet. He blocked her path, his big male body filling her vision and all of her senses. When she tried to dodge him, his hands came down firmly on her shoulders, holding her still.

"Talk to me, Arabella. Tell me what this is about."

"My family." She couldn't contain the shiver that rocked her when she thought about what they might be enduring because of her, possibly at this very moment. "Massioni promised me that if anything ever happened to him, he'd have them killed."

Ettore's scowl deepened. "Your father might have something to say about that. Your brother, Consalvo, too."

She gazed up at him, shaking her head in misery. "My father's dead. So is Sal. I guess you didn't know. How would you, right? You left and never looked back."

He flinched as if her words stung as much as a slap. Yet when he spoke, there was only quiet, patient concern in his deep voice. "What happened?"

"It was Sal," she said, still wounded by her brother's fall from grace—and the betrayal that followed. "Three years ago, my father made the mistake of turning over the vineyard to Sal. Things didn't go very well. He was careless with the books. Worse than careless. None of us realized how deeply in debt the business was—or why—until Sal's mate, Chiara, confided in me about his gambling. She was worried for him, and for the future of their infant son. But it was already too late. Sal got mixed up with bad people, the worst of them being Vito Massioni."

Ettore blew out a sharp curse. "The idiot. Sallie owed him money?"

"A lot of money. More than any of us could pay. By the time we learned what he'd done, Massioni was out of patience. He tortured Sal, nearly killed him." Bella took a fortifying breath. "My brother was scared and desperate, in fear for his life. He couldn't have been thinking clearly...

At least, that's what I've had to tell myself in order to forgive him for what he did to me."

She watched Ettore's eyes darken with grave understanding. "Your brother is the reason you're with Massioni?"

She nodded. "Vito showed up at our Darkhaven one night, along with a dozen armed men. He wasn't there to negotiate. The men shot my father in front of all of us. Sal was going to be next. He made all kinds of promises, offered to give Massioni the house, the vineyard—everything he could think of. None of it appealed to Vito, of course. He had plenty of property, plenty of money. Then Sal looked at me."

"No." Ettore's voice dropped to a low growl. "Jesus, he didn't."

Bella swallowed. "Sal told him about my gift for scrying. He told Massioni to imagine how much richer he could be if he had the ability to see the future. Sal promised that I was worth ten times as much as the debt he owed. In the end, I'm sure he was right. Massioni took me away that night, after giving his men the order to kill Sal."

Ettore's eyes were no longer dark, but crackling with shards of amber that ignited with his rage. As he spoke, the tips of his fangs glinted bright white behind his lips. "That cowardly son of a bitch. If your brother were alive right now, I'd fucking kill him myself." He reached up to touch her face and she could feel the power of his fury beneath the tenderness of his fingers.

"It doesn't matter anymore. I did what I had to in order to survive. Chiara and my little nephew are what matter most to me. They're the reason I stayed with Massioni. He held their lives ransom to make sure I never crossed him or tried to get away."

"Well, he can't hurt anyone now," Ettore said. "As of tonight, Vito Massioni's either dead or damned close to it."

"No. You don't understand." She stepped back, shaking her head. She wished she could stand there all night under the warmth of his caress, but her dread was only intensifying by the moment. "You don't realize what you've done, Ettore. He gave instructions to his entire criminal network to hunt down Chiara and Pietro if anything ever happened to him. If he's dead, so are they. Or they will be soon."

Ettore studied her for a moment before hissing a tight curse. "Your brother's widow and her boy—are they still at the vineyard?"

She nodded.

"Fuck. That's three hours in the other direction." He stared at her, grim but resolute. "If we push it, the Pagani should get us there in under two."

"Does that mean you'll help me?"

"To my last breath, Arabella." He cupped her face in his strong palm, his eyes blazing with determination and something deeper. Something that lit a dormant hope in her chest and made her veins tingle with heat.

She knew he felt the same kindling of emotion too. It was there in his glittering eyes, and in the lengthening points of his fangs.

He may have abandoned her without explanation a decade ago, but all of the attraction and need that had existed between them was still there. Still burning inside both of them.

"Come on," he said after a long moment, his voice rough. "We'd better go."

CHAPTER 5

They made it to Potenza in just under two hours, thanks to clear late-night roadways and the seven hundred horses at work inside the Pagani's massive engine.

Savage turned onto a narrow two-lane and headed for the Genova family vineyard even before Bella pointed to give him directions. He had been born in the same southern province of Italy, and, like her, he had spent the better part of his youth traipsing around the volcanic soil foothills of the region's imposing Mount Vulture.

Unlike Bella, however, he had no family of his own. Whoever his parents were, they'd been gone from his life soon after he was born. Abandoned when he was just a baby, he'd been raised in one Darkhaven orphanage after another until he was old enough to take care of himself.

He thought he'd found something close to family when he met Bella's brother, Consalvo, at university and the two became fast friends. He had regarded Sal like a brother, helped work the vineyard with the family as if it was his own.

For a long time, he had actually believed he'd found someplace to belong.

He *had* belonged...until his desire for Arabella had been found out and he'd been informed by her father that he was no longer welcome there.

Not good enough for his daughter.

Bella deserved something better.

Hell, Savage wouldn't argue that, even now.

But as he glanced over at her and watched her lovely face turn ashen with dread on their approach to the long gravel drive that led to the homestead at the base of the mountain, he felt a wave of possessiveness—and protectiveness—he could not deny.

And he felt guilt too.

For leaving her the way he had, for letting her think he didn't care.

For not being present to ensure that she never knew a moment of pain or heartache or fear.

All the things he could see playing across her features now.

Because of him.

She sucked in a sharp breath when she spotted the ominous-looking, empty black sedan parked halfway up the drive to the rambling villa. "Oh, no. Ettore, we're too late."

He clamped his molars tight, holding back the curse that leaped to his tongue. She was right. It didn't look good.

A plan formed in his head—a risky one, but the best option he had.

He didn't dare ditch the car with Bella inside it, and damned if he was going to let her out of his sight for as much as a second.

"Slide down as far as you can," he told her. "Don't move, Bella. Not unless I tell you to."

She shot him an anxious glance but did as he instructed.

He swept off his black knit skullcap and tossed it aside. Instead of keeping his cautious pace up the meandering drive, Savage gunned the engine, letting the tires chew up the dirt and dust as he roared all the way to the homestead.

Up ahead in the dark, a pair of Breed thugs in black suits were prowling the perimeter of the house and surrounding grounds. Shit. They were both carrying semiautomatic pistols and looking short on patience. Maybe that was a good thing where Bella's family members were concerned.

Savage threw the Pagani into park but left the engine running. Since his attire could raise questions he didn't want to answer, he would have to employ his unique brand of obfuscation in order to get him past the other males' suspicion.

Using the Breed ability that served him well in his stealth line of work, he conjured an illusion that turned his tactical gear into a black suit and altered his face and hair color. Then he pulled his own semiauto 9mm and climbed out of the car as if he had every right to be there.

"Jesus Christ," he muttered loudly as he stalked toward the goateed man out front. "Where the fuck are the other guys?"

The henchman scowled. "What other guys? Far as I know, me and Luigi were the only ones called out for this job. Who the hell are you?"

"Backup," Savage said, giving the man a look of disdain. He called out to the second man, a thick-necked mountain of a male who was just coming around from the rear of the farmhouse. "What the fuck's taking you so long, Luigi? You find that bitch and her brat back there?"

Luigi shook his head as he started jogging over to meet them. "Not yet. They must've cleared out before we got here."

Savage grunted. "Good."

He popped a round into each man's skull before either of them could react. The two would-be killers dead on the ground, he jogged back to the Pagani. Arabella was still hunkered down on the floor in front of the passenger seat like he'd instructed her. Good girl.

He opened the door. "It's okay. Chiara and your nephew aren't here and the two men sent to find them won't be looking for them anymore."

"Thank God." She lifted her head, pushing herself up to peer into the darkness where Massioni's men lay unmoving in the grass near the house. "But Chiara wouldn't have known to run away. There wouldn't have been time to get very far, especially with a three-year-old in tow." She glanced up at him, worry—and a small glimmer of hope—in her soft brown eyes. "But I think I might know where they are."

Savage held out his hand to assist her from the car. Gathering up the long skirt of her dress, she ran past the dead Breed males with Savage at her side. They entered the sacked villa and she headed immediately for the sampling room at the back of the expansive house. An immense wine cellar was attached to the room, its floor-to-ceiling wine racks filled with bottles of nearly every vintage the vineyard had ever produced.

"Over here," Bella said, walking to the far wall.

The bottles housed in those racks looked to be the oldest in the collection. Most of them were covered in a fine layer of dust. Pulling a sliding wooden ladder toward her, she climbed up and reached for one of the highest bottles in the old rack. Instead of pulling the aged bottle of Aglianico out, she twisted it clockwise.

It wasn't a bottle. It was a lever to a secret chamber.

One narrow section of racked wine popped open soundlessly.

Bella swung a glance over her shoulder at him. "My father had this panic room installed during the wars after First Dawn twenty years ago."

She started to duck inside. Savage caught her by the arm. "Stay close to me, Bella. If anything happens to you, I couldn't..."

He let the thought trail, but his touch lingered longer than necessary. She gave him a curious look, then nodded.

They stepped inside the unlit, cavernous room. Large oak barrels, shelves of paper supplies, and chunky, hand-hewn wooden tables made the secret chamber appear to be nothing more remarkable than a workroom for the vineyard.

Bella reached to turn on a light switch just inside. "Chiara?" she called softly. "Are you in here? It's me, Arabella."

A small whimper sounded from somewhere behind the barrels. Then a petite, pretty brunette emerged from the shadows, her dark-haired toddler son held protectively in her arms. "Bella!"

The two women raced to each other, embracing amid Chiara's tears and Bella's quiet assurances that she and Pietro were okay now. That they were safe.

Savage stood back from the emotional reunion, all too conscious of the fact that every minute they delayed here was one more minute they risked being discovered. They were fortunate that only two of Massioni's henchmen had been dispatched to the vineyard. That didn't mean there wouldn't be more sent to sniff around and make sure the job was finished.

The dead Breed males in the yard would be ashed by the morning sun, but whoever sent them would be waiting for them to return or report in.

And now that he was thinking about daylight...

It was late, and all too soon it would be dawn. They were too far afield to make the drive back to the command center before the sun rose and ashed him, too, which meant he needed to find them somewhere secure to settle in for the night.

Grabbing his phone, Savage called the scrambled line at the Order in Rome to apprise them of the situation. He'd already ignored more than one call from base demanding the status of the mission. He'd have hell to pay when he got back, no doubt. Probably right now too.

Trygg's dark growl greeted him on the other end. "Having a good time out there?"

Savage grunted. "There's been a slight change of plans."

"No shit? Was that before or after you jeopardized the entire mission in order to chase after some former tail?"

Okay, so maybe he deserved that. He definitely deserved it. But Trygg didn't understand, and Savage didn't have time to explain it right now. "Her name's Arabella Genova. I had to go back in for her and get her out of there. You're going to have to trust me on that."

"Not my trust you need to worry about," Trygg said. "Commander Archer's on a call with Lucan Thorne in D.C. as we speak. They weren't happy to hear you went AWOL in the middle of an op."

"Yeah, well, I got the job done."

"You sure about that? You verified Massioni blew up with his villa, right?" When Savage let the question hang a second too long, Trygg hissed a low curse. "You didn't verify. Jesus, Savage. I hope to fuck she's worth it, man."

He glanced over at Bella. Yeah, she was worth it. Her life—the relief and happiness he saw in her face right now—was worth everything.

"If I fucked up with Massioni, I'll handle it. Right now, I need to find a safe house for the day. I've got two Breedmates and a three-year-old Breed male with me here in Potenza right now. I need to make sure they're somewhere secure."

"Two females and a kid? I'm not gonna ask," Trygg muttered. He went silent for a moment, then heaved a surly sigh. "How far are you from Matera?"

Savage knew the town, had prowled the ancient streets and subterranean caverns of the old settlement more than a few times in his youth. "It's not far. An hour, give or take."

"Get there. I know somewhere you can go." Trygg gave him quick instructions, landmarks to guide him to where he needed to go once he arrived. From the sound of it, his comrade wasn't sending him into the touristy heart of the historic town, but down into the Paleolithic *sassi*—the neighborhood of ancient limestone caves that clung to the steep walls of Matera's central ravine. "Take the old stone steps behind the church. Follow the path on the left. Someone will be waiting to meet you and take you to a safe shelter."

"Who am I looking for?"

"A Breed male with long black hair and obsidian eyes. His name is Scythe."

"Scythe? Sounds like a real hospitable guy."

"You didn't ask for hospitable. You asked for someplace secure, and that's where I'm sending you."

"Point taken," Savage drawled, reminded that Trygg was nothing if not literal. The deadly, unsociable male dealt in absolutes, whether it came to combat or conversation. "What I'm saying is, you're sure about this male, this Scythe?"

"Completely."

"Care to elaborate?"

There was a long silence, then Trygg finally said, "He's my brother."

CHAPTER 6

Bella hated to let go of Chiara and Pietro, but Ettore's grave look as he ended his call to the Order left no question that they weren't totally out of danger yet.

"Come on," he said, walking over to collect them. "We can't delay here much longer. It's best if we get moving."

"Back to Rome?"

"There isn't time for that now. It'll be daylight in a few hours. My driving skills tend to suffer when I'm crispy."

She smiled wanly, but it was hard to find any humor in the risks he was taking for her tonight. For all of them now. And she could tell from the tone of his voice that the urgency to move on wasn't motivated only by his Breed aversion to ultraviolet rays. His concern went deeper than that.

"You think he's still alive, don't you?"

A tendon pulsed in Ettore's square jaw. "If he's not dead, I promise you I won't rest until he is. But first I need to make sure you and your family are somewhere secure. My comrade in Rome is arranging for someone to meet us in Matera. We'll have shelter there for as long as we need it."

As Bella and Ettore spoke, Chiara stepped forward with her young son clutching her hand.

Ettore glanced at the boy who was looking up at him warily. He crouched down to his level and placed his hand lightly on the child's shoulder. "You were very brave, keeping your mother safe in here until we arrived. Good work, Pietro."

He nodded shyly at the praise, and Bella's heart squeezed to see the little boy's fear melt away under Ettore's gentle treatment of him.

"How long will we need to stay away?" Chiara asked hesitantly.

Ettore's gaze met Bella's as he stood up. She knew that heavy look, what it meant. The two killers who'd shown up tonight hadn't succeeded, thanks to him, but it was almost certain there would be more behind them. The old vineyard and the rambling house where Bella was raised might never be safe again. Then again, it hadn't truly been safe in years. Not since Massioni entered their lives.

Combing her fingers gently through her little nephew's dark hair, Bella met Chiara's gaze. "We'll figure all of that out later. Right now, we need to do what Ettore says, okay?"

"Yes, of course. May I gather a few things for Pietro before we go? I promise I'll hurry."

Ettore nodded and Bella glanced down at her red gown and bare feet. "I don't suppose you have anything in your closet that would fit me, do you?"

Chiara smiled warmly. "You can look for something in your own closet, *sorella*. I kept your room just as it was on the day you were taken, in the hopes that you would come home again one day."

The kindness of that gesture—the sisterly love from her brother's widow—put a lump in Bella's throat. "Thank you."

She pulled Chiara into a brief hug before Ettore brought them all out of the panic room and back into the empty villa to prepare to leave.

A few minutes later, Bella was dressed in a pair of dark jeans and flats and a black T-shirt. Chiari held Pietro in one arm, a small bag containing his favorite blanket and toys and sundry other necessities slung over her other arm. Ettore took the bag from her and headed outside, leading the way.

"We have to leave the Pagani," he said, bypassing the two-seater sports car. "There's not enough room in it, but we also need to avoid drawing attention. I don't like the idea of taking Massioni's men's vehicle, but I can ditch it after we get to Matera in case anyone's looking for it."

"I've got a truck out back," Chiara said. She pointed to the barn behind the house. "It's not fast, but it'll get us where we're going. And it's plain enough that it won't turn any heads along the way."

Ettore considered for a moment, then shrugged. "Sounds better than our other options."

They retrieved the rust-spotted old pickup truck and climbed in, Bella sandwiched on the narrow bench seat between Ettore and Chiara and Pietro.

It was impossible to ignore the heat of Ettore's thigh pressed against hers as they drove off into the thinning darkness. Being this close to him again, her senses overwhelmed with the warmth and strength and scent of him, Bella knew a contentment—a feeling of security—that had eluded her for so long she hadn't recalled what it was like to feel safe and protected.

She hardly realized how badly she'd craved that feeling until now. With him.

Chiara and Pietro must have felt some degree of safety now too. They had both dozed off just a few minutes into the drive. No doubt the late hour and the stress of what they'd endured tonight had left them exhausted, but Bella knew their peaceful breathing had much to do with the man who'd surely saved their lives.

Bella glanced at Ettore in the soft light of the old truck's dashboard. His eyes were fixed on the open road, one hand slung over the top of the steering wheel. He seemed deep in his own thoughts until the weight of her gaze drew his attention. He looked her way, and although she was embarrassed to be caught staring at him, she couldn't pretend she hadn't been.

"Thank you for helping them," she said quietly. "Thank you for helping all of us tonight."

He gave a small shake of his head. "There's no need to thank me, Bella. I would do anything for you. Don't you know that?"

No, she didn't know that. For all she knew, she'd meant absolutely nothing to him. Not ten years ago. Certainly not all this time later. "Why did you do it, Ettore? Why did you leave and never come back? Was it because of something I did?"

"No." His answer came swiftly, his brows furrowing in a scowl. "Christ, no. You didn't do anything at all. Tell me that's not what they let you believe…"

"They?" A sick feeling opened up in the pit of her stomach. "You mean my family? You mean my father and Sal?"

His silent stare was confirmation enough.

"Tell me," she prompted. "What did they do?"

He glanced back at the road. "They were only looking out for your best interests, Bella. They noticed we were growing closer—they noticed my interest in you as a woman—and your father wasn't pleased. Neither was Sal, actually."

"Are you saying they pushed you away? No… Surely they would not. Are you saying they didn't want us together, so they forced us apart?"

Anger clawed up the back of her throat. She could hardly stand the thought of what their interference had caused her. To think she had wept over her father's murder. To think she had wept for Sal, even after he'd betrayed her to Vito Massioni.

But selling her out to that criminal thug hurt less than knowing the two men she trusted the most all her life had actually betrayed her even more egregiously long before then, when they stole her chance at a future with Ettore.

He slanted her a sober look. "They loved you, Arabella. Your father wanted to make sure you found a male who could provide for you, give you all the things you deserved in life. Your father and Sal both wanted only what was best for you."

Her answering scoff was brittle. "Look how that turned out."

"They couldn't have known how things would end up," he gently assured her. "But I wish I had known. I wish the Order had been on to Vito Massioni years ago, so I could've killed the bastard before he had the chance to lay a hand on you."

"It could've been worse," she admitted quietly. "I endured his temper sometimes, but at least I avoided his lust."

When Ettore glanced at her, there was surprise in his gaze, and more than a little relief. "You mean, he never—"

"Never," she said. "I told him my gift for scrying would only last as long as I was a virgin. Since I made him wealthy with my visions, he apparently decided he enjoyed collecting his money more than he would enjoy abusing me."

He smirked. "Clever girl. Except for one thing."

She felt a blush creep over her cheeks at the reminder.

She wasn't a virgin. She had given that part of her to Ettore. It had been their one and only time together.

The next night, he was gone.

"Fortunately, Massioni never doubted me. I think he might've eventually, but he had other women to slake his needs."

"Thank God," Ettore muttered. He frowned, his hazel gaze turbulent with stifled fury. "What about your visions, Bella? Did you never see any hint of your brother's troubles in your scrying bowl?"

She shook her head. "I don't see visions that relate to myself or the people I care for. My ability has never worked like that."

Which was why she'd never seen Ettore either, although it hadn't stopped her from trying to find him with her gift over the years he'd been gone. But her scrying had never found him.

Not even as he'd planned for and carried out his attack on Vito Massioni.

She dearly hoped Ettore had been successful, because if Massioni were alive to get his hands on her now, his punishment would be beyond brutal.

Ettore's mouth flattened into a grim line. "I never should've agreed to leave, no matter what your family wanted. It wasn't their decision to make. I didn't understand that until after I was gone." He reached over and stroked her cheek. "I should've come back for you, Bella. I'm sorry I wasn't there."

She turned into his caress, feeling no animosity toward him, only gratitude. And an affection that went far deeper than that.

Far deeper than the desire she felt simply for being seated so closely beside him, his comforting touch lingering against her face.

"You're here now," she said, pressing a soft kiss to the center of his palm.

His eyes flickered with sparks of amber light as her lips met his skin. She only meant the contact to be one of gratefulness and caring, but she felt the jolt of awareness too.

Her chest tightened, heat spreading across her breasts, licking down to her core.

Oh, yes, she still cared for him.

She wanted him.

Memories of stolen kisses and secret, tender embraces filled her head. She'd had only one night with Ettore, naked in each other's arms, but she had held it close to her heart ever since.

Neither the cruelty of time nor fate had diminished anything she felt for him. To the contrary, it had only made the craving deepen. It had only made her recognize how keenly she had felt his loss all this time.

And how profoundly happy she was to be reunited with him now.

Even if in a shadowed corner of her heart she dreaded that fate wasn't nearly finished with them yet.

CHAPTER 7

Savage didn't know how he'd managed to endure more than an hour in the truck, seated so close to Bella. Her thigh had rested against his the whole trip, contact that had distracted him, soothed him...aroused him beyond reason.

It sent his mind spinning back in time, to another evening drive they'd taken together on vineyard business. The one that had ended with both of them undressed and tangled together on a blanket under a midnight blue sky streaked with shooting stars.

"Come on, Ettore! Isn't it amazing?"

She grabbed a bottle of the newest Aglianico from the wooden cases in back of the truck and started running up the side of the nearby hill. He watched her go, her long legs bare and her curvy backside clad in grape-stained, faded denim shorts. He was always in a state of arousal around her, but seeing her dance away from him under the thin moon glow turned his cock to granite.

"Bella, you'd better come back. I don't think this is a good idea." *Nevertheless, he pulled an old wool blanket from behind the seat and jogged after her.*

She helped him spread it out on the cool grass, then pulled him down next to her. "Here, open this." She handed him the bottle and a corkscrew.

"I don't drink wine," he reminded her as he pulled the cork out with a soft pop. None of his kind did, but she knew that well enough.

"Do you ever wish you could? Even a taste?"

"No." He had never craved wine, but then he watched her tip the bottle to her lips to take a sip and he knew a thirst unlike any he'd ever known. Her throat worked as she swallowed, her head tipped back, drawing his eyes to the creamy column of her neck.

He cleared his throat, searching for his voice as his fangs punched out of his gums and his vision began to fire with amber. *"Your father and Sal are expecting us back at the vineyard."*

She slowly brought the bottle down from her mouth and set it in the grass. Her lips were wet, as dark as cherries from the wine. Long black lashes framed the solemn pools of her eyes. *"Do you want to go, Ettore?"*

He knew it as the chance it was—his only hope to stop this need for Bella before it went too far. They had been circling this moment for weeks. Hell, from the moment he first walked on to the Genova property.

Fleeting glances. Brief touches. Shared laughter. Then, later, after he'd fought his attraction for as long as he could, there had been a kiss, a few stolen embraces. Followed by heated caresses that had left both of them in flames.

But she was an innocent, just eighteen years old to his twenty-five.

Even worse, she was the Breedmate sister of his closest friend.

The last thing he should be doing was sitting beside her in the starlight, staring at her throat and wishing he was a better man. One with honor enough to lie and say he wasn't out of his mind with desire for her.

"What do you want, Ettore?"

"You."

He took her down beneath him on the blanket and unwrapped her as reverently as a precious gift. Each breathless moment was seared into his senses, from her soft moans as he kissed and licked and sucked every tempting inch of her…to her shuddering cries as he entered her virgin body and introduced her to an even deeper pleasure as the sea of shooting stars skated overhead.

Savage groaned at the uninvited recollection and the need it stoked in him even now.

By the time they reached the ancient hillside town of Matera, his body was rife with desire, his cock so hard it was a wonder he'd been able to drive.

His palm still burned from the sweet kiss she'd placed there.

His veins throbbed with hunger for her—a hunger that was startlingly more intense than simple desire. If he'd imagined that their years apart would cool his feelings for her, that tender kiss to the center of his hand had obliterated all hope of that.

Holy hell, he was in trouble here.

He should be thinking about his duty to the Order—and about the mission status that was uncertain at best—yet his mind was wrapped around Arabella Genova.

So was his heart. Although to be fair, that part of him had been hers for a lot longer than his life had been pledged to the Order.

How many times had he considered defying the wishes of her father and brother to go back and beg for her forgiveness and take her away with him forever? How many human blood Hosts had he drunk from, wishing it was Bella's vein that was nourishing him instead, her Breedmate blood ensuring that she would always be his?

Now, all he had were regrets.

He only hoped he could somehow get the chance to make things right. But first he needed to make sure she was safe.

"This way," he told the women, after leaving the old truck in a church parking lot as Trygg had instructed.

Carrying Chiara's bag so she could focus on her child, Savage placed his hand at the small of Bella's back and brought them to a flight of well-worn stone steps on the other side of the church. The stairs descended away from the quaint hotels and restaurants near Matera's city center, into the thickly settled community of limestone dwellings that appeared to grow out of the walls of the broad ravine.

Waning blue moonlight and the golden glow of random lanterns and street lamps illuminated the uneven trail Trygg had given them to follow. At the predawn hour, there were no tourists on the tangled network of stone paths and meandering steps of the *sassi*. The ravine was quiet, nothing but the sound of their footsteps on the dusty old cobbles and the occasional jangle of a sheep's bell from the flock starting to awaken on a grassy flat across the way.

Savage followed the path to the left, as he'd been told, which took them toward what appeared to be the low-rent section of the Paleolithic-era neighborhood. White limestone residences with the occasional flower box in their window or potted plant outside the door gave way to an unlit stretch of cobbles lined with rustic domiciles in various states of neglect, most with weeds and cactus sprouting out of their cracked and crumbling walls.

"Stay close," Savage advised the women as he led them deeper into the settlement. "We should almost be there now."

A few minutes later, just as Trygg had described, his brother waited up ahead on the walkway. At least, Savage hoped the immense, black-haired Breed male was Scythe.

As they approached, Savage walking protectively in front of Bella and Chiara, the other male lifted his head and swung a glance in their direction. Long ebony hair hung several inches past his shoulders, and a trimmed black beard outlined the grave set of his mouth. The male's eyes, as dark as jet, narrowed on Savage across the distance.

Yep. Definitely Scythe.

Savage nodded to him in greeting. Scythe's face remained expressionless within his curtain of dark hair. Dressed in a black leather trench coat that covered more black clothing beneath it, the male looked every bit a cold-blooded killer.

Which was saying something, coming from Savage, a warrior whose stock-in-trade was dealing death.

At Savage's back, he heard Bella suck in a shallow gasp.

"It's all right," he told her, touching her arm in reassurance. "This is who we're supposed to meet."

Without introduction, Scythe turned and started walking away. Apparently, he was as people-friendly as his brother. So long as the male was trustworthy and his safe house was secure, Savage would give the lack of social skills a pass.

"Let's go," he said, pausing to press a kiss to Bella's forehead. "We'll be safe here, I promise."

They followed Scythe to one of the last cave houses on the path, a squatty residence devoid of windows and accessible through a door that was reinforced with an iron grate. Savage wasn't expecting much as the other Breed male opened the door and let them inside, but it turned out the place only appeared forbidding and neglected from the outside. They stepped into a comfortable, if minimalist, dwelling with hand-hewn furnishings, arched stone ceilings, and warm, rug-covered floors.

Once they were inside, Scythe motioned for them to follow him farther into the place. More rooms were burrowed out of the rock of the ravine, connected by snaking tunnels large enough for both Breed males to walk through at their full height.

"I don't generally have guests," Scythe announced, sounding none too pleased. His voice was low and dark, almost a snarl as he strode ahead of them, his words echoing off the walls. "There is a small bed in the chamber to your right, and a larger one in the room at the end of this corridor. Make use of them as you wish."

Savage glanced at Bella. "You and Chiara take the beds. I don't need to sleep."

It was true enough. As Breed, he didn't require a lot of rest, but he doubted his thoughts would give him much peace anyway. To say nothing of his body, which was still thrumming with want of Bella.

She looked as if she meant to protest his sacrifice, but her sister-in-law was teetering on her feet and Pietro hadn't lifted his head since they left the truck. "I'll go help them settle in."

Savage remained in the passage as the women departed for the room. When he glanced at Scythe, he found the male watching Chiara through narrowed eyes. A dark scowl creased his brow.

"Trygg didn't say anything about a child being in danger."

"He didn't?" Savage frowned. "I'm sure I mentioned the boy when I spoke with him."

Scythe grunted. "Yeah. I'm sure you did too."

The cryptic response intrigued him. "Is it a problem?"

Scythe didn't answer, which told Savage far more than any words ever could. "If you or the females need anything, let me know."

Okay, conversation over apparently. Savage held out his hand to the other male. "Thank you. I owe you for this, and I won't forget it."

Scythe stared at his outstretched hand for a long moment. At first, Savage didn't understand why. Then he saw it—the severed stump at the end of the other male's right wrist where there had once been a hand.

And there was something else unusual about Scythe that he'd missed until now as well.

Around his *dermaglyph*-covered neck was a circle of mangled, vicious looking scars. By the severity of them, Savage had to guess that the Breed male had nearly lost his head at some point in his life too.

Since Breed genetics could heal all but the most catastrophic of injuries, Scythe must have been starving for blood or already half-dead from some other cause at the time this wound was inflicted.

Scythe shrugged. "We'd been raised to think we were invincible. It made many of us reckless. Not many survived after we got our first taste of freedom."

"Freedom from what?"

"From our collars."

The newsflash took Savage completely by surprise. He gaped at the obviously lethal, clearly antisocial Breed male. "Are you telling me that you were born a Hunter?"

Looking at him now, it made sense. As far as assassins and stealth operatives went, they didn't come any deadlier than the Hunters—first generation Breed males who'd been bred off the same Ancient sire and raised to be merciless killers by the Order's chief adversary. To keep his scattered army of perfect assassins obedient, Dragos had outfitted each of them with an ultraviolet collar that discouraged defiance or escape. Punishment was instant and final.

Dragos's secret program had been in operation for decades before he was taken out by Lucan and his warriors twenty years ago. As for the Hunters themselves, they were all but legend among the Breed now, with only a handful known to exist.

Evidently, Savage was looking at one of them.

He met Scythe's shark-black stare in question. "Trygg said you were his brother."

"He is. As are the others."

"Others?"

Scythe acknowledged with a curt nod. "The other lost boys. The dozens of young Hunters who escaped their collars when Dragos was killed."

CHAPTER 8

Ettore and their intimidating host were just parting ways as Bella stepped out of the bedroom where Chiara was resting with Pietro. She hesitated until the immense black-haired male had walked off before she approached.

Ettore glanced her way, a look of lingering astonishment in his eyes.

"Is everything all right with your friend?" she asked.

He grunted, raking a hand through his loose blond waves. "I wouldn't exactly call Scythe a friend just yet, but yeah, we're good."

Bella registered the name with an inward shudder. It was certainly a fitting moniker for the curt, menacing-looking Breed male. "If Scythe's glower is anything to go by, he doesn't seem happy to be saddled with houseguests."

"Are you kidding? That is his happy face." Ettore's grin flashed, revealing the twin dimples that had never failed to charm her. "How are Chiara and Pietro?"

"Exhausted. They're already asleep."

"You should be too," he said, his voice dropping to a tone of tender concern. His hand rested warmly on her shoulder. "Come on. Let's get you settled in the other bedroom."

It all seemed so surreal, being in this strange place, feeling safe despite the fact that she was on the run from an evil man and his network of criminal associates.

Ettore did that for her. She had always felt safe when she was with him. The guns and blades bristling from the belt that circled his waist had nothing to do with how protected he made her feel. It was him, the man, who had always been able to put her at ease.

As much as he aroused her.

Her skin still felt too warm, too tight, as they paused together at the chamber's open doorway. Everything they'd said in the truck, the stolen caresses they'd shared in those brief moments of semiprivacy earlier tonight, now hung between them like a wound that needed tending.

Ettore seemed to feel the same awareness that she did. The heat radiating from him was palpable, his touch at the small of her back light, yet searing. She wanted to feel his hands on her everywhere, not just in comfort or reassurance, but in passion.

He cursed as his eyes met hers, his hazel irises dark but glittering with flecks of amber. "For God's sake, don't look at me like that, sweetheart. I'm hanging by a thread here."

"I am too." She couldn't resist reaching up to him, letting her hands skim the firm muscles of his chest. "I've been hanging by a thread since you showed up at our vineyard with my brother all those years ago, Ettore."

His heart was thundering. His pulse slammed against her palm, hammering like a drum. He searched her gaze for a long moment, his breath rolling in deep, panting gusts.

The curse that boiled out of him was sharp, hissed between his teeth and fangs. "I wasn't expecting any of this. My first duty is to the Order. I have a mission to carry out. Until I'm certain I've completed it, I shouldn't be thinking about anything else. Not even you. Hell, especially not you."

"Of course. I understand." She glanced away, weathering a sting she hadn't seen coming. "Ettore, I didn't mean to suggest—"

He took her hand and hauled her against him, silencing her with a kiss. When he drew back from her lips, his gaze had gone molten. "I have no right to be thinking about anything but my duty to the Order. That's what I keep telling myself, Arabella. But then I look at you and none of those other things matter."

She swallowed, watching the fire dance in his eyes. His pupils were narrowed to thin black slits, and his fangs surged even larger behind his parted lips. The sight of his transformation sped her pulse, while at her hip, the hard steel of his arousal sent a current of hot need licking through her senses and straight into her core.

"I walked away once," he snarled. "God help us both, I don't think I can ever do it again."

His name was a jagged sigh on her lips as he grasped her face in his palms and covered her mouth with his once more. Kissing her so deeply she could hardly find her breath, he walked her backward into the chamber with him, kicking the door closed behind them with his boot heel.

Something wild had been unleashed in him. She saw it in his eyes, heard it in the rough scrape of his voice. And now all of that unhinged desire was pouring into her through his kiss.

"You're mine," he murmured against her mouth. Her moan of confirmation evidently wasn't enough. "Say it, Arabella. Let me hear it."

"Yes." Oh, God. She could hardly hold the desire that chased through her. Every hot sweep of his lips over hers, every carnal thrust of his tongue, inflamed a need in her that was swiftly burning out of control. "Please, Ettore. I need you. I need to feel you inside me."

His answer was an animalistic, purely possessive snarl. Pressing her down onto the narrow bed, he stripped away her clothing then quickly removed his own. Part of her wanted him to take things slowly—give her time to savor every nuance of the rock-hard, beautifully formed body she still saw so often in her most fevered dreams.

But the desire they had for each other had been denied for too long.

Too much precious time had been stolen from them already.

She was desperate for him. More than anything, she needed to feel his skin against hers and know that this was no dream now. That he was real. That he was hers again.

Always, she amended silently, allowing the wish to live in her heart as he settled himself atop her.

His eyes blazed as he watched her, his hand moving between their bodies to tease and stroke her sex. His fingers slid through her juices, a groan ripping out of him as he cleaved her folds and found the slick entrance to her body.

"You're already wet for me," he murmured, a grin tilting the edges of his wicked mouth. "Damn, you're soft, Bella. So beautiful. So fucking hot."

She couldn't bite back her whimper of pleasure, both at his praise and at the intensity of her arousal for him. He teased her sensitive flesh, taking her mouth in another deep, soul-searing kiss. She felt him test her tightness with his fingers, starting with one, then adding another, his thumb working a profane magic on her clit.

There had been no one since him, and the euphoria of being naked with him now, in his arms after so much longing, was too much to bear. Her orgasm rushed up on her unexpectedly, far too wild to hold back. She clutched his shoulders as her cry tore out of her throat. Arching off the mattress, she rode the wave to its crest, grinding shamelessly against his hand as the bliss poured over her.

"Open your eyes, baby," he coaxed her as he continued to pleasure her with his fingers. "I've waited too long to see this look on your face again. I swear, Bella, you've only gotten more exquisite."

She caught her lip between her teeth as the aftershocks rippled along her nerve endings, while beneath the pleasure another climax was already beginning to build. "Ettore, please…"

He knew what she needed. Shifting his weight, he positioned himself between her spread thighs. Her body was more than ready for him, slick and hot and open. Yet it was still a shock to feel the impossible thickness of him as he pushed the head of his cock inside her, then thrust to fill her with the hard length of his shaft.

"Bella," he uttered tightly, "you have to tell me if I'm hurting you."

"No." She shook her head, even as tears welled in her eyes. "Oh, God…it feels so good. I thought I remembered, but this…"

"I know, baby." He started to move within her, rocking slowly at first, each stroke taking him deeper, pushing further inside her, until she wasn't sure where he ended and she began.

"Ah, love," he murmured. "Your body is so tight around me. So damned perfect. I can't—"

His words were lost to the feral groan that ripped out of him. Caging her between his forearms, he drove inside her faster, deeper, untamed in his need. His handsome face contorted with the ferocity of his thrusts, his fangs so enormous they filled his mouth.

Bella's gaze fixed on those diamond-bright points as he crashed against her. She couldn't get enough either. She wanted all of him. Not just this moment and the wish that it might last. She wanted forever with Ettore Selvaggio.

After just one time together and ten long years in between, he was still the only man she craved.

In her heart—to the depths of her soul—she knew he was the only man she would ever love.

CHAPTER 9

Savage didn't fully understand the depth of his mistake until he was buried within Bella's velvet, wet heat. She moaned and sighed as he rolled his hips against her. Her hands roamed his back, her fingernails skating down the valley of his spine, scoring him as he pushed her toward the peak of her release.

Damn, she was lovely. Sweetly angelic, yet sexy as hell. She always had been, but now there was a strength in her too.

There was a power inside her, one that had been forged in the fire of what she'd endured the past three years. No longer the sheltered innocent, but a resilient woman who knew what she wanted and wasn't afraid to take it.

And, incredibly, what she wanted was him.

Still.

The realization stunned him, humbled him. Made him want to hold her close and never let her go.

One taste of her a decade ago had ruined him for any other woman.

Now, every cell in his body was hammering with the need to make her his alone.

In flesh and vow.

God help him, he wanted to claim her in blood too.

He wanted that with a ferocity he'd never known.

Not true, he corrected. He had wanted Bella as his blood-bonded mate even then. Ten years of absence from her had only solidified that resolve.

He loved her, and blood bond or not, he knew he would destroy any male who thought to take her away from him now.

"You're mine, Bella."

He growled the words as he pumped into her, knowing they sounded more like a demand than pledge.

They were both. They were his purpose for breathing, and he couldn't pretend they were anything less.

Not now.

Not when she was coming apart in his arms, her fingers digging into the muscles of his biceps as she cried his name and shattered with the force of her orgasm. The tight walls of her sex vibrated along his cock, tiny muscles gripping him like a slick fist as wave after wave coursed over her taut body.

He watched her come, trying to slow his own release just so he could revel in the pleasure he was giving her. But his need owned him. This female owned him, and trying to temper what she stirred in him was like trying to cage a wildfire.

He took her mouth in a deep kiss, drinking up her little sighs and moans as her climax began to ebb. When her eyelids slowly lifted, she gave him a blissful smile that he would kill to see on her lips for the rest of his life.

His voice was gruff, raw. "You're mine."

"I always have been," she whispered.

Ah, Christ. That tender admission was more than he could bear.

Pleasure seized him, pushing his hips into a fevered tempo. Each thrust took him deeper, made his hunger for her coil tighter, testing its already razor-thin leash.

Bella moved beneath him, meeting every hard stroke, taking him even deeper as she lifted her hips and wrapped her long legs around him.

Her hands roamed his face and shoulders, caressing him, worshipping him. The knot of his orgasm gathered at the base of his spine, wringing a sharp groan from between his clenched teeth. Blood pounded in his temples, in his cock…in the deadly lengths of his fangs.

"Oh, God," Bella gasped, tipping her head back as the flush of another release swept over her skin. "Ettore…I can't hold on. You feel too good."

He was beyond words now. He was only instinct and need, pure male. Utterly consumed by the remarkable female in his arms. He responded with a triumphant growl as she cried out beneath him. He couldn't stop his hips from moving, nor his blood from pounding with the overwhelming urge to claim his female in every possible way.

The urge became a mantra as his orgasm sped toward its peak.

He didn't realize he was staring at her throat until he heard Bella's soft voice filter through the haze of his blood-tinged thoughts.

"Yes," she said. "Yes, Ettore. I want it too."

When he met her gaze, he found her brown eyes steady and unafraid.

So full of love, it staggered him.

He knew he should turn away, be the stronger one.

He should give her this choice when they both were clear-headed and fully able to process the ramifications of what a bond would mean. One taste of her blood and he would feel her in his veins for as long as either of them lived. He would know her deepest emotions as his own—every joy and sorrow, every pleasure or pain.

And if she should die before him, he would be cursed to feel that too.

The bond was irreversible.

Unbreakable.

Eternal.

Concepts that had never entered his mind with another woman were all he could think of now that he was here with Arabella.

He loved her.

To his soul, he had loved her all this time. And the part of him that was more than mortal wasn't willing to wait another moment to claim her. That possessive, primal part of him wanted to bind her to him irrevocably.

Forever.

There was no place for logic in it, no room for regret.

There was only need.

Only love.

He roared with the ferocity of everything he felt, and as his release took hold of him, Ettore lowered his mouth to Bella's neck and sank his fangs into her tender flesh.

CHAPTER 10

If the bliss of making love with him had nearly wrecked her, it was nothing compared to the pleasure she felt at the sudden, sharp penetration of his fangs into her carotid.

Bella gasped at the piercing pain, feeling his bite all the way to her marrow. But that initial jolt gave way to a pleasure that defied description as his lips fastened over her skin and he drew the first sip of blood from her wound. Heat raced through her veins like rivers of quicksilver, all of her senses—every fiber of her being—drawn toward the pulse point that now flowed beneath Ettore's mouth.

Each suckling tug, every erotic sweep of his tongue, confirmed what she had already known.

She was his.

If she hadn't been before, the connection he had just activated between them ensured she always would be. He could never take another as his Breedmate so long as his bond to her was intact. For him, there would only be her.

The joy that understanding gave her was almost too much to bear. It filled her heart, even as it awakened something raw and primal inside her.

"You belong to me now, Ettore." She tunneled her fingers through his hair, holding him to her throat as he drank. "Mine."

He moaned, still rocking atop her, their bodies intimately joined. His strokes intensified along with the suction of his mouth against her vein.

The combined sensations flooded her with desire, stoking her need all over again.

"So good," he murmured, his deep voice as rough as gravel, his breath rushing hot against her throat. She felt his tongue sweep over the twin punctures, sealing them closed.

He lifted his head to watch her now. His eyes were glowing as bright as coals, gazing at her with such a ferocity of emotion it stole her breath. She had never seen his fangs look so sharp and unearthly. She licked her lips, hungry to feel them at her throat again.

Everywhere.

He was ferocious and otherworldly, the most magnificent man she'd ever seen.

His wicked mouth curved as he caressed the side of her face and the tender skin where his bite had been. "I can feel you inside me, Bella. I feel your blood in my own veins, in every cell of my body. And I feel your pleasure. I feel how badly you need me to make you come again."

As if to punctuate, he thrust long and slow and deep, a rumble of satisfaction vibrating through him as she cried out in helpless ecstasy.

"My sweet Bella," he said, lowering his head to kiss her forehead, her cheek, her parted lips as she sighed. "I wish you could feel how much I love you."

"Show me," she whispered, reaching up to trace her fingers along his rigid jaw, her gaze drifting to his fangs. "Let me taste you now, Ettore. Give me your bond."

She didn't have to ask him twice.

On a snarl, he brought his wrist up to his mouth and bit into it. Blood dripped onto her breasts, hot splashes of crimson that inflamed her dark thirst for him as he guided her mouth to his wounds.

She sealed her lips over the punctures. The first drop of blood on her tongue felt like a kiss of flame. She moaned, both in shock and in thirst.

She lapped at his skin, astonished at the intense rush of heat through her body as she drank from him. Ettore's blood felt alive with a wildness and strength she could barely comprehend. As powerful as an electric charge, each sip blasted into her body, into her cells…into her soul.

There was no fear left in her. No doubt. Everything peeled away, leaving only their love. This connection that nothing, and no one, could sever.

And beneath the contentment she felt as she sipped from Ettore's vein was a deeper blooming of desire.

It was the most erotic thing, to drink from him as he moved inside her, watching her with those eyes that burned everything away except the bond they now shared.

She didn't think her body could withstand another hot race toward climax, but Ettore's blood had unleashed something animal inside her. Something fierce and demanding. Something violently carnal.

"Ah, fuck, baby." He groaned, the tendons in his neck straining as she suckled his wrist and writhed beneath him. "I know. I can't be gentle now either."

Pulling his wrist away from her, he quickly sealed the wounds then flipped her over onto her stomach. One strong arm slid beneath her, hoisting her backside up to meet him as he slammed home from behind her.

He took her swiftly, aggressively, giving no quarter until they both were fully spent and collapsed on the bed in a sated tangle of limbs.

She didn't know how long they lay there, wrapped in each other's arms, their bodies slick with sweat and blood and the musky scent of their lovemaking. Bella could have stayed there for hours. Days. Forever.

She groaned when he rolled away, bringing her with him.

In the adjacent bathroom, the water began to run in the tub at Ettore's mental command.

Bella rose off the bed with him, smiling as he caught her in his embrace and pressed a tender kiss to her forehead.

She drew back, searching the banked embers of his gaze. "That was...amazing."

He inclined his head in solemn agreement. "Yes, it was. More than amazing."

She traced one of the *dermaglyph* swirls on his chest. "So...where do we go from here?"

He grunted, a smile playing at the edges of his sensual mouth. "To the bathtub for starters. I've made a mess of you."

"No, Ettore." She slowly shook her head. "You've made me whole."

His expression intensified, sparking a soberness that she could feel now, in his blood. In her own blood too, as it throbbed heavily in her breast and in the pulse points that all craved his bite.

"Ah, Bella. God, I love you," he murmured. "But I don't know where we go from here. Back to Rome to begin with. From there, we'll have to figure it out. Right now, I only know that I need you with me."

It was all the promise she needed. Him. With her. Together.

She could hardly believe this was her new reality.

Tipping her chin up, he kissed her with reverent care. Then startled her when he scooped her into his strong arms and carried her to the bathroom. He stepped into the tub with her, sinking down into the water with her straddled against him.

Bella sighed into the comfort of his arms and the softly lapping pool around them. "This is heaven," she murmured, resting her head on the muscled pillow of his shoulder. "I've never been so happy. I never thought I would be."

Ettore tenderly caressed her, his hands wet and warm and soothing as he bathed her. She started to drift, her mind relaxing as she watched the little ripples dance in the bath water.

The vision came on so suddenly, she flinched.

It formed beneath the clear surface—horrific, bloody, violent.

She saw a Breed male covered in mangled, melted skin. Dark soot and grime smeared all over his shoulders and burned head. He held a screaming human in his jaws. The man's throat was torn open as the predator siphoned his blood in gulp after greedy gulp.

"Bella?" Ettore's voice was flat with dread.

He had to feel her shock. Her terror.

His hands shook as he pulled her away from him so he could see her face. Her gaze was still riveted on the water, her mind still caught in the hideous vision.

"Sweetheart, what is it? Tell me what's wrong."

She could hardly find the words.

Because at that moment, the Breed male in her mind's eye lifted his ruined head. His furious, blazing amber eyes seemed to reach out for her through the water.

"It's him," she murmured. "Massioni. He's alive."

CHAPTER 11

Bella's vision weighed on Savage like a ton of bricks parked on his chest, a weight that was only increasing in the hours since she'd described what she'd seen in the water. The very thing he'd dreaded, the mistake he'd made in not making sure he had finished the job, was soon coming home to roost. He had no doubt of that.

Unfortunately, Bella hadn't been certain if she'd seen Massioni in the immediate future, or days—even weeks—from now.

Nor did it matter.

The son of a bitch had survived the blast that should have killed him.

Vito Massioni was alive, and that meant Savage had failed in his mission for the Order.

He could only pray he hadn't failed Bella in the process.

And to make certain of that, he was doing the only thing he could think of to ensure their safety.

"Everyone ready to go, sweetheart?"

Bella nodded as she strode toward him from the back bedroom. "Chiara will be right behind me. She's having a bit of trouble with Pietro. The poor thing has been having nightmares most of the day."

"Understandable," Savage said. "The kid has been through quite an ordeal. You all have." He drew Bella under the shelter of his arm. "We need to be on the road to Rome as soon as the sun sets. It's only a few hours away, but the sooner I get you and your family there, the better I'll feel."

She peered up at him, stroking his tense jaw. "You're sure your comrades won't mind taking us in for a while?"

"You're my mate, Bella. Chiara and Pietro are my family now too. The command center may not be a suitable home for a child, but somehow we'll find a way to make it work."

Her gaze was tender on him. "You're a good man, Ettore."

"I want to be," he said. "For you. And that means making sure you're as far out of Massioni's reach as possible. At least until I can finish him for good."

Savage seethed with the urge to fix his fuck-up personally and painfully with the bastard. There was a time when he would have.

Before Bella reentered his life, he'd thought nothing of charging into the fray of a dangerous situation to take out a target. He'd never had a death wish, but as a warrior pledged in service to the Order, his life had been expendable if it meant the difference between success or failure of one of his missions.

All that had changed now. Bella and he were bonded. Now, if he were injured—if he were killed—she would feel his anguish as if it were her own.

She would suffer everything he did, just as he would endure her every pain or fear.

So, no matter how viciously he wanted to make Vito Massioni pay for every hour of every year he'd held Bella prisoner for his own gain, Savage had to exercise caution. He had to be sure he didn't fail—with her or with the Order.

She rested her head against his chest, where the heavy pound of his heartbeat throbbed. "I'm scared, Ettore."

"Don't be," he murmured, placing a kiss on the top of her head. "I'm not going to let him get you. I'm not going to let him get Chiara or her son either."

"I know you won't. But I'm scared for you." She drew in a shallow, ragged breath. "If I ever lose you again—"

"You won't." Guiding her gaze up to his, Savage urged her to see the resolve in his eyes. She had to feel it in her blood now, through the bond that would join them forever. He slid his hand around her nape and brought her to him for an unrushed kiss that ensured she felt all of the love and promise that he held for her in his heart.

He could have kissed her for hours, and he swore to himself that he would, once he made sure she and her family were safely returned to Rome.

Sensing they were no longer alone, Savage turned his head and found Scythe standing there. Christ, the male might be immense and formidable, but he moved like a wraith.

He held out his left hand, a vehicle starter in his palm.

"What's this?" Savage asked, pivoting to face the former Hunter. The key fob was for a Range Rover—a new one, by the look of it. Scythe handed it to him.

"The truck you arrived in might get you where you're going, but this will be better."

"I left that vehicle half a mile away at the church. How the hell did you know what we were driving?"

Scythe didn't answer, and Savage figured there was a lot about the reclusive male and his methods that would remain a mystery. Instead of pressing him, Savage slipped the welcome gift into his pocket.

"Thank you."

Scythe gave him a faint nod.

"We're ready!" Chiara called from behind them. "I'm sorry to keep you waiting."

The petite brunette had her son's little hand grasped in hers as she approached from the other end of the corridor. As they drew closer, Savage felt a cold shift in the air. He didn't realize what it was until he looked at Scythe and saw that the male had gone utterly still. His onyx eyes were stark, almost haunted, beneath the harsh slashes of his black brows.

Chiara must have felt the chill too. She glanced up nervously at Scythe, practically tugging dark-haired Pietro along when the boy's steps began to slow in front of the big Gen One.

But the child didn't seem to have any fear for the sinister-looking male. His feet halted in front of Scythe, his little head tilting up to stare in unabashed awe. "How'd you hurt your hand?"

Chiara and Bella both sucked in their breath. Hell, even Savage felt a jolt of unease as Scythe's hard gaze slowly descended to look at the boy. When he spoke, the male's deep voice was as unreadable as his stoic face.

"I tried to help someone a long time ago."

By the male's grave tone, Savage assumed his hand wasn't the only thing Scythe lost.

"Come on, Pietro." Chiara gave her son's hand a small tug. She looked up at the big male, her cheeks flaming with color. "I'm sorry. He's just starting to learn about manners."

Scythe shrugged vaguely, but his bleak eyes lingered on the pretty Breedmate. "It's all right."

Savage cleared his throat. "We should get moving. It's past sundown now, and we have a lot of time ahead of us on the road."

As he spoke, the faint sound of a woman's scream went up somewhere in the distance outside the *sassi*. Scythe heard it too. His dark head jerked to instant attention.

Just as another shriek sounded—this one closer and belonging to a man.

A man who was screaming for his life.

Savage's blood iced over with dread. "What the fuck?"

Scythe drew a phone out of his leather trench coat and brought something up on the display. His curse was guttural, vibrating with fury.

"Rogues," he said grimly.

He turned the device so Savage could see it. On the screen was live video from several different cameras positioned in Matera's city center. The surveillance showed humans racing in all directions, while a group of Rogues—he counted half a dozen in just the few seconds he watched—poured into the streets on the attack.

"Oh, my God," Bella gasped, her terror-filled eyes rooted to the small display.

It wasn't the first time in recent weeks that a city had been overrun by blood-addicted vampires. Thanks to Massioni's proliferation of Red

Dragon, the narcotic that had turned scores of the Breed into Bloodlusting animals, violence like this was becoming almost epidemic again in many parts of the world.

Savage cursed viciously.

So much for leaving any time soon.

He wasn't about to risk Bella or anyone else's life by heading out into the chaos running rampant outside their safe house. And the idea of letting Matera's innocent population be slaughtered by blood-addicted predators was more than he could stand.

He met Scythe's fathomless black stare and saw the same resolve in him.

"You got extra weapons somewhere in here?"

The male gave him a curt nod.

More screams rang out in other parts of the town. More death coming closer by the minute. If the Rogues weren't stopped, it wouldn't take long before their attack moved down into the ravine.

Savage turned to Bella. He pulled one of his pistols from his weapons belt and placed it in her hand. "You ever shoot one of these?"

"No." She shook her head vigorously, but the worry he felt spiking through her blood was there for him. "Ettore, what are you—"

"Take it," he ground out fiercely, giving her a quick demonstration on how to take off the safety. "You aim this at anyone who comes to the door that isn't me or Scythe. And take this too." He unclipped a sheathed dagger from his belt and handed it to her. "That blade is titanium. It'll ash a Rogue in seconds flat."

He hoped to hell she never got close enough to one of them to use either of the weapons, but he wasn't taking any chances.

"Stay put, you hear me?" He grabbed her close, imploring her with his eyes and the hard, desperate pound of his heart. "I'll be back for you as soon as I can."

"Promise me."

He dragged her against him and kissed her—a brief, but impassioned confirmation that he wasn't about to lose her when they were so close to finally having a future together.

It wasn't easy to release her.

But as the terrorized screams of Matera's citizens continued to ring out, he knew he had little choice.

He turned to Scythe, now his unlikely ally. "Let's do this."

CHAPTER 12

The screams carrying down into the *sassi* from the city above only seemed to worsen in the few minutes after Ettore and Scythe had gone.

Those terror-filled shrieks—many of them agonized, final cries—left Bella shuddering and heartsick. Frightened to her marrow.

"We're going to be all right," she told Chiara and her frightened little boy, hoping her uncertainty didn't show in her eyes. As much as she trusted that Ettore was a capable warrior—Scythe too—they were only two against what was easily three times as many Rogues.

If anything happened to Ettore...

"You love him, don't you?" Chiara's voice was gentle, sympathetic.

"I love him more than anything in this world. I've loved him since I was a girl, back at the vineyard." She absently lifted her hand to the side of her neck, where she could still feel the claiming heat of Ettore's bite. "We're mated, Chiara. Our blood bond is only hours old."

"Oh, Bella." Chiara hugged her close. "You deserve this kind of happiness. You of all people deserve it."

Did she?

Bella couldn't help thinking that if not for her gift and Vito Massioni's want of it, Chiara and Pietro would not have been pawns at his mercy all these years. If not for her, Massioni would be dead—finished by Ettore in his mission for the Order.

If not for trying to rescue her from Massioni's villa, Ettore would already be back in Rome with his comrades, not swept into more violence and death.

High-pitched shrieks sounded again from somewhere outside.

"Momma!" Pietro whined, clutching at Chiara in wide-eyed alarm.

She picked him up and shushed him with tender words, rocking him. "It's okay, *piccolo*. Momma's here."

Bella reached out to stroke the little Breed male's head. "Why don't you both go relax in the back bedroom? It'll be quieter there."

Sheltered deeper into the cave dwelling. Away from the sounds of chaos and slaughter outside.

"You're sure?" Chiara gave her a dubious look. "I don't like the thought of leaving you alone to wait out here."

"Go," Bella gently encouraged. "I'll be fine. And soon Ettore and Scythe will be back."

Another sharp cry rent the night, startling Pietro. He started to cry softly against his mother's shoulder. Finally, on an apologetic nod, Chiara relented and turned to head back to the other room.

Bella took a seat in the living area, eyeing the weapons Ettore had given her. The gun and dagger rested on the side table next to her. She wished she were skilled enough to help him in some way. Feeling helpless made her antsy, made her mind spin from one disturbing thought to another.

She got up to pace the rug, worrying about Ettore. And the more she worried, the more she wondered if this random Rogue attack was actually random at all.

What if Vito Massioni had something to do with it?

She didn't want to think about the vision she had scried earlier, but the truth was his hideous face had been seared into her mind ever since.

And as much as she dreaded the idea of glimpsing him again, she needed to see if she could learn anything more that might help Ettore and the Order prepare to destroy him.

Taking the gun into the small kitchen with her, she retrieved a rustic stone bowl and filled it with water from the sputtering tap. Although Scythe didn't require mundane food or drink for nourishment as one of the

Breed, his modest home had apparently been outfitted for human residents.

She stared into the bowl of water, trying to ignore all of the pain and death taking place outside her shelter. She focused all of her concentration on the clear pool, but nothing happened.

She tried again, praying for something.

Anything.

But the water gave her nothing.

Her gift refused to comply.

"Dammit." She heaved a sigh, closing her eyes and lowering her head into her palms.

When she opened them again, she did see a face reflected in the water.

Vito Massioni's hideous, disfigured face. His unblinking eyes stared back at her, the amber glow of them furious. Insane. Murderous.

His jaws were open, baring the twin daggers of his elongated fangs.

"Hello, Arabella."

Oh, God.

No.

She screamed and wheeled around, horrified to find the Breed male standing behind her. Her hand shot out to grab for the gun, but Massioni was much faster. With barely a sweep of his arm, he sent the weapon flying into the other room.

She tried to scramble out of his reach, but he grabbed a fist full of her long blonde hair and yanked her back. She crashed against him, her stomach turning at the foul stench of soured blood and death that clung to him.

"Didn't I warn you never to cross me, Bella?" His arms wrapped around her, strong as steel. His breath was hot and rank as it wormed into her ear. "Didn't I tell you there was nowhere you could run that I wouldn't find you? Your family too." He clucked his tongue, a revolting, wet sound. "Did you think I was so careless that I wouldn't take steps to make sure of that? The tracer on Chiara's truck led me straight to you. The Rogues ensured that the warrior from the Order would have no choice but to leave you unattended."

Nausea swamped her, not only from the horror of their mistake, but from the repulsiveness of Massioni's nearness. She moaned, struggling in vain to break loose. "Let me go!"

He chuckled. "Stupid girl. Didn't I tell you there would be pain if you deceived me? Now, there will be death."

Bella struggled and fought, but it was no use. Even severely injured from the blast that should have killed him, Massioni was inhumanly strong.

He was also deadly, even though his burned, mangled skin was raw, open wounds still seeping on his forearms despite the massive amount of blood he had likely consumed in his efforts to heal.

Bella's gaze fixed on the worst of the wounds that mangled the flesh of his arms. Maybe there was a tender spot on this dragon after all. Her bile churned, but she pushed past it to dig her fingers as deep and as savagely as she could into the ruined muscles and tendons.

He howled in anguish—and when his grasp loosened in reflex to the pain, she threw herself out of his grip. Stumbling to the floor, she scrambled away into the living area, hope surging through her.

But it was short-lived.

Chiara rushed out of the far chamber. "Bella? Oh, my God!"

Her scream when she spotted Massioni brought Pietro out of the bedroom behind her.

What happened next occurred so quickly, Bella could hardly comprehend it.

One moment, Massioni was doubled over in agony and anger. The next, he had Pietro by the wrist, holding the little boy up like a prize. Like a slab of meat caught on a butcher's hook.

Massioni's amber eyes burned even brighter in his rage. He snorted and sniffled, his lips peeling back from his teeth and fangs. There was a deep madness in his transformed gaze. In his feral, blood-stained face.

Oh, shit.

He really was crazy. Worse than crazy, but she hadn't realized it until now.

He had drunk too much blood since he escaped the blast.

Vito Massioni was lost to Bloodlust.

He was Rogue.

"You shouldn't have done that, Arabella. Now, you're really going to suffer."

His tongue slid out, snakelike, as he eyed the Breed child that dangled from his grasp. Then he looked back at her as she slowly got to her feet from her stumble into the other room.

His head cocked at a chilling, exaggerated angle. "I think we'll start by letting you watch me rip this boy's heart out and eat it in front of you both."

CHAPTER 13

"I don't think so, asshole."

Savage held a semiauto in his hand as he stood in the open doorway, his eyes lit up with fury, his fangs pulsing with the need to shred Vito Massioni to pieces.

He and Scythe had split up after leaving the *sassi*, working the attack from both ends of the city in order to contain the situation as best they could. Savage had just ashed his third Rogue of the night when all of a sudden it felt as if his heart was about to burst out of his chest in ice-cold terror.

Bella's terror.

Their bond had told him instantly that she was in danger. He hadn't been prepared for what he saw as he entered the *sassi* safe house and met with the hideous, Bloodlust-afflicted creature facing him now.

"Let the boy go, Massioni."

Savage would have opened fire already if Bella wasn't standing between him and a clear shot at the slavering Breed male.

Besides, in Massioni's current condition, he was as volatile as a human on PCP. Putting him down cleanly would take a lot more rounds than Savage had left in his pistol.

Or a titanium dagger.

Unfortunately, he'd buried one a few minutes ago in the skull of a Rogue who'd ripped the throat out of a nun inside one of Matera's old churches. His other blade he'd given to Bella.

He saw no trace of the gun or the knife he'd given her.

And there wasn't time to consider alternatives so long as Massioni had little Pietro hanging painfully by his wrist while Chiara wept and pleaded for mercy on her son.

Massioni sneered at Savage. "Done chasing rabbits so soon, warrior? Here I'd been looking forward to taking my time with these three."

"You heard me. Put the boy down."

Instead of complying, he raised Pietro higher, until the child's rib cage was level with Massioni's open maw. Saliva dripped from the tips of his fangs. "Put down your weapon, warrior."

Savage didn't move. He didn't as much as blink. Holding his 9mm steady, he only hoped Massioni would believe his bluff.

"Bella," he said calmly. "Move out of the way, baby."

Massioni growled. "Don't you take even one fucking step, Bella, or the next thing you'll hear is this brat's screams as I punch a hole through his sternum with my fist."

Chiara sobbed. Bella looked equally miserable, but she held herself together. She stared at Savage, shaking her head as if to warn him away from doing anything rash.

Well, fuck that. He would do anything to get her out of this, but damn if he wanted to forfeit an innocent child's life to accomplish it.

He saw little choice but to try to catch Massioni off guard.

In a split-second move, Savage took his shot, hitting the Breed male's forearm.

Massioni hissed as the bullet bit into his ravaged flesh.

As Savage hoped, he lost his grip on Pietro. The boy dropped to the floor, unharmed.

But then, just as quickly, Massioni snatched up Bella and hauled her against him like a shield.

She screamed. Arms trapped at her sides, she struggled in vain to break loose. The monster who held her only chuckled, seeming to delight in her terror. His glowing gaze was wild with madness. And dangerously smug triumph.

Savage couldn't contain the nasty curse that exploded out of him. He'd never known this kind of fear. He'd never felt the kind of bleak horror that raked him as he watched his mate sag into a resigned slump in her captor's arms.

Massioni tilted his head, those insane amber eyes studying Savage too closely.

"What's this?" he taunted. "Why, you look more than worried for this bitch, warrior. Am I taking something you thought belonged to you?"

"Let her go."

He held his weapon steady on his target, but he knew damned well he would never pull the trigger. Not when he was staring at Bella's beautiful, fear-stricken face.

If anything happened to her—for crissake, if she died right here at Massioni's hands—he would burn the whole world down around him.

"Please," he said woodenly, too afraid of losing her to care if he had to beg. "Let her go."

Massioni's eyes narrowed on him. "You've fucked her."

Savage bristled at the other male's crudeness. He wanted to flay him just for uttering the words.

A bark of laughter erupted from between the male's cracked and blistered lips. "Holy hell. You love her. Don't you, warrior?"

Bella made an anguished sound in the back of her throat. She shook her head at Savage, and as their eyes connected and held, he didn't so much feel fear in their bond, but a strange and steely determination.

"She's no good to me now," Massioni muttered. "Her gift was the only thing of value to me. You've ruined it." He shrugged. "I might as well kill her now."

Massioni gripped her chin in his soot-blackened, blood-stained fingers. He yanked her head back, and Bella's sharp cry tore into Savage.

Her pain was real.

But her terror had galvanized into something else.

Something that told Savage to trust what he was feeling, not what he was seeing.

"All right." He relaxed his stance, lowering his weapon. "All right, you son of a bitch. You win."

Massioni stilled. Confusion swept over his feral features. His hold on Bella relaxed—ever so slightly.

It was all the opportunity she needed.

Twisting in the slackened cage of his arms, Bella drew the dagger she'd been concealing in her hand and drove it hard and fast and mercilessly into the center of his chest.

He staggered back, a look of shock on his face.

Until the poison of the titanium began to seep into his corrupted blood system. He howled, his face constricting in disbelief and agony. His body convulsed, collapsing to the floor.

Savage was at Bella's side in no time, pulling her close to him—holding her tight as the Rogue that had once been Vito Massioni began to disintegrate into a puddle of sizzling, melting flesh and bone.

In a few moments, there was only ash where his body had been.

He was dead, and Bella was safe.

Chiara and her son had come through the ordeal uninjured too.

As Savage held Bella in his embrace, he glanced to the door where Scythe had now entered. The former Hunter strode inside his house, his black gaze taking in the signs of struggle and the pile of ash still crackling on the floor. Then he looked to Chiara and Pietro, the pair of them huddled together nearby, and something crossed the remote male's face.

Relief, Savage thought.

And maybe something more.

Regret?

Whatever it was, the emotion was there and gone in an instant.

He gave Savage a sober nod, whether in confirmation of what he'd allowed him to see just then, or in acknowledgment of their teamwork tonight, Savage wasn't sure.

He might have tried to decipher it, but right then, with Bella warm and alive in his arms and his heart full to the brim with love for her, the only thing on his mind was the well-being of his woman.

His brave, beautiful mate.

He couldn't contain himself from dragging her to him for his kiss.

She resisted a little, drawing back on a small groan. "Ettore, I'm a mess. I have his blood on me…his foulness."

"That won't stop me from kissing you," he told her gently. "Nothing is going to stop me from doing that ever again."

He pulled her closer, wrapping her in his embrace as he brushed his lips over hers in a slower claiming, a tender joining of their mouths that still had the power to inflame them both—even after the ordeal they had just endured. Perhaps because of it too.

But she was right. She had been through hell with Massioni. Not only tonight, but for the past three years as well.

Now that the monster was no more, Savage wanted to erase all trace of him from Bella's life.

He swept his tongue across her soft lips on a groan that promised more. With Chiara quietly tending to her son, Savage lifted his head to look at Scythe.

"If you don't mind, I'd like to go draw a bath for my lady."

"Actually, I'd prefer a shower," Bella interjected, glancing up at him wryly. "No more baths, at least not for a while."

Savage chuckled. "Baby, whatever you want, it's yours."

"You, Ettore." Her soft brown gaze turned serious as she reached up and held his face in her warm, courageous hands. "You're all I want. You are all I'm ever going to need."

"You have me," he murmured quietly. "You have every part of me, sweet Bella. You always have."

They kissed again, his love for her soaring in his chest, in his veins. Through their bond.

Her love twined with his, and the depth of their connection was so profound it nearly brought him to his knees.

He didn't care that they had a small audience in the room with them. He didn't care who knew how completely he adored Arabella.

Loved her.

Desired her.

He wanted the whole world to understand that she was his.

And he was hers…in all ways.

Forever.

CHAPTER 14

"Keep kissing me like that, female, and I may decide to keep you here permanently."

Bella laughed and gazed up at Ettore, both of them now dried off and dressed after taking their time to clean up together. "Live in a *sassi* cave house and make little Breed babies? Sounds just about perfect to me."

Ettore paused. "Is that what you want?"

She smiled, lifted her shoulder in a faint shrug. "The cave is optional."

The sound he made as he wrapped his arms around her was one of joy and wonder. Even reverence.

"Do you have any idea how much I love you, Arabella?"

"I do," she said. "Because I feel it inside me. I hope you can feel even a fraction of the love I have for you, Ettore."

His rough moan was confirmation enough, but he kissed her anyway. Their union was so precious to her, she truly would have stayed right there with him forever if he asked it of her.

But Chiara and Pietro were waiting in the living area outside.

And Ettore's comrades with the Order in Rome were awaiting his return too.

Bella knew his duty was on his mind as he led her out to join the others. He'd been in touch with the command center in the hours since Massioni's death, both to inform them of the situation in Matera and to explain that he would be coming back to Rome with his Breedmate and her kin.

He threaded his fingers through hers as he brought her out to the main part of Scythe's home.

The signs of the earlier confrontation were gone now. Chiara was sweeping up the cold ashes from the floor, while Pietro sat on the rug nearby. He had a little toy in his hand—a carved lion made of stone. Scythe stood back from the boy, his black eyes haunted somehow as he watched him play with the miniature creature.

Bella's heart squeezed at the sight. When Scythe abruptly glanced up, she felt intrusive somehow. As if she had invaded private, long-buried thoughts that the forbidding Breed male had no intention of sharing.

Ettore held up the key that Scythe had given him earlier tonight. "Are you sure the Rover is ours?"

He gave a firm nod. "Keep it. If I have need of another vehicle, I have ample resources to get one."

"All right." Ettore inclined his head. "We should get moving, then. We have a lot of road ahead of us if we mean to make it back to Rome before sunrise."

Scythe grunted, contemplative. "Through my brother, Trygg, I'm aware that the Order has more than its share of trouble these days. If you or your comrades ever have need of more hands on deck—" The sober male actually smirked now. "Or even just one hand—then I trust you'll let me know."

Ettore chuckled. "I will. Thank you."

Scythe extended his good arm to him. The two males exchanged a brief left-handed shake. Then Scythe turned his fathomless gaze on Bella.

"Take care of each other."

"We will," she replied. And whether the intimidating Gen One wanted it or not, she rose up on her toes to kiss his beard-darkened face. "Thank you, Scythe. For everything you've done for us."

He stepped back without a word or acknowledgment, yet despite his reticence, she knew in her heart that she and Ettore had made a friend. If needed, they had a lethal, lifelong ally.

Chiara and her son as well.

Bella watched as her brother's widow collected her child from the rug where he was playing. She whispered something into Pietro's ear, then the boy shyly stepped over to stand in front of Scythe. In his pudgy fingers was the carved animal.

"Here," he said, offering it back to the larger male.

"You keep it," Scythe said, his deep voice toneless. "I've held on to it for too long. It's yours now."

Chiara smiled, gathering her arm around her little boy's shoulders. "I don't know how to thank you for giving us shelter," she murmured.

"No thanks is needed. It's enough to know that you and your child weren't harmed."

"No one's going to harm them anymore," Ettore added. "When I spoke with the command center, they informed me that the explosion at the villa the other night killed all of Massioni's lieutenants. His network is in shambles. My comrades and I are already making plans to crush his organization to the ground. No one will be coming after Bella or any of her family anymore."

Chiara's relief was clear in her eyes. But there was a note of hesitation there too. "I'm glad to hear that," she said. "Because I've decided that I don't want to go to Rome."

Bella frowned. "What? Then where—"

"The vineyard is my home, *sorella*. That's where Pietro and I belong."

Although it made sense, the thought of leaving her family behind still put a pang of sadness in her breast. Ettore must have registered the spike in her emotions. His fingers came to rest lightly under her chin, tipping her face up to meet his.

"Do you want the same thing, love? To go home to the vineyard, instead of living with me at the command center in Rome?"

"The vineyard hasn't been my home for a long time. Where you are, Ettore, that's my home now."

Because of him, her family was safe now.

Because of him, she had everything she'd ever wanted—all she needed—right here in her arms.

They said their final good-byes to Scythe, then drove his black Range Rover back to the vineyard in Potenza.

Hours later, with Chiara and Pietro settled again in their home, Ettore took Bella's hand and walked her out under the starlight.

She saw his gaze drift to the sleek blue Pagani that had brought them to this place two nights ago. It seemed like forever since he'd stormed into her life again and whisked her away from the villain who had held her.

Now, she and Ettore had forever waiting for them in their new life together.

She couldn't wait for it to begin.

He gestured to the sports car. "You don't suppose Chiara has any use for that, do you?"

"Hmm. Probably not," Bella replied with mock contemplation. "The Rover would be more practical. Not to mention it might give Scythe a reason to come around and check on them from time to time."

Ettore grunted. "I've got a feeling that might happen either way."

She smiled. "You may be right about that. Still, a sports car won't get much use out here at the vineyard. And Pietro is still years away from truly appreciating that kind of machinery."

"Shame to let a perfectly good Pagani sit unappreciated."

She smiled up at him. "And it'll certainly get us back to Rome a lot faster."

Ettore smirked. "Faster to Rome means faster into my arms again. And into my bed."

"I like the sound of that," she said, arching her brows.

"Then let's go."

He playfully smacked her backside, and they both raced down to the waiting car. They climbed in beneath the lifted gullwing doors, and in seconds the Pagani rumbled to life.

Ettore took her hand, bringing it up to his lips. "Ready for the ride of your life?"

"Oh, yes." Bella smiled. "I'm ready for anything with you."

* * * *

Also from 1001 Dark Nights and Lara Adrian, discover MIDNIGHT UNLEASHED.

Sign up for the 1001 Dark Nights Newsletter
and be entered to win a Tiffany Key necklace.

There's a contest every month!

Go to www.1001DarkNights.com to subscribe.

As a bonus, all subscribers will receive a free
1001 Dark Nights story
The First Night
by Lexi Blake & M.J. Rose

Turn the page for a full list of the
1001 Dark Nights fabulous novellas...

Discover 1001 Dark Nights Collection Four

ROCK CHICK REAWAKENING by Kristen Ashley
A Rock Chick Novella

ADORING INK by Carrie Ann Ryan
A Montgomery Ink Novella

SWEET RIVALRY by K. Bromberg

SHADE'S LADY by Joanna Wylde
A Reapers MC Novella

RAZR by Larissa Ione
A Demonica Underworld Novella

ARRANGED by Lexi Blake
A Masters and Mercenaries Novella

TANGLED by Rebecca Zanetti
A Dark Protectors Novella

HOLD ME by J. Kenner
A Stark Ever After Novella

SOMEHOW, SOME WAY by Jennifer Probst
A Billionaire Builders Novella

TOO CLOSE TO CALL by Tessa Bailey
A Romancing the Clarksons Novella

HUNTED by Elisabeth Naughton
An Eternal Guardians Novella

EYES ON YOU by Laura Kaye
A Blasphemy Novella

BLADE by Alexandra Ivy/Laura Wright
A Bayou Heat Novella

DRAGON BURN by Donna Grant
A Dark Kings Novella

TRIPPED OUT by Lorelei James
A Blacktop Cowboys® Novella

STUD FINDER by Lauren Blakely

MIDNIGHT UNLEASHED by Lara Adrian
A Midnight Breed Novella

HALLOW BE THE HAUNT
A Krewe of Hunters Novella by Heather Graham

DIRTY FILTHY FIX by Laurelin Paige

THE BED MATE by Kendall Ryan
A Room Mate Novella

NIGHT GAMES by CD Reiss
A Games Novella

NO RESERVATIONS by Kristen Proby
A Fusion Novella

DAWN OF SURRENDER by Liliana Hart
A MacKenzie Family Novella

Go to www.1001 DarkNights.com for more information.

Discover 1001 Dark Nights Collection One

FOREVER WICKED by Shayla Black
CRIMSON TWILIGHT by Heather Graham
CAPTURED IN SURRENDER by Liliana Hart
SILENT BITE: A SCANGUARDS WEDDING by Tina Folsom
DUNGEON GAMES by Lexi Blake
AZAGOTH by Larissa Ione
NEED YOU NOW by Lisa Renee Jones
SHOW ME, BABY by Cherise Sinclair
ROPED IN by Lorelei James
TEMPTED BY MIDNIGHT by Lara Adrian
THE FLAME by Christopher Rice
CARESS OF DARKNESS by Julie Kenner

Also from 1001 Dark Nights

TAME ME by J. Kenner

Go to www.1001 DarkNights.com for more information.

Discover 1001 Dark Nights Collection Two

WICKED WOLF by Carrie Ann Ryan
WHEN IRISH EYES ARE HAUNTING by Heather Graham
EASY WITH YOU by Kristen Proby
MASTER OF FREEDOM by Cherise Sinclair
CARESS OF PLEASURE by Julie Kenner
ADORED by Lexi Blake
HADES by Larissa Ione
RAVAGED by Elisabeth Naughton
DREAM OF YOU by Jennifer L. Armentrout
STRIPPED DOWN by Lorelei James
RAGE/KILLIAN by Alexandra Ivy/Laura Wright
DRAGON KING by Donna Grant
PURE WICKED by Shayla Black
HARD AS STEEL by Laura Kaye
STROKE OF MIDNIGHT by Lara Adrian
ALL HALLOWS EVE by Heather Graham
KISS THE FLAME by Christopher Rice
DARING HER LOVE by Melissa Foster
TEASED by Rebecca Zanetti
THE PROMISE OF SURRENDER by Liliana Hart

Also from 1001 Dark Nights

THE SURRENDER GATE By Christopher Rice
SERVICING THE TARGET By Cherise Sinclair

Go to www.1001 DarkNights.com for more information.

Discover 1001 Dark Nights Collection Three

HIDDEN INK by Carrie Ann Ryan
BLOOD ON THE BAYOU by Heather Graham
SEARCHING FOR MINE by Jennifer Probst
DANCE OF DESIRE by Christopher Rice
ROUGH RHYTHM by Tessa Bailey
DEVOTED by Lexi Blake
Z by Larissa Ione
FALLING UNDER YOU by Laurelin Paige
EASY FOR KEEPS by Kristen Proby
UNCHAINED by Elisabeth Naughton
HARD TO SERVE by Laura Kaye
DRAGON FEVER by Donna Grant
KAYDEN/SIMON by Alexandra Ivy/Laura Wright
STRUNG UP by Lorelei James
MIDNIGHT UNTAMED by Lara Adrian
TRICKED by Rebecca Zanetti
DIRTY WICKED by Shayla Black
THE ONLY ONE by Lauren Blakely
SWEET SURRENDER by Liliana Hart

Go to www.1001DarkNights.com for more information.

About Lara Adrian

LARA ADRIAN is the *New York Times* and #1 internationally best-selling author of the Midnight Breed vampire romance series, with nearly 4 million books in print and digital worldwide and translations licensed to more than 20 countries. Her books regularly appear in the top spots of all the major bestseller lists including the *New York Times*, *USA Today*, *Publishers Weekly*, Indiebound, Amazon.com, Barnes & Noble, etc.

Lara Adrian's debut title, Kiss of Midnight, was named Borders Books best-selling debut romance of 2007. Later that year, her third title, Midnight Awakening, was named one of Amazon.com's Top Ten Romances of the Year. Reviewers have called Lara's books "addictively readable" (Chicago Tribune), "extraordinary" (Fresh Fiction), and "one of the best vampire series on the market" (Romantic Times).

With an ancestry stretching back to the Mayflower and the court of King Henry VIII, Lara Adrian lives with her husband in New England, surrounded by centuries-old graveyards, hip urban comforts, and the endless inspiration of the broody Atlantic Ocean.

Connect with Lara online:

Website - http://www.laraadrian.com/
Facebook - https://www.facebook.com/LaraAdrianBooks
Twitter - https://twitter.com/lara_adrian
Pinterest - http://www.pinterest.com/laraadrian/

Discover More Lara Adrian

Midnight Unleashed
A Midnight Breed Novella
By Lara Adrian

Coming October 10, 2017

Return to New York Times and #1 international bestselling author Lara Adrian's "addictively readable" (Chicago Tribune) Midnight Breed vampire romance series with a pulse-pounding novella of paranormal seduction and dangerous thrills, where an icy immortal beauty and a lethal Gen One Hunter must confront a powerful enemy while struggling to deny the irresistible calling of their blood.....

On behalf of 1001 Dark Nights,

Liz Berry and M.J. Rose would like to thank ~

Steve Berry
Doug Scofield
Kim Guidroz
Jillian Stein
InkSlinger PR
Dan Slater
Asha Hossain
Chris Graham
Pamela Jamison
Fedora Chen
Jessica Johns
Dylan Stockton
Richard Blake
BookTrib After Dark
The Dinner Party Show
and Simon Lipskar

Made in the USA
Middletown, DE
30 June 2019